Greythorne

WITHDRAWN

Greythorne

CRYSTAL SMITH

Fitchburg Public Library
5530 Lacy Road
Fitchburg, WI 53711

HOUGHTON MIFFLIN HARCOURT

Boston New York

Copyright © 2020 by Crystal Smith

All rights reserved. For information about permission to reproduce
selections from this book, write to trade.permissions@hmhco.com or to
Permissions, Houghton Mifflin Harcourt Publishing Company,
3 Park Avenue, 19th Floor, New York, New York 10016.

hmhbooks.com

The text was set in Bembo Std.
Map art by Francesca Baerald

Library of Congress Cataloging-in-Publication Data
Names: Smith, Crystal, (Crystal Campbell), author.
Title: Greythorne / by Crystal Smith.
Description: Boston ; New York : Houghton Mifflin Harcourt, [2020] |
Series: Bloodleaf trilogy ; [2] | Audience: Ages 14 and up. |
Audience: Grades 10–12. | Summary: As the people of Achlev struggle
to survive the instability fueled by Dominic Castillion, Aurelia is
determined to save them and her loved ones at any cost.
Identifiers: LCCN 2019029206 (print) | LCCN 2019029207 (ebook)
| ISBN 9781328496317 (hardcover) | ISBN 9780358246312 (ebook) |
ISBN 9780358376620 (international edition)
Subjects: CYAC: Fantasy.
Classification: LCC PZ7.S644636 Gre 2020 (print)
LCC PZ7.S644636 (ebook) | DDC [Fic]—dc23
LC record available at https://lccn.loc.gov/2019029206
LC ebook record available at https://lccn.loc.gov/2019029207

Manufactured in the United States of America
DOC 10 9 8 7 6 5 4 3 2 1

4500794978

To Carma—
For reading every draft,
no matter how rough

GREYTHORNE
Manor & Village

Achlevan
Camp

RIVER URSE

Greythorne
Village

Old Mill

Mercer's
Shop

Greythorne Manor

To the
Continent

Stella Regina

PART ONE

CONRAD COSTIN ALTENAR, EIGHT YEARS OLD AND THE ASCENDANT

king of Renalt, was humming to himself in time to the creaks and jolts of his carriage. It was an old Renaltan folk song, meant to be sung in a melancholic minor key: *Don't go, my child, to the Ebonwilde, / For there a witch resides . . .* Everyone knew the first verse, but he much preferred the lesser-known second, which described a phantom horseman:

> *Don't go, my child, to the Ebonwilde,*
> *For there a horseman rides.*
> *His stallion's mane is silver flame*
> *With night-black coals for eyes.*
> *Don't go, my child, to the Ebonwilde;*
> *Please stay here warm in bed.*
> *If you see him, child, in the Ebonwilde,*
> *You just might lose your head.*

As Conrad hummed, he fiddled with a new toy: a pointed puzzle box with nine sides and a series of intricate buttons and latches that had to be pressed and turned in just the right order to open a hidden compartment with a prize inside. It was from his sister, Aurelia, an early gift for his upcoming coronation, now only two days away. Convinced the box concealed candy, Conrad had been poring over it for the duration of his Renaltan tour. He wanted to have it figured out before the excursion reached its end, and though Greythorne—the final stop and chosen location to begin his coronation procession—was only a few miles away now, he was sure he could have the puzzle cracked and the candy consumed before they pulled onto the drive.

As he concentrated harder, his humming tapered off.

Push, turn, twist, twist, tap, and then . . .

Nothing.

"Bleeding stars," he cursed before glancing around the empty carriage to reassure himself that no one had heard. But his only companion was his own reflection, which gazed back at him from the mirrored panel on the other side of the carriage.

Onal, the crotchety old woman who'd spent the last five decades serving as the royal family's physician and most trusted adviser, always said foul language was a clear sign of a weak mind. It was something of a joke, however, as she possessed an impressive vocabulary of vulgarity of her own and made liberal use of it. But while *she* was above reproach—mostly because no one ever dared reproach her—his own behavior was being closely observed and chronicled. That's what this tour had been all about: showing the people of Renalt that their young king was capable and ready to lead. *They're looking for reasons to remove you,* Aurelia had warned at their parting. *Don't give them any.*

He wished that she could have accompanied him on this venture, though he knew it was better that she was keeping her distance. If he wanted the people to accept his rulings, they first had to accept his rule. Best not to remind them of his ties to a blood witch suspected of bringing down Achleva's capital.

Not that Aurelia was too frightened to face her detractors; she wasn't afraid of anything. Not intolerant townsfolk or falling cities or blood spells or being alone. Not even the dark.

He gulped and found himself moving the carriage curtain aside to peer up at the black clouds gathering in the sky above. A storm was coming and, on its heels, nightfall. He sent a mildly remorseful prayer up to the heavens: *Most Holy and Merciful Empyrea, I'm sorry for swearing again. Please let us arrive at Greythorne before it gets too dark.*

He didn't used to be afraid of the dark, but in the last months, it seemed like the blackest nights heralded the bleakest events. It was in the dark that Toris had tricked him into betraying Aurelia; it was in the dark that Lisette was torn from him, never to be seen again. And it was during the darkest night he ever knew—the night of the black moon—that his beloved mother took her last breath.

Nothing good ever happened in the dark.

A deep, rolling rumble of thunder rattled the floorboards, and the carriage suddenly slowed to a stop. There was a knock at the door. His appointed regent, Fredrick Greythorne, poked his head in and yelled over another slow groan from the sky, "A storm is coming, Majesty. This road has been known to flood in heavy rain."

Fredrick's brother and new captain of Conrad's personal guard, Kellan Greythorne, was waiting behind him. He said, "We can push through or find higher ground off the path until it blows over."

Conrad leaned out of the carriage. They'd come upon the hawthorn thickets that surrounded the Greythorne property. The journey was close to its end now, and how long could the storm last, anyway? Probably just a squall, summer's last fit of anger before handing over its post to autumn. It would probably tire itself out within the hour. The obvious choice would be to just pull off the road until it did, but they were so close to the welcoming fires of Greythorne, and it was going to be night soon.

"We keep going," Conrad stated. "We push through."

"As you wish," Fredrick said, exchanging glances with his brother, and Conrad could see that they'd both have preferred the other option. But their king had given an order.

The horses pounded the path at breakneck pace until the rain started falling, coming down in heavy sheets. The carriage squelched through mud that, in minutes, became a mire. Conrad, bracing himself in a corner, felt the whole contraption sinking lower and lower into the sludge as the noises outside grew louder, until the cries became shouts and the carriage stopped with a heaving lurch, sending him toppling.

Conrad scrambled back onto his seat, craning his neck to peek through the crack between the curtain and the window sash.

There was no one there.

The road was deserted, the horses and guards all gone. There was no rain, either; it was dry and quiet, with just the whisper of a slight wind across a hazy, red-tinged twilight.

"Hello?" Conrad called into the empty expanse, his voice trembling. "Anyone there? Fredrick?" He gulped. "Kellan?"

He wanted to retreat into the carriage, to huddle and hide until his men returned from . . . wherever they had gone. But what if something was wrong?

Aurelia would never cower in a carriage and wait to be rescued.

She'd be the first one on the ground, heading boldly toward the danger, letting nothing stand in her way.

If Aurelia could be brave, so could he.

He put one gold-slippered foot to the dirt, then the other, pulling his butter-colored brocade coat after him before abandoning it, disgruntled, on the floor of the carriage. If he was going to play the role of the hero, he didn't want to look like a foppish fool doing it. The pointed shoes and high silk stockings were embarrassing enough. He would have much preferred to save the day while wearing the sterling mail and cerulean cape of a Renaltan soldier, or the long, dark coat Zan used to wear that made him look baleful and brooding, but this would have to do.

Everything was unnervingly still, as if all the insects and animals were pausing to watch what he would do. He pulled the clear glass knife from its sheath—a luneocite blade that had also once belonged to Aurelia. He'd found it among her things and decided to make it his own; the knife was small and looked fragile, like Conrad himself, but it was actually sturdier than steel. Having it on his belt made him feel stronger, too.

Ahead on the road, he saw something move. A trick of the strange crimson light, he thought at first, but then it moved again.

He squinted. "Hello?" he asked the silence.

The figure seemed to form itself from silver smoke and murky shadow, beginning as a wispy outline but quickly coalescing into a substantial, looming shape that towered over him. Conrad's eyes widened, fingers becoming slick on the handle of his small knife as the shadow further sharpened, becoming not one entity but two.

He was face-to-face with the characters of his silly folk song: a gray-cloaked rider atop a ghostly horse.

If you see him, child, in the Ebonwilde, / You might just lose your head.

"Bleeding stars!" he yelped again, swiveling on the toes of his pointed shoes and diving into the shelter of the hawthorns lining the road.

The net of branches and their needle-like spines lashed his clothing as he plunged through them. He could hear hooves behind him, coming closer and closer with each passing second. The thick-woven thatch was nearly impenetrable even for his slight shape; it should have been impossible for anything larger. But when Conrad cast a glance over his shoulder, he saw the gray rider and his silver steed pass through the thicket like smoke through a sieve.

As he ran, the hawthorn changed form too; soon, the thicket became a hedge that parted before him, revealing a cobblestone path. He took one corner, then another. Right, then left, then right again. It was a maze—Greythorne's maze. And the horseman seemed to be herding him toward the old church enclosed in the heart of it. Outside the hedge, lights winked from the windows of the familiar estate, beckoning like beacons.

He dashed forward while the horseman followed, coming closer and closer. The bells in the church tower were chiming a discordant song as Conrad swiped at the thorny tangles standing between him and the safety of the sanctorium. He strained to remember the path Kellan had taught him, turning left, then right, left again, back and forth and around again, through the twists and spirals, losing ground every time he had to backtrack after a wrong turn.

They came to the center at the same time. The horse screamed and the rider reached out from the flying folds of his colorless cloak for Conrad as he scrambled for the sanctorium steps.

For a moment, all stopped. Both figures were crystallized where they stood for the space of one heartbeat, maybe two, before the church bells went silent and everything—the ground, the air, the fabric of reality—seemed to splinter apart in a searing flash and a roaring pulse of power.

On the road into Greythorne, the rain ceased as abruptly as it started, and in the distance, the travelers could hear the bells of the Stella Regina beginning to chime the hour. Fredrick Greythorne checked in on his young charge to make sure he wouldn't be frightened by the violent lurching of the carriage as they pulled it from the mud. But when he opened the door, he found Conrad fast asleep inside, surrounded by a slew of crumpled waxed candy papers, his golden hair tousled into unkempt knots and his shoes and satin stockings in dirty tatters. He had drifted off to sleep clutching his strange, nine-sided puzzle box.

My opponent was a merchant of middle age by the name of Brom Baltus who had stopped at the Quiet Canary Tavern hoping to acquire some female company and play a couple of rounds of Betwixt and Between before hauling his goods — a cartload of apples, cheeses, and fine wines — the final stretch of his route. It was to his great misfortune that he sat down at the card table with me; when I was done with him, he'd be lucky to leave with enough coin left to hitch a ride home to his unhappy wife, let alone purchase an hour or two of a Canary girl's precious time. I'd have hated to rob them of good business, but from the smell of him, none of them were likely to mind.

Brom leaned forward to lay down his second-to-last play. His smug grin revealed a mouthful of tobacco-stained teeth. "Sad Tom," he said, pushing the card toward me. "Time to up your wager, miss, or call the game."

I frowned at the card and its depiction of a despondent, droopy-eyed lad clutching a withered four-petaled daisy. It was a surprisingly savvy move for a man who had accidentally singed his mustache try-ing to light his pipe not five minutes earlier. I'd already put down all the collateral I'd planned on staking—twelve gold crowns earned over two months of careful card-game conquests—and had little left with which to improve the pot. If I failed to provide Sad Tom with something to cheer him up, I'd lose all of it, and the cart of goods besides.

I hesitated only a moment before reaching into my pocket and retrieving the last thing of value left to my name: a fine white-gold ring set with an exquisite clear-cut stone. I hadn't worn it for months, but somehow I could not bring myself to lay it away in a jewelry box. Even now, as I placed it in the center of the table and the stone caught the candlelight and bounced it back in a thousand rainbow shards, I felt a keen sense of trepidation at the possibility of its loss. But I had plans to keep, costly plans, and Brom's goods would go a long way toward covering the costs.

"Finest Achlevan jewel crafting," I said. "Pure luneocite stone, skillfully cut and artfully set."

"And what makes you think it's worth—?"

"It used to belong to the late queen Irena de Achlev," I said. "It's engraved with her initials and the de Achlev seal." I steepled my fingers and leaned forward with a cocky tilt to my head, eyes still shrouded beneath my dark hood. "Imagine what the ladies at court in Syric would pay for such a souvenir."

Brom's eyes were gleaming—he knew exactly what kind of price it would fetch. Relics of the fallen de Achlev dynasty had become hot commodities among Syric's social elite. And to have belonged to the last queen . . . the ring was worth double the pile of coins on the table. I said calmly, "Surely Sad Tom is not so sad anymore?"

"Indeed not," the man said with a smirk. "Wager accepted. Make your next play, little miss."

Little miss. If a man had placed that selfsame wager, it would have been met with suspicion. This fool would have at least asked himself, *What kind of hand would warrant such an extravagant offer?* But because I was a woman, and a young one at that, Brom Baltus saw the move as a signal that he'd already gotten the better of me. That he'd forced me into a corner and I'd naively cast out my last line in desperation just to stay in the game.

What had Delphinia said? *You don't play the cards; you play the player.*

We were still two moves from the finale, but I had already won.

I waited for Brom to settle into his self-assuredness, using my next turn to play the Fanciful Blacksmith, resplendent in his great brown beard and frilly petticoats, hammering happily away at his forge. My opponent did just as I thought he would and mistook the balance card for a schism card and played Lady Loveless over the top of it. He sat back in his seat with a sneer, certain that he'd just secured his success.

"Lady Loveless has just sent your Blacksmith into the furnace," he said. "Time to pay up."

"Ah," I said, "but the Blacksmith stands on his own. He has no need for Lady Loveless's approval." I allowed myself a tiny hint of a smile. "Which means I have one more card to play."

I made a slow, deliberate show of turning over my last card, taking far more satisfaction than necessary in Brom's changing expression—disinterest followed closely by chagrin, shock, and dismay—as he realized what I'd done.

Staring up at him was the Two-Faced Queen.

The card depicted two versions of the same woman, one with night-dark hair against a snowy background, the other with ice-white hair against a deep black wood. They echoed each other in the exact same position, as if the line dividing them and bisecting the card was a mirror. And indeed, the card itself acted like a mirror, reflecting the players' own plays back onto them. My cards had all been balance cards, while his had been schism after schism. He had, in effect, annihilated himself.

I plucked the ring from atop the pile of coin and twirled it around my fingertips, allowing myself a single moment of melancholy before returning it to my pocket. "Now, then," I said, brusque and business-like, "where shall I collect my winnings?"

While Brom went to complain about me to the tavern's proprietor, Hicks, I went upstairs to my tiny room to stash some of my winnings away. It was little more than a closet, my room—especially when compared to the lavish accommodations occupied by the Canary girls just down the hall—but it had a big window overlooking the front entrance of the tavern and the wide, grassy expanse of the Renaltan provinces beyond. I experienced bouts of panic sometimes if things got too dark or quiet; this room and the bustle of this building suited me just fine.

The Canary girls did not understand my stubbornness at keeping the room despite being able to afford a bigger one after my winnings began to accumulate, but then they were always fretting after me. The girls were easy to like, and despite my early reticence, we became fast friends. They coached me in card-playing strategies, and during my card games, they'd sometimes drop hints about my opponents' hands. In return, I'd slip them a few coins whenever their hints proved to be especially valuable. They'd all been born with different names, but when, one by one, they came to work at the Quiet Canary, they each went through the process of choosing a new one for themselves. Lorelai, Rafaella, Delphinia, and Jessamine were what they went by now, names that had a lovely glint to them; saying them together felt like letting brightly colored jewels drip through your fingers.

Built at a crossroads between four of Renalt's remotest provinces, the Quiet Canary was always busy with dealings both above the table and below, as much a haven for the honest merchant as it was for the cutthroat highwayman. It was set just far enough from Syric to make it inconvenient for the capital to police, but central enough to make it an easy waypoint for merchants and travelers crossing from one side of Renalt to another. It was a place where you could be whoever you wanted to be, and no one would second-guess you or even care. They knew exactly who I was, but they never made me feel any different for it.

Delphinia was coming down the stairs with a client as I was going up. "Evening, Delphinia, Father Cesare," I said to them as we passed.

"You're in fine spirits. Had a good night, did we?" Delphinia asked.

"I did," I said. "You were right about using the Two-Faced Queen. Brom Baltus didn't even see it coming."

Delphinia's smile faded just a little. "Be wary of that man, Aurelia. He's a mean one—not someone to be trifled with."

I assured her, "He's aggrieved, of course, but Hicks will have him on his way in no time."

Hicks, bless him, had developed a disinterested languor in his years as proprietor at the Quiet Canary. If no one was dead or dying, Hicks preferred to be left to his hobby of whittling toys and trinkets, like the puzzle box I'd bought from him to give to Conrad. He certainly wasn't going to lift a lazy little finger to interfere with the results of a fair round of Betwixt and Between.

Delphinia did not look convinced, but I turned to Father Cesare. "Any news for me today?"

The soft-spoken priest began feeling around in his robe. "Yes, my dear," he said. "As a matter of fact, a parcel arrived at the sanctorium this morning, addressed to you from one Simon Silvis. It's why I came tonight." At Delphinia's smirk, he added, "Well, one of the reasons."

"Simon?" I asked incredulously. In the aftermath of Achlev's fall, Simon had decided to retreat into the solitude of the abandoned Assembly Hall, telling us that he preferred to dedicate the remainder of his years to quiet study, free from the daily sorrows and strain of a kingdom at war with itself. That he chose to retire to the one place in the world that could not be found by those who did not already know its location was significant; he wanted to be left alone. I could hardly blame him, but I never thought I'd hear from him again. "Why would he send something for me to you?"

Father Cesare handed me a small parcel and said, "It happens more often than you'd think. We at the Stella Regina sanctorium are well-known for our . . . discretion . . . in certain matters. We keep a more open mind than most of our fellows, especially those of the judicial

arm of the faith." He raised his eyebrows meaningfully; he was refer-
ring to the Tribunal.

I untied the twine from the package and pulled off the paper.
Inside was a book of indeterminate age, bound in leather dyed a deep
emerald and inlaid with a pale rose-gold design that looked like spindly branches. I cracked it open and began to slowly thumb through
the delicate pages. They were filled with archaic drawings of circular
patterns and strange figures, annotated in a tongue I didn't recognize.

"I don't understand," I said finally. "Why would Simon send me
this? I can't read it."

"I'm the sanctorium archivist." Cesare leaned over, lifting his
spectacles from the chain around his neck to squint at the book. "I'm
not as well-read as an Assemblyman, to be sure, but I don't think it is
immodest to say that I do have a knack for ancient vernacular. Ah, yes!
This is written in the pre-Assembly dialect preferred by the female-
led clans of the Ebonwilde. About 450 PA would be my guess."

"You're saying that that little book is two thousand years old?"
Delphinia gaped.

"Maybe not the book itself, but the language in which it's written,
yes. Give or take a few hundred years, yes."

"But what does it *say?*" I turned another page to find three human-
like outlines overlaid on one another, each inked in a different color.

"I could make out only a few of the words," Cesare said. "Let's
see . . . *Life.* Or *flesh,* maybe? *Sleep. Soul* . . ." He shrugged. "The
translations aren't exact, and I'm rusty. But I do have a few texts back
at the sanctorium that might help you with translation. If you want to
come by before the coronation tomorrow."

I stiffened but forced a smile. "Perhaps I will, if I decide to attend." I slipped him one of my new-won coins. "Thank you for bringing this to me," I said. "I know it's a long way to travel just to drop off a book." I glanced at Delphinia. "I'm glad to see you making good use of your trip."

"Oh, it is always a pleasure ministering to the faithful here at the Canary," Father Cesare said, his stout arm around Delphinia's waist. "Shall I buy you another drink, my dear, with this new wealth?"

Her red-currant lips curved into a smile. "If you *must*."

Back in my room, I tucked Simon's unusual gift into my satchel next to the bloodcloth that still carried a round, rust-colored drop of his blood before spreading my winnings out across the desk to count them. I almost had enough saved now. As soon as the coronation was over and Conrad was officially installed as king with Fredrick as his regent, I would be able to buy a room on the *Humility,* the ironically named pleasure boat owned by Dominic Castillion. The floating fortress of Achleva's self-proclaimed new king was renowned for its beauty and brutality. It was of an unusual design, powered not by wind or rowing but by coal and steam from great furnaces housed in the ship's belly, freeing up room for ballrooms and banquet halls and baths on the decks above while malnourished and mistreated prisoners toiled in oven-like heat below.

The first coins I'd won at the Canary had all gone to procuring a copy of the ship's plans from an Achlevan refugee who came through, got wildly drunk, and claimed he was formerly employed as a shipbuilder by the Castillion family and had helped the ambitious noble-

man build his fleet. Even if it was an embellishment of the truth—
or a complete fabrication—I paid him ten silver coronets to reproduce diagrams of the ship on the back of the elegant Canary-stamped
stationery Lorelai had ordered in sheaves to pen elaborate and illicit
letters to her favorite lovers.

The man had re-created the *Humility*'s schematics from his memory while completely stewed, but the sketches were startlingly intricate and full of minute details suggesting a deep familiarity with the
ship's layout. I decided to operate on the assumption that his claims
were true and spent the last eight weeks studying the drawings to
memorize every crucial detail, every weakness. As the vessel was protected by a fleet of well-armed fighting ships, the only way to get to
it was to buy my way aboard and attend the balls and feast at the banquets. Though the idea of that disgusted me, I'd do whatever it took
to end his ill-conceived attempt for Achleva's crown.

The man was a monster, and I would not rest until he and his
ship met their final resting place at the bottom of the cold Achlevan Sea.

There was a soft knock at the door. "It's open," I said, sweeping
my ship notes and coins into the top desk drawer alongside some of
my favorite past prizes: a silver hand mirror, bottles of perfume from
the continent, and jewelry too pretty to sell and too outlandish to
wear. As an afterthought, I took the luneocite ring from my pocket,
setting it on top of the pile before closing the drawer. If I didn't have
it with me, I wouldn't be tempted to wager it again.

I shut the drawer and moved to sit on the bed just before Jessamine
poked her head inside.

"I have something for you," she said, sweeping her wealth of auburn locks over one shoulder, her brown eyes bright. She had to stoop to enter, nearly hitting her forehead on the low-hanging eaves of the steeply pitched ceiling. "I don't know how you stand this," she said. "I really don't."

"I'm almost a full head shorter than you are," I pointed out.

"An infant would still find this room stifling," she said, settling next to me. "And that window, and the noise . . . How do you sleep?"

"I don't sleep much," I admitted. "And when I do, I rest better with people nearby, coming and going . . ."

"Oh, yes," Jessamine said, "You do *so* love people."

"I like knowing they're there," I said. "I don't need to be best friends with them."

"Stars save me," Jessamine said, dimpling, "you are a strange creature."

"So you've brought me something." I brightened. "Is it more Halderian chocolate? Please tell me it's more Halderian chocolate."

"Not chocolate," Jessamine said. "Better." She pulled a bottle from behind her back — it had already been uncorked.

"Wine?" I suppressed a smile. "I can't drink with you tonight, Jessa. I've got somewhere to go."

"Not just any wine," she said. "*Sombersweet* wine."

My eyebrows shot up. "Where, exactly, did you get that?"

"Brom Baltus has a dozen bottles in his cargo. It costs a fortune, but it is worth every penny."

"I guess that means *I'm* now the proud owner of a dozen bottles of sombersweet wine, as I just won his entire cart of goods at Betwixt and Between."

Her mouth dropped open.

"You can take what you want," I said. "I'm mostly interested in the apples and dry goods."

"I'm not worried about whether or not you'll share your sombersweet wine, Aurelia. I'm worried about Brom Baltus. That's a man who doesn't like to lose. And he especially won't be happy about losing *everything*."

"Delphinia said much the same thing." I shrugged. "His hurt pride is hardly my problem." My gaze shifted from the drawer with my savings back to the bottle in her hand. "How much did you say sombersweet wine would sell for?"

"Double, maybe triple, one of the Canary's own bottles."

I did the calculations in my head. That would give me *more* than what I needed; I could move my plans up by a month at least. I suddenly felt light with relief.

"Perhaps we should celebrate my acquisition," I said, taking the bottle. "Is this going to give me hallucinations?"

"Oh, come now, hallucinations? It's just supposed to make things glitter a little." She watched me take a swallow. "Anything?"

"Afraid not," I said. "No glittering. Are you sure that Baltus didn't lie? Sombersweet is rather hard to come by; not many would know if it wasn't legitimate."

"I guess I'd better drink this whole thing and see what happens," she said wryly. "Best to know for sure."

"I'll ask you for your appraisal tomorrow morning," I said, rising to reach for my wool cloak, which was hanging from a peg by the door. Then I stopped, staring at the mirror over my desk. "Did you see that?" I asked Jessamine.

"See what?"

"My reflection. For a second there, it looked . . . different. Not quite like me, exactly."

She said excitedly, "Maybe the wine causes hallucinations after all. What did you look like? A mermaid? A goblin?"

"No," I said. "I looked like me, but my hair was darker. Almost black." I gave a self-conscious laugh.

"I've always thought you'd look ravishing as a brunette," Jessamine said. "And I've got the dyes we'd need. Just say the word . . ." She winked.

"The same dyes that turned Rafaella's hair green last month?" I smiled. "Thank you, but no."

"It was only for a few days!" Jessa protested. "And her bookings went up wildly. She's even thinking about trying it again."

"Rafaella could have no hair at all and still get bookings," I said, settling my cloak over my shoulders and lifting my satchel over my arm.

"True," Jessa agreed. "Where are you off to?"

"None of your business," I replied.

She grinned widely. "Tell Kellan Greythorne I said hello."

I was in the stable, hitching my newly acquired cart to my horse—a dependable, stout mare named Madrona—when I first sensed Brom watching me, hovering just outside the building. I'd already unloaded most of the wine bottles, except for one I tucked into my sack, a gift for the coronation celebration tomorrow, even if I would not be there. Hicks had taken the rest of the bottles to the cellar, leaving me alone in the dark outbuilding.

"I know you're there," I said, latching the cart's bellyband around Madrona's midsection. "If you were planning on ambushing me, you've already lost the element of surprise. Might as well just get it over with now." To Madrona, I said, "How's that, girl? Nice and snug?" I gave her head a fond scratch. "Good girl."

Brom shambled into the doorway, hunching his shoulders forward to make himself look more intimidating. "You're a cheat," he growled. "A filthy, whoring cheat."

"Filthy?" I shook my head. "Only one of us deserves that description, and it certainly isn't me. I'm not a whore, either—I lack the natural talent. Now, a cheat? I *have* been known to bend a few rules when the occasion calls for it. Usually, that's when I come up against an especially witty and cunning challenger." I gave him an unimpressed glance. "Alas, that was not the case today."

He lunged for me, his eyes wide and shot with red, but I quickly sidestepped and sent him toppling into the stall. His anger fueled mine, and I could feel the magic respond in the blood curling in my fingertips as he scrambled to his feet and grabbed a horsewhip from where it hung looped on a hook.

He gave a few test lashes, cracking the whip into the air, a menacing grin starting over his face as he approached. The girls were right—Brom was the type to harbor a grudge.

Don't use magic, I told myself as my blood continued to roil in response to the threat. *Don't use magic.* But even after four months of abstinence, the urge had not faded in the slightest, no matter how much I tried to remind myself that a single spell could mean my death.

Giving up magic had been a necessary sacrifice: though the events of Aren's tower didn't kill me, the illness that plagued me for weeks afterward came close more than once. Simon hypothesized that I'd used more magic than my body could have created on its own, and that I was being forced to repay a debt of blood with every spell I attempted to cast, no matter how small. There was a chance the effects could fade with time, he suggested, but I could not afford to find out.

Still, as Brom came nearer, I wondered what difference there was between using magic and dying, and *not* using magic and dying.

When he got close enough to strike, I raised my arm to protect my face, letting the lash bite through the fabric of my sleeve instead. It coiled around my forearm like a snake, but I breathed through the sting and caught hold of the leather, ripping it from his hands with a sharp tug. The lash would leave a weal on my arm, but at least he hadn't broken the skin; it was always harder to keep the magic in check when blood was already flowing.

Deprived of his weapon, Brom swiped at me instead, wrapping his thick arms around my torso and pulling me down into the dirt and the hay that lay scattered on the stable floor. Though drunk and clumsy, he twice outweighed me, and rage lent him a frothing, brutish might. He pinned me to the ground, spittle clinging to the singed yellow whiskers of his mustache. I gagged.

"I'll kill you," he said, clamping one meaty paw around my neck to allow the other to procure a dirty blade from his boot. As I gasped for air and thrashed under his crushing bulk, he said, "That's the reward for witches and thieves." And he held the knife over me, ready to plunge it into my chest.

My voice scraped past the clamped passage of my throat with the last dregs of air left in my lungs. "I'm not a thief." And just as my sight began to dim, I found his eye with my thumb and drove it deep into the socket.

He screeched in pain, and I used the moment to kick him off and roll away, pulling myself up with the apple cart's wheel. Just as soon as my feet were beneath me again, he came at me with the knife, swiping and slashing wildly, half-blind but wholly committed to my obliteration. I ducked, but one of his swings caught the canvas tied across the apples, sending dozens of them spilling through the slash and across the ground.

"*Bleeding stars,*" I cursed furiously. I'd have to make quicker work of this conflict, if only to avoid losing any more of the precious cargo. Madrona, however, was delighted at the unexpected gift and watched the rest of the fight placidly munching one apple after another.

Brom was already coming at me again, but I kicked him square in the chest before swinging my fist hard against his face. My technique was short on refinement, but what I lacked in finesse, I made up for in fervor, as the fire that so often surged in my blood could be burned off in a misbegotten battle almost as effectively as in a blood spell.

Almost.

Brom had his hand to his nose, which was gushing blood, thick and bright crimson. I hated that I could feel magic in *his* blood, too—dim and distant, but undeniable. The longer I abstained from using my own blood, the louder the call came from the blood of others. But to use unwilling blood was unconscionable; indeed, the Assembly had considered it the most egregious of trespasses, the only rule a blood mage could never break without damaging his own soul.

For centuries, Cael had used the Tribunal's murders to provide himself with an unlimited supply of unwilling blood; I'd have rather died than take even the smallest step in his direction. Which meant I had to know when to call a fight I might otherwise have won.

"*Stop!*" I said as Brom made to charge again. "I'll give you the ring. Just let me take the cart."

He smiled through the blood, which was now coating his teeth, outlining them in crooked red lines. "Why would I take your trinket and leave without my cargo when I can just kill you now and get them both? And a pocketful of gold crowns besides?"

He jabbed the knife toward my belly at an angle that would have slid up under my ribs. I ducked to the side, grabbed his arm, and cranked it behind his back. He wrenched it back with a yowl, and we struggled over the knife for several seconds before I lost my grip on his arm. It snapped free of my grasp and popped back in his direction like a slingshot. He jumped back to keep the knife from slicing his belly, his heavy body slamming hard against the wooden beam behind him and the pitchfork that had been hanging from it. He slumped, glassy-eyed, impaled on the tines that were aligned with the back of his skull. They'd decapitated him internally, severing the connection between his spine and his brain; his death was immediate and utterly irreversible.

Through my shock, I thought for a second that I saw a wisp of his spirit. But if it did form, it was whisked away too quickly for me to witness it. This was how it was now; ever since the tower, there were no ghosts left in my world. No more spirits. No hauntings. At times like this, I was grateful I didn't have to deal with a vicious specter so soon after vanquishing its corporeal counterpart. But often, the lack of lingerers made the world seem less crowded but lonelier.

I was still catching my breath, staring at Brom's scarecrow corpse, when I saw a man in the doorway of the stable. I moved back.

Hicks frowned, disapproval faintly marking his otherwise expressionless face. "Bother," he muttered gruffly. "I just cleaned these stalls."

"It's not what it looks like," I said. "It's not what you think . . ."

"Brom done kilt 'imself is what I saw." Hicks pursed his lips. "His wife'll be right pleased. Some o' the girls, too."

I gaped at him.

"Get on w'ya, girl," Hicks said, shooing me away. "Yer interferin' w' my cleanin'. I'll send word to his missus. You get them goods to th' ones what needs 'em."

✶

The camp was built just outside of Greythorne Village, a makeshift collection of tents to house the Achlevan refugee families who'd come to Greythorne looking for work. Before their capital was destroyed and their country went to war with itself, they were healers, merchants, craftsmen, scholars . . . Now they were working the hardest, most backbreaking jobs Renalt had to offer to keep their families fed.

Things were slightly better in Greythorne than in other communities of Renalt. The fertile fields were well suited to growing flax for linen and raising sheep for wool, and over the decades, these advantages had given way to a thriving textile industry. But Greythorne's population was small, and it had always struggled to keep the production on pace with the demand. But despite the increased output that came with extra help at the spinning wheels and beside the coloring vats, the residents of Greythorne Village remained cold and unwelcoming toward their new neighbors. Prejudice is more resilient than the strongest dye; the villagers' hands were now free of callus and stain, but their hearts were not.

Inside the uneasy camp, my cart and I were painfully conspicuous.

In front of one sputtering fire, a listless mother rocked a squalling infant. At another, a little boy tapped a rock with a stick in a slow, lethargic rhythm. A man of indeterminate age and drooping shoulders dragged a bundle of damp firewood between the tents while a dog with patchy fur and protruding ribs panted after him.

Not one year ago, they'd lived behind Achlev's walls, untouched by raging tempests or invading armies, by fire or famine or the whims of the ferocious sea. I wasn't the one who had destroyed the city, but I'd tried to stop the destruction and failed. And the instability that came afterward, stoked by the conquest-minded Dominic Castillion, pitted nobleman against nobleman, city against city, with the innocent populace caught in between.

There was guilt to be had in that, and penance to be paid.

I stopped the cart in the center of the camp and unhitched it from Madrona while several pairs of mistrustful, uneasy eyes watched me from the tents.

"There're apples in here," I announced to the air. "And some grain; cheeses, too." When no one responded, I took Madrona's reins. "Take whatever you need," I said, backing slowly down the path to the village.

"You shouldn't feed 'em," a voice said next to me. "They're strays. Feed 'em once; you'll never be rid of 'em. Unseemly, it is, seein' a young Renaltan lady like you out alone this time of night, in such a place." She eyed my trousers and boots. "And dressed in such a way."

"And you are?" I asked with as much cordiality as I could muster.

"Lister. Prudence Lister."

"You're out rather late yourself, are you not?"

The woman grunted, shouldering a pole with a stringer of small fish dangling on its end. "If my circumstances was different, I'd not be caught dead out here. But a woman's got to eat. And now that old Mercer's given my job away to these lazy Achlevan loiter-sacks"—she spat on the ground—"I fish or I starve, simple as that."

"I'm not sure what you—"

"I been Mercer's best dyer for well on thirty year before he cast me aside for that lot." She jerked her head toward the camp behind us. "He shut down my old dyeworks, too; said with the Achlevan mordant techniques, we don't have to use urine no more! How is all that fancy fabric gonna keep its color if ain't no pee used to set it? Bah!" She held up one knobby hand, inspecting it in the moonlight. "My hands is barely stained no more," she said ruefully. Then, "You're lucky I came by when I did, to walk you to the village so as you don't come across any more Achlevan miscreants. Where you headed, anyway, girl?"

"Mercer's, actually," I said smoothly. "To pick up an order."

Her mouth puckered as if she had tasted something sour. "Mistake," she said gruffly. "Mercer's cloth is no good anymore. You don't know what kind of filth those Achlevan hands will have left on it—"

"Not urine, at least." My tone was clipped. "Good night, Mrs. Lister."

She gave me the same glassy-eyed gape as the gudgeon at the end of her pole. Without another word, Madrona and I left her by the well at the center of the village square and continued down the road toward the clothier's textile shop. When I looked again, she was gone.

It was now several hours past the setting of the sun, and most of the shops had shuttered for the night, the windows dark, the buildings brooding. I was surprised to see lights winking in the windows of the old millhouse on the outskirts of town; it had sat empty for ages, ever since a new mill had been built farther up the River Urso.

I tied Madrona up at the gate outside Gilbert Mercer's shop before making my way up the walk to pound at the door. A voice came from the other side, "We're closed!"

"Mr. Mercer," I called, "I've come to pick up the cape I commissioned? I've brought the money I owe."

At that, the locks began to jingle and the door swung open. Gilbert Mercer was a man of late middling age dressed in fine fabric stretched too tight across his midsection, his cheeks glowing a rosy color that gave him a jolly appearance but probably meant he drank too much.

"Ah, my lady! I was beginning to wonder if you'd show! I finished your project weeks ago."

"My apologies, Mr. Mercer, for the lateness, both in my coming and of the hour. I hope it's not too much of an inconvenience."

He patted my hands. "Nonsense, nonsense! No inconvenience. It's always a pleasure to work with your family, my dearest Princess."

"You were my mother's favorite, you know. She'd wait by the window for your parcels; she swore by your fabric, refused to sew with anything else."

"She was a treasure, your mother," Mercer said fondly. "Taken from us too soon, Empyrea keep her."

My breath hitched. "Yes. She was."

I waited at the front while he shuffled past the bolts of folded linens and wools into the back of his shop. While he rummaged for my order, I tried to make small talk. "Met a woman named Lister on my way over to you."

From the back, he said, "Prudence, yes. She's none too happy with me these days, I'm afraid."

"She says you fired her to hire some Achlevan refugees."

He returned with a parcel in his arms, eyeing me warily. "They do beautiful work," he said. "Their spinning, weaving, dyeing . . . I've increased my production twice over since taking them on. I would never have let Prudence go, but she was so abusive to them . . ."

"You don't have to justify anything to me, Mr. Mercer. I'm thankful that they've found work. I wish there were more in Renalt like you."

"It would be one thing if I was employing refugees out of the goodness of my heart, but I am not. I am simply capitalizing upon a boon that landed on my doorstep. They work harder than anyone I've ever had in my employ. And what work they do . . . It's exquisite. Look here." He waved me to a wire form upon which hung a dress of burgundy shot with silver, shimmering in the lamplight. The cut was simple; there were no lavish trims or intricate embroideries, but it didn't suffer from the lack. Indeed, adding anything else might have detracted from the loveliness of the fabric. "I've been importing raw silk from the isles for decades," Mercer said, "but I've never been able to render it into such magnificent cloth as this." Then, noticing my captivation, he added, "It looks to be about your size."

There was a time when I had a closet full of dresses not unlike this one, and I'd hardly worn them. What did it say about me that, now that my life was more suited to breeches and boots, I wanted a dress? I could hardly muck around the Quiet Canary dressed as a creature of the court and expect anyone to take me seriously.

Still . . . it *was* beautiful.

"What are you going to wear to your brother's coronation tomorrow, my lady?"

I made myself turn from the dress. "I wasn't planning to attend."

If he disapproved, he didn't show it. "Have you any other occasions coming soon that would call for such attire? It would suit you marvelously, I must say. And I would give you an excellent price."

Even at a discount, it would cost a mint. But I'd had a windfall earlier today; what better way to use those extra coins? If half the reports of the *Humility*'s extravagance were to be believed, I'd need the proper attire to set a single foot upon the deck.

At once dark as blood and silver as a blade, the dress was perfectly suited to assassinating a usurper.

"I'll take it," I said.

3

Mercer was wrapping the dress in a second parcel when he saw me taking a peek at the first. He said, "It turned out quite well, I think. Though I don't know why you'd want to use an old worn-out cloak to start with," he said, "when you could have had it made up new."

"It has history," I said as the package fell open. I let my hand run across the familiar blue fabric, given new life.

It was Kellan's old soldier's cloak, the one that had comforted and kept me warm during the darkest days in Achleva, now a resplendent coronation cape for Conrad. It was newly emblazoned with his king's crest, a shield bearing the Renaltan fleur-de-lis, flanked by a heraldic stag and hare.

Mercer's work was just as good as my mother always said it was: he had rendered the seal flawlessly in gold thread, adding ermine trim to the cape edges. A gold clasp with the same seal was fixed onto the front, a new symbol for the king of a new Renalt.

It would lend a sense of legitimacy to a ceremony that lacked the traditional trappings of a king's ascension. The official coronation pieces—crown, scepter, mantle—were out of our reach in the Ren-altan capital, Syric. The Tribunal, fractured as it was after Toris's death, had locked down my family's castle and turned it into a fortress, using the city's occupants as a deterrent against any attack we might consider. We could not storm it without causing civilian casualties, so we let the Tribunal scurry, ratlike, to the safety of its gilded nest. There were near-daily reports of the jockeying made by the remaining magistrates as they scrambled to hold power within their diminished regime. The names of the front-runners changed constantly—Magistrate Connell one day, Johns the next. Followed by Michaels, and eventually Orryan. Then Bachko, Arceneaux, Santis . . . too many to keep track of. It was my sincere hope that they'd slowly destroy themselves, saving us the trouble.

We'd made it clear to the people that Conrad would rule from his regent's holdings at Greythorne; he did not need a castle to be king. Dressing the part, however, certainly couldn't hurt.

I tallied up my coins as Mercer tied the two parcels together. "I'm just short," I said in dismay. "I'll have to have you put the dress back." I sighed. "Unless you'd take a bottle of wine as payment." I set the offering on the table in front of him, hopeful.

"Sombersweet wine?" He put his hand to his chest. "My dear . . . I'll owe you another dress for that!"

"If you'd prefer the coin, I can come back another day . . ."

"No, no, child. This will be sufficient, to be sure. On one condition, that is." He smiled broadly and produced two glasses from under the table. "Share a drink with me?"

I took the long way to the manor, skirting the perimeter of the village to walk off some of the effects of the wine. I hadn't seen Conrad in weeks, and I didn't want to be tipsy for our reunion.

The farmers' fields outside the village were in the last interval of growth before harvest; the cornstalks waved high above my head, protected from crows by a crude poppet wearing a horse-head mask probably salvaged from last year's Day of Shades. Beyond them, pumpkins were beginning to show the burnish of orange across the ribbed curves of their rinds, grown fat under the late summer sun. The night wind was brisk, and as it kicked up, I could hear the creak of the weathervane atop the mill as it spun in its rusty flange to point north.

The old mill, once a formidable building, was now crumbling beneath the weight of time. The water wheel no longer turned. It hung at an odd angle, the river lapping hungrily at it as it passed, waiting for the day the water would finally claim it. The thatch of the roof was patchy and thin, barely stretched over the braces, which jutted out like ribs.

The windows were filmy, but even several layers of grit could not fully dampen the light of the lamps within. A new shingle was hung over the door, carved with a rudimentary picture of a spindle. The inside was lit with low-burning lamps, and through the windows, I could make out the shapes of a dozen women, bent over spinning wheels and looms. While the village slept, these women carried on, toiling long into the night.

I remembered Mercer's words: *They work harder than anyone I've ever had in my employ. And what work they do . . . It's exquisite.*

I wondered, just for a moment, what life was like for them before

I destroyed their city. And then I hurried past, adding it to my list of questions that still hurt too much to ask.

The Renaltan flag was flying over the steep peaked roofs of Greythorne, announcing to all—including me—that King Conrad was in residence, returned from his tour. Somewhere inside those warm, welcoming windows, my brother was preparing for tomorrow's festivities, surrounded by courtiers and well-to-do callers. The great Greythorne stables would be full to the brim with the horses of visiting dignitaries, and a variety of carts and carriages lined either side of the long drive from the village square to the manor's main front door.

If I wanted, I could walk up those stairs. I could let my cape be taken, have my name announced. I could claim my place at Conrad's side as his regent. I could guide him into adulthood. That's what my mother would have wished for.

But I didn't.

Instead, I took a sharp turn to the left, cutting through the flower gardens and around to the eastern side of the grounds, and tied Madrona's reins around a garden post. "Wait here," I told her, hoisting my satchel, and giving her a pat. "I'll be right back."

From the road, Greythorne looked much like any other provincial manor: a house of dark timber and light stone, fondly watching over the little village and the rolling hills from a throne of well-tended flower beds and manicured shrubs. But as I circled around back, it became clear that the house, as lovely as it was, was built to serve as sentinel to another, more stunning site beyond: the elaborate hawthorn-hedge maze that spiraled like a bursting star from the white walls and black-slate roof of a renowned sanctorium built by the fourteenth-century monk Saint Urso.

The church of the star queen. The Stella Regina.

The sanctorium's imposing bell tower loomed as I wound my way through the narrow, overgrown paths of the maze, muttering a litany of blasphemies each time I found myself at another impasse. I thought I knew the labyrinth well enough that cutting through it to the back entrance of the manor would be easy, but I was still buzzing from the wine, and it had been a few years since I'd last traversed it. Everything looked different at night, too. Bigger. More ominous.

The maze was spooky enough already, littered as it was with unsettling statues: a narrow-eyed fox, an owl on a naked branch, a child holding a doll.

They used to terrify me. I'd been through enough now to know there was nothing to fear from immobile marble, but even so, there *was* something discomfiting about the maze and its stony occupants: an agitation, almost—as if they were somehow out of place. Lost.

Using the bell-tower spire to orient myself, I eventually found my way to the back end of the sanctorium. The entire wall was stained glass, an intricate depiction of the Empyrea descending in human form to rain fire upon heretics and sinners. The glass faced west so that the light of the setting sun would shine through it and bathe evening supplicants in the Goddess's mighty glow.

The front of the sanctorium faced east, toward Greythorne Manor, the bell-tower spire reaching high above the red-painted doors. A small plaza had been built at its base, where a fountain of still water was watched over by the stone likeness of Urso, the man who'd built all of it: the maze, the sanctorium, the statues, even the settlement that would one day become Greythorne. Fixed in the center of the mirror-like pool, he gazed into a hidden beyond with a look of melancholy longing, one hand cupped, the other extended as if reaching out for something. There was a plaque at his feet, but I had to lean over the water to get close enough to make out what it said.

In memory of Urso,
artist, architect, visionary.
1386–1445

A tendril of my hair slipped from over my shoulder and into the water, disturbing the perfect stillness with soft ripples. When they quieted, my reflection had changed.

It wasn't me. Or rather, it was—but a different version of myself. Gone were my ashy hair and silver eyes; the girl staring back in my place had hair like night and eyes like an angry ocean.

Then she spoke, whispering in my own voice.

One or the other. One or the other. Daughter of the sister, or son of the brother.

At the red moonrise, one of two dies.

I stumbled away from the fountain's edge just as the carillon bells housed in the cathedral's spire began to chime, heralding the midnight hour and the passage of one day to the next.

When the bells had quieted, I forced myself to look once more into the pool, but the apparition was gone. The reflection was mine again.

I rocked back on my feet. I'd heard that sombersweet could induce hallucinations. I just hadn't expected them to be so unnerving.

"Aurelia?"

"Bleeding stars!" I whirled around to find Kellan staring at me, arms folded. I put my hand to my chest. "Did you have to sneak up on me? I think my heart stopped!"

"I didn't sneak up on you. I said your name three times before you heard me," he replied. "I was doing a sweep of the perimeter when I saw your mean old nag making a feast out of the vegetable garden and knew you had to be around somewhere." He stopped, looking from me to the Stella Regina's bell tower. "Did you go . . . to *church?*"

"No," I said adamantly, adjusting the pack across my shoulder. "I was using the maze to get to the manor's back entrance. Wanted to get in to see my brother without alerting any of the rest of your guests."

"Really? Through the maze? I seem to recall once finding you huddled up in a corner of it, scared out of your wits."

"I was ten," I said. It was how Kellan and I first met: My mother, baby brother, and I had come to celebrate the Day of Shades festival at the end of the harvest, when old legends claimed the line between the living and the dead was the thinnest. And while there *were* plenty of spirits walking the world that night, it was the living that frightened me. Ghosts I knew. But I was unprepared for the costumed parade, where the townsfolk donned garish, oversize animal heads of plaster and paper, painted with fiendish smiles and hungry eyes. When one of them leered at me, howling in manic laughter, I had bolted straight into the hedge maze.

It was Kellan, then twelve years old, who found me hours later, crying and miserable, in a remote corner of the labyrinth.

He'd held out his right hand and said, "Don't be afraid. I know the way out. I'll see you to the end."

At the sight of us emerging from the maze, my mother showered him with thanks and praise of an equal volume to the scolding she gave me.

He began his soldier's training the next day; Mother had insisted upon it. Kellan was to be my personal guard. If she couldn't always be there to keep me from trouble, she'd enlist someone who could.

That moment, in this maze, had entwined our lives forever.

The repercussions of that event were visible even now: he was dressed in a soldier's uniform, but his cloak was the sleek gold of the captain's mantle instead of the lieutenant's cobalt blue. It was embroidered with the Greythorne family's hawthorn crest, intertwined with the limbs of a gryphon rampant. To anyone else, it would appear to signify his fidelity and fierceness in serving the king—which was true. But I knew the idea for the gryphon came from the charm I'd given him before we breached Achlev's wall five months ago. Choosing it for his cloak was Kellan's furtive way of acknowledging me as well. It was a nod to our shared history and bond, however tenuous it could still sometimes be.

He wore the new color, and the responsibility of the position it accompanied, with a stoic regality that made me wish, not for the first time, that I could go back to that long-lost moment when the thing I wanted most in the world was for him to love me.

"You were going to sneak in?"

"That was the plan, yes."

"Did the plan include attending any of tomorrow's festivities?"

My silence was all the answer he needed.

He clasped his hands behind his back—his soldier's pose. "Conrad misses you," he ventured carefully, watching me closely to gauge my reaction; we'd had this conversation before.

"You know why I stay away," I replied quietly. "I do it *for* Conrad."

"I don't think it's for Conrad," Kellan argued. "It's *never* been about Conrad. It's about you. And what happened to Zan."

"Don't," I warned.

"I've kept quiet. Kept my distance. Let you grieve. But you can't keep going like this forever. There are people—real, live, *actual* people—who need you."

I wouldn't look at him, but that didn't stop him from taking my hands. His were beautiful: chiseled and strong, with long and graceful brown fingers. They were the working hands of an equestrian and swordsman, but they looked like they should have belonged to a musician.

He paused for a second before venturing, "I sent a few men to Stiria Bay."

I yanked my hands away. "*No.* Kellan, you know that—"

"They brought back this." He took out a small folded kerchief and pulled the corners away carefully, revealing a fierce bird formed of gold and gemstones. "Aurelia." Kellan gently placed the kerchief and charm in my palm. As he moved, I could see his charm—a brother to this one—peeking out from beneath the collar of his uniform. The gryphon: Fierce, noble, loyal. Just like its bearer.

I looked down at the glimmering, jewel-studded wings of the charm in my hand.

The firebird: Beautiful. Devastating. Doomed to die, but blessed with rebirth.

And Zan *had* died and been reborn. I just wished I'd known how excruciatingly short his second chance would turn out to be.

I took a deep breath. "Did they find this with his . . . ? Did they make sure it was properly . . . ? Or perhaps . . . ?"

Body. Buried. Burned. All words I couldn't bring myself to say aloud.

"It was found washed up on shore with the rest of the debris from the wreck. There were no other . . ." Kellan swallowed, looking away. ". . . Remains."

I shoved the firebird back into his hands, suddenly desperate to remove it from my sight.

"Aurelia, don't do this to yourself," Kellan said. "You have to come to terms with all of this. You have to put it behind you so that you can heal. And come home."

"That's *enough*." There was a scythe-like sharpness to my tone; I had no interest in hearing his opinion on what my grief should look like. "I will look in on Conrad, and then I will take my leave."

"Back to the tavern, so you can continue gambling for scraps?"

"Where I go and what I do is my business, not yours."

"It used to be. Your safety was my concern—my *only* concern— for years!"

"Well, you're a captain now. Sworn to protect the king, not me. You have been released from my service."

"But not from our blood bond. Or have you forgotten about that?"

That quieted me. Of course I had not forgotten about the consequences of the bloodcloth ritual. It was always in the back of my mind.

Kellan continued, "Your life is not just yours. Perhaps you should take a little better care of it. No more gambling. No more plotting revenge against Castillion. You owe no allegiance to Achleva. You're not their queen. Zan was *barely* a king when he died. Let them solve their political problems on their own. I know you want to go back there, but right now . . . it's *dangerous*."

"You think I should just turn a blind eye to suffering? No change in regime comes without cost to the poorest and most vulnerable. Nor can we expect the unrest to limit itself to Achleva's borders. I mean —you've got a camp of refugees living right outside your window!"

"Better to have them here than you there. My men brought back stories of gangs on the streets. Militias. A vigilante, calls himself the Horseman, inciting people to violence . . . Fredrick has already helped King Conrad draft a decree offering asylum to Achlevans with useful skills—"

"And what about those who don't? Those who are too young, or too old, or too sick . . . are we going to tell them to go back the way they came? Back to the gangs, the militias . . . ?"

He paused. "If you *really* cared about what happens to the refugees, you'd be at court with your brother and Fredrick, advocating for them, working to enact laws that could *actually* help them, here in Renalt."

"You tell me I'm unsafe among the sheep and propose that I go wander among the wolves as an alternative?" I could hardly bridle my contempt. "The court is no friend to anybody. They want Achleva to burn so they can pick over the bones for trinkets to wear in their hair or on their wrists."

"Your own brother has to sit with them every day."

"It's not his blood they hunger for!" I snapped. "He's *safer* without me there. You all are."

I pushed past Kellan, moving toward the maze's exit path. Anger had sobered me considerably; I'd be able to find my way out with my eyes closed now.

"Zan wouldn't want this life for you," Kellan called after me.

His pronouncement sang like an arrow through the night air, finding its mark in my back, through my heart.

"Good night, Kellan," I managed. "Enjoy the coronation."

They said that Zan probably went softly, that he didn't suffer. That Stiria Bay was mercifully cold and he would have felt no pain, that his end would have been almost sweet. But I'd had ghosts show me their drowning deaths before, and they were neither soft nor sweet.

After the tower, I'd been so sick. So heartsore. I'd only just learned that use of magic was destroying me and that I'd have to give it up forever. I'd only just lost my mother . . .

No. I'd *killed* my mother. Traded her life for Zan's. I had intended to be the one who died on the tower, but what did my intentions matter? Mother died because of me.

It wasn't Zan's fault either. He didn't choose for me to break into the borderland of death and drag him back into the material world. That was all on me too.

It all happened because I allowed myself to love Zan. I allowed *him* to love *me*.

I was born of bloodleaf, was I not? A poison. I tried so hard to help people, to make a difference, but I only ever made things worse. And just like bloodleaf, whatever small good I worked could never match the magnitude of the havoc I'd wreak trying.

For every one life saved, two must be lost.

Six weeks after the fall of Achlev, I told Zan to go on that tour of Achleva's western coast with Baron Aylward and Baron Ingram. I told him to parley with Castillion. Forge an alliance with this rising force, the upstart lord of Achleva's snow-clad, northernmost province. *Make him your right hand. Keep him close,* I said. *We need strong people on our side.*

And I was *relieved* when Zan chose to go. And even more relieved when he suggested he go without me.

For a few days, at least, I wouldn't have to look at him and remember that, for him, I'd killed my mother.

For a few days, I wouldn't have to wonder if I'd make the same choice again, if I had to do it over.

Empyrea save me, what an idiot I was. What a starsforsaken *fool.*

It was hard, keeping myself apart from the people I loved, but it was easier than watching them hurt because of my presence in their lives.

I found Conrad sleeping, snoring softly, in the large, well-appointed chamber that Lord Fredrick and his wife, Elisa, had so generously relinquished for him when he came to Greythorne.

Cocooned in a pile of pillowy blankets, Conrad was dozing with both small hands around the puzzle box I'd commissioned from Hicks. I'd filled the box with sugar-dusted cinnamon drops, knowing Conrad would love both the puzzle and the prize. And indeed, he now slept with it tucked under his chin, as if it were a plush toy and not an oddly angled box with two pointed ends. I moved it over to the other side of him—even in his sleep, his grip on the thing was firm—and could hear something sliding around inside. It was heavier than candy; he must have solved the puzzle, eaten the candy, and refilled the box with some other childhood toy.

I touched his hair lightly, glad to see him holding on to a little piece of whimsy, and only slightly jealous of his peaceful slumber. I hadn't had a full night's rest since Achleva; my sleep was plagued with troubling dreams.

The dreams varied in subject and duration but were all exactly the same in their sharpness—so close to resembling reality, I often didn't realize the difference until I woke. Mostly, the dreams were just short revisitations to simple moments from my childhood, like getting scolded by Onal for knocking a portrait off the wall in the Hall of Kings, or watching Mother softly hum while she composed a letter at her desk.

Other times, though, the dreams took decidedly darker turns. In one, I found myself standing outside an unfamiliar cottage, listening to screams coming from inside. I'd scramble from one opening to another—door, window, cellar entrance, window—but they were all sealed shut. My body was too tangible to pass through the walls but too insubstantial to turn a knob or pick a lock. I could do nothing but listen and wait. Eventually, the screams would subside into an awful silence, and I would bolt awake, ears ringing.

The Screaming Dream, terrible as it was, was one of the easier ones. The Bleeding Dream, the Drowning Dream, and the Nothing Dream were all much, much worse. I sometimes woke from those drenched in sweat, or coughing up imaginary water, or unable to move my arms or legs for endless, agonizing minutes after becoming fully conscious.

Conrad sighed sweetly and deeply, shifting around in his blankets before settling back into deep, rhythmic breathing, one cheek rosy from being pressed against the pillow.

He'd been through so much, grown up so fast . . . and he was carrying the burden of new responsibility with an admirable degree of dignity and grace. But he was still only an eight-year-old child, one whose world had been upended in just a few short months. He'd lost his home, his surrogate sister, his mother . . .

One or the other.

My head snapped up at the sound. There was a mirror hanging on the far wall of the bedchamber in a heavy silver-gilt frame that was higher than the four-poster bed was tall. In it, Conrad looked exactly the same, but I was changed once more.

My dark-haired reflection spoke again, in a soft, papery whisper.

At the red moonrise, she rasped, *one of two dies. The firebird boy or the girl with star-eyes. If it is he, the crone will be free. If it is her, the crone is no more. One or the other. One or the other. Daughter of the sister, or son of the brother. At the red moonrise, one of two dies.*

I stumbled out of Conrad's room and headlong into Kellan, who'd come up the stairs after me. "Aurelia," he began in surprise, glancing at the guards posted on either side of the door, "are you all right? Is Conrad—?"

"Conrad's fine," I managed to choke out. "It's just . . . just . . . some dust in the air, caught in my throat."

I hurried down the hall and around the corner with the guards' eyes on me, Kellan on my heels. I barely made it out of their line of sight before I was on my knees, my spluttering coughs turning into great heaves.

"Aurelia?" Kellan pulled me to my feet as doors down the hall began to open and curious faces of the coronation guests began to peer out, courtiers mostly: Lord Gaskin, Marquess Hallett, Lady Parik. "You're not well. Come on. This way." As he passed, he announced to the watchers, "Go back to sleep, all. Nothing to worry about."

He took me to his own room and laid me down on his bed while he went to fetch Onal. My coughs had subsided, but I felt weak and wrung out, shaking like a skeletal leaf in a bitter breeze, breaths coming quick and shallow, scraping past my raw throat.

I glimpsed myself in the mirror at the end of Kellan's bed. My doppelganger was gone, and the only face looking back at me was my own. Not that it was a comfort; I looked wretched. Waiflike. Wasted. Wild. A creature of tangled hair and dark-circled eyes. And despite the chilling sombersweet-induced apparition, the most troubling thing I'd seen all day was my own unrecognizable reflection.

Zan wouldn't want this life for you.

But it didn't matter what Zan would have wanted. Because Zan was dead and gone, and he'd taken the Aurelia I used to be with him.

I woke before sunrise to find Onal sitting on the side of Kellan's bed.

"I was told that you weren't feeling well." She had a satchel slung over her bony shoulder from which she began pulling an eclectic mix of tonic bottles, setting them one by one on the table directly across from where my head lay on the pillow so that I could see exactly what she was doing. I was well-versed in her concoctions, and of this assortment, each new option was more rancid than the last. She watched my face as she lined them all up, gauging my revulsion. *If you're not sick enough to want the remedy,* she used to say, *you're not sick at all.* This was her way of threatening me back to health.

"I'm fine," I said.

"Kellan said you retched all over the hall. That doesn't sound like 'fine.'" She paused. "Are you using magic again?"

"I didn't use magic, Onal. Not last night nor any other time since Stiria, four months ago." I took a deep breath. "It wasn't magic . . . just a bad reaction to sombersweet wine. Whoever said those hallucinations were pleasant was almost certainly lying."

"You were drunk?" Her disapproval was palpable.

"I had one glass with Gilbert Mercer when I picked up Conrad's coronation cape."

Her disapproval deepened. "You couldn't handle *one glass* of wine?"

"If I didn't know any better, I'd say you're more disappointed in my inability to hold my liquor than in the idea that I got completely soused and lost my dinner in the middle of the hall."

"I'm shocked and saddened." She shook her head and *tsk*ed. "One glass. I thought I raised you better." Then she shrugged. "Lucky for you, the cure for your malady is time, rest, and water."

I threw off my blankets. "All of which can be done far, far away from here."

"It's coronation day," Onal said. "And everyone already knows you're here." She stared at me from over the wire rims of her glasses.

"Including Conrad, who was very excited to see you'd bought yourself a dress for the occasion."

"Bleeding stars," I muttered. "I left both parcels in his room last night, didn't I?"

"You certainly did."

"I don't suppose there's any getting out of it now," I said.

"At this point, *not* going might make people wonder where your allegiances lie."

"I've gotten very tired of worrying about what other people wonder."

"This is the life you were born to, whether you like it or not. Just remember: your absence is just as notable as your presence. And, at least, if you're there, you have more control over what ideas they come away with." She gave me a scrutinizing stare. "A bath has been drawn for you in the next room. Please, for the love of the Holy Empyrea, wash some of that dirt off your face and make sure your hair is twig-free before you set foot in public. And here." She put a bottle of one of her remedies down on the table. "This will ease your recovery a little, I think."

I picked up the bottle and popped the cork, giving the contents a sniff before setting it back down. "This is rat poison."

"Nonsense. It's simple chlorella elixir."

"I know what chlorella elixir smells like. This is not it."

"Oh, yes. Chlorella elixir is in the blue-violet bottle; now I remember. Curse these aging eyes." Her tone was regretful, but her smile was not. "Though many of the ingredients in this are very healing. Except for the cyanide, of course."

"Except for that." I crossed my arms. "Did I pass the test?"

"Well enough."

"What would have happened if I didn't recognize the poison?"

"You'd have died a very painful death, most likely. But it would have been your own fault, really, for not remembering your lessons."

"Onal, it's been ten years or more since my herbology lessons."

"Then it's a good thing you didn't forget. But if you would like to resume your education in herbology and give yourself something to do besides feeling sorry for yourself, I could possibly be convinced to take you on again as a pupil."

"You think that making me memorize which roots cure nausea and which act as laxatives is going to help *me* feel better?" I gave a mirthless laugh.

"It's an important distinction," she said. "And yes. I do."

"Why? What could you possibly know about how I feel right now?"

"You're a fool, girl, if you think you're the only one in the world to be hurt by love. Or its loss." Her pinched lips twitched ever so slightly. "I've lived a good long while, young lady. I've seen and experienced more than you could ever dream. It's because of my infinite wisdom and patience that I will, this once, choose to overlook your impudence and not simply do away with you and tell everyone it was an accident."

"That would be so much more believable if you hadn't just attempted to dose me with rat poison."

She pointed the bottle at me like a scolding finger. "Get up. Get dressed. Get to work."

"And do what?"

She dropped the bottle into her bag and said, "Whatever it takes. You want things to be different? Work to make them different. Work until your back aches and your fingers bleed and everything hurts so bad, you forget the pain in your heart." Quieter, she added, "You can't ever outrun something you carry inside you. Don't waste your time trying."

I tipped my head sideways, really looking at her. This woman had practically raised me, and I was struck by how little I really knew about her. She was outspoken and irascible, quick to share her opinions, and yet somehow never talked about herself, not really.

She grew uncomfortable under my gaze and went to the door. "You have until noon to wash and dress in a chemise. Your lunch will be delivered here then—unless you'd rather attend the banquet? Ha, I thought not. At one, a maid will help dress you. At two thirty, another will attend to your hair. And at four, another will come to powder your face and put some color into those pasty cheeks of yours. Hopefully, you'll be somewhat presentable in time for the procession, which will start at five."

"You think I require *eleven hours* to become 'somewhat presentable'?"

"At least. A week would have been better, but we have to work with the circumstances we've been given. And all of this is assuming you won't simply change back into your slovenly farmer's wear and escape into the wild the instant I leave this room."

"Well," I said, reluctantly eyeing the dress laid out on the bed, "if the king desires my presence at his coronation, I suppose I have no choice but to stay. Are *you* going to be there?"

She scoffed. "Are you jesting? I wouldn't be caught dead."

✸

The dress I'd bought from Mercer was even more beautiful in the daylight, the color of ripe raspberries shimmering in morning dew. It fit me exactly, too, sweeping in a wide arc from one shoulder to the other, creating a perfect parallel to the cut of my clavicle.

The housemaid Onal had bullied into helping me was a reticent, reluctant girl named Nina; she tugged and teased my hair into a half-dozen of the most current styles, only to nervously unpin it as many times more, afraid Onal would find the work unsatisfactory. After the seventh failed attempt, I thanked and dismissed her, letting my hair tumble loosely over my shoulders instead.

Zan liked it that way the best, free to be lazily twirled between his fingers.

I was trying to banish those painful thoughts when Kellan knocked softly and entered.

"I was supposed to be drinking with Jessamine tonight," I said with a sigh. "She'll be sorry I stood her up."

"I've met Jessamine," Kellan said, "and I think she'll manage fine without you."

He came to stand behind me as I studied my reflection in his tall, gilt-edged mirror.

"I brought something for you," he said. "A final touch."

He moved my hair aside and lifted his hands over my head. Strung between them was a black velvet ribbon, upon which hung a single ornament: Zan's firebird charm. Paired with the crimson dress, the gems became incandescent, sparking fire with the slightest turn.

The firebird settled into the hollow of my throat as Kellan said, "It's not my place to tell you how to feel. I know that. But I know what this meant to him. And to you."

"Thank you," I said with as much sincerity as I could muster.

"I've got to get back to the party," he said. "Father Cesare said that you should head up to the sanctorium before the procession begins. He has a book he wants to show you."

I nodded, secretly relieved. In Syric, the coronation procession wove in and out of the streets, running from the castle to the Grand Empyrean Basilica on the other side of the city, a five-mile journey with the citizenry gathered on each side to cheer and cast flower petals under the feet of the processional participants. I'd never seen it myself, as my father ascended to the throne many years before I was born, but I heard the stories from my mother, who'd describe the events in intricate detail while I absorbed every word with bright eyes.

This would be a procession in miniature, winding through the maze from Greythorne Manor to the steps of the Stella Regina; a nod to tradition, at least, on aging cobble instead of gleaming silver stone, scattered with leaf litter rather than rose petals. The Stella was no Grand Basilica, but it had a simple, exquisite kind of beauty: white marble pillars and crimson doors, crowned by a gleaming black roof. And it had a lauded place in royal history: Praying at the Stella Regina before the end of the Renalt-Achlevan war, King Theobald said that the Empyrea herself had come to him in a dream and commanded him to offer the next female heir of his line to the next prince of Achleva. It was, in a sense, the birthplace of the treaty that would one day bind my fate to Zan's.

Though I could hear voices and laughter coming from the direction of the banquet hall, I turned gratefully in the other direction; there was not much I wanted to do less than go rub shoulders with the same people who'd witnessed my reckless attempt to save Simon at the last banquet I'd attended in Syric. I slipped out the back service entrance into the cool afternoon air.

In preparation for the procession, the monks of the Stella had tied blue ribbons into the hedges along the proper path to the church so that no one would get lost on the way in. I wished they'd been there the night before but was glad enough for them now. I was only a few steps in, however, when I heard someone come up behind me.

"Aurelia?"

I turned to find my brother at the mouth of the maze. He was wearing the new cape I'd left at his bedside, his dark golden curls gleaming against the cobalt blue of the fabric. He also wore a doublet of gold brocade and a shiny new pair of gold-buckled shoes.

I hugged him quickly. "Don't worry, little brother. I'm not leaving. I'm just heading up to the sanctorium a little early. I'm going to talk to Father Cesare and then pick out my seat. Don't want to risk getting stuck behind Lady Gaskin and that three-foot bird's nest she calls hair." I felt a sharp jab in my ribs. "Ouch! What is—"

He had been holding the narrow, point-ended puzzle box when I hugged him. He quickly hid it in his tunic and went about brusquely straightening and smoothing his cape and clothes. "Aurelia," he said, more businesslike than a child carrying around a toy had any right to be, king or not, "I am not worried that you won't be there tonight. I know you will be. I needed to talk to you because . . . Here. Take this." He looked over both shoulders to make sure we were alone before thrusting an object into my hands.

It was my luneocite dagger. I'd laid it away in one of my trunks after Simon forbade me to use more magic; Conrad must have rifled through my things to retrieve it.

"Conrad," I said, sucking in a breath, "why do you have this? It's not supposed to be—"

"It's *important,*" he said insistently. "Just keep it with you. I mean it." His eyes, when they met mine, were grave.

I palmed the knife, quickly tucking it in the pocket of my dress. "You *know* I can't use it. Why . . . ?"

"Just do it," Conrad said. "I have to be getting back before they start wondering where I am—Stars, they've been watching me like *hawks*. Keep it with you," he said again before hurrying back the way he came, toward the manor. "You're going to need it."

The Empyrea was usually depicted as a white winged horse, but the Stella's slate roof, white walls, and red doors were designed to honor the Goddess's human beauty as described by King Theobald: hair black as night, lips the color of a blood-red rose, and skin white as fresh-fallen snow. The gaudy, gilded halls of the Tribunal's Grand Basilica were lined with depictions of angry angels and paintings of vengeful spirits; the Stella, in its simplicity, was its complete opposite. It was almost peaceful.

Inside, the hall was cavernous and quiet, filled with white light from tall windows. A balustraded balcony circled the marble aisle of the nave, which was lined on each side by mahogany pews. A berobed figure was bent over the lectern next to the altar, where a floral crown waited atop a velvet pillow. With the real crown jewels locked away by the Tribunal, the Stella's monks had created a stand-in headpiece made of symbolic plants: leaves of olive and laurel entwined with late-blooming hawthorn blossoms.

Behind the altar sat the heavy golden chair that would act as the throne to which the king would ascend. Less ornate chairs flanked it on either side: seats for Conrad's regent, Fredrick Greythorne, and his wife, Elisa. Plus another for Conrad's chosen captain, Kellan.

I wasn't sure if I was sad or thankful that there was no chair on the dais meant for me.

My heels clicked on the tile and reverberated through the airy rafters. The man at the lectern looked up with a start. "Oh, hello, child," Father Cesare said, hurriedly attempting to hide a tall bottle behind an altar cloth. "Reviewing the script again. Just trying to keep my lines fresh in my mind," he said.

"Why, Father, are you nervous?"

He wiped a bit of sweat from his brow with a handkerchief. "A little," he confessed. "I've been giving sermons here for near on three decades. But I've never had so many gentlefolk in attendance to watch, nor ever presided over a ceremony as . . . auspicious . . . as this one."

I eyed the bottle he had attempted to hide. "No doubt the Canary's wine will help you through it," I said, smiling. "Is that sombersweet?"

"Jessamine sold it to me," he said. "Bought five bottles for the

Day of Shades. It's very good, though. Not sure it's going to make it that long."

"Be careful with it," I warned. "It has some unfortunate side effects."

He laughed and closed the book on the lectern. "I am very glad you decided to come, my lady. When we spoke last night, I felt sure you intended to stay away from the celebration."

"When we spoke last night, I did intend to stay away."

"The young lord Greythorne can be persuasive, I'll admit."

"Stubborn, you mean."

"Yes, that too."

I smiled. "Kellan said you had a book to show me. I assume you found something that might help me decipher Simon's . . . gift?"

"Yes, yes. It is in my study. This way, if you please." I followed him into the north transept hall, past the iron-grate door demarcating the end of the sanctorium's public space and the entrance into the private living areas belonging to the Ursonian monks, then through a side room that was empty save for four simple cots lined up in a row.

Over his shoulder, Cesare said, "The young lord Greythorne was here when I got in this morning. I think he must have slept on one of the pews."

"That was my fault. He let me take his room. He should have stayed in there with me, but he's too genteel for his own good."

"Well, he could have taken my cot. I *had* intended to return last night, but Delphinia kept me very late and then convinced me to stay. Thought it best to rest at the Canary and get a fresh start this morning. She has an insatiable thirst—"

I put up a hand. "Please, you don't have to describe—"

"—for *knowledge,*" he finished. Then he gave a good-humored shrug. "And other things, too, of course. But in those matters, I must confess, I am more student than teacher."

On the other side of the bunk room was the door to the library and study. Sheaves of paper and ink-stained quills littered every surface not occupied by stacks of books. And books were everywhere —lining the shelves, piled into waist-high towers, wedged into every corner.

I walked past the bookshelves, observing the titles in turn. "So where is this book you told Kellan about?"

"Not there," he said, and turned to the only section of wall not covered by shelves or stacks of books. Then he tapped it in three seemingly random places. To my surprise, the wall swung open, revealing a secret closet behind it, where even more books were stashed. "We keep the most precious of our collection in here, and all of Urso's writings. He was a seer, did you know? Normally, such a gift would have been persecuted by the Tribunal, but even they could not deny that it could come only from the Empyrea herself. In fact, they spent many years trying to get their hands on our collection." He smiled. "They could never find it, though. Urso saw to that." Cesare selected a book from the top, blew a cloud of dust from its cover, and passed it over to me. Then he closed the closet again, and it disappeared so completely into the wall, it was as if it had never been there.

I looked down at the book in my hands.

Mane Magicas, it read. *Early Magics.*

Cesare said, "It's written in a mix of archaic pre- and

post-Assembly dialects. I assume you're familiar enough with post-Assembly language?"

"*Satis scio,*" I replied. *I know enough.* "How did you come by this book?" I asked. "No sanctorium in Syric would so much as dare . . ."

He smiled and patted my hand. "The monks of the Order of Urso have long been friends to witches. A tradition passed on from Saint Urso himself. He built little secrets into all of his work. Some small, like that compartment, for hiding books on witchcraft. And others large enough to hide witches themselves." He gave me a thoughtful look. "Apologies if that term is offensive; I forget sometimes that real magic users prefer more respectful titles."

"I'm not offended by it," I said. "Simon once told me that 'witch' was a coarse term, and that the Assembly preferred to call themselves mages. But the Assembly is gone now, and I was never one of their number. I have no reason to adhere to their nomenclature." I paused. "You knew I was a witch?"

"Oh, child," he said gently, "everybody knew. We watched to see what would happen to you, but we had hoped that your position and parentage could protect you. Much to our shame, we were wrong."

"What could you have done," I asked, "if my circumstances were different?"

"We have our ways." He smiled, gesturing widely. "Saint Urso designed dozens of buildings in this province. The Stella, the manor, the maze. Even"—his eyes twinkled—"a certain tavern situated conveniently at the crossroads between the east-west and north-south highways of Renalt."

I lifted an eyebrow. "The man who created the Stella Regina also built the Quiet Canary?"

Cesare nodded. "The continuity of his work is more in the structural elements of his designs and less in the superficial, outward appearances."

"You're saying the Canary has secret hiding places as well?"

"It does indeed. Not that I'd be able to find them; they are not included on any diagrams or plans. Safer that way." He motioned to the chair behind his desk. "Sit. Read awhile. When the bells chime, you'll know that the procession has arrived. You remember how to open the compartment?"

I nodded.

"Good. Make sure it gets put properly away," he said. "Even in these new times, it is better to be safe than strung up on the Tribunal's gallows."

He left me in the warmth of the study, two books spread open before me. It was slow going at first trying to find printed symbols in *Mane Magicas* that matched the intricate scrawlings in Simon's book. The first breakthrough was when I recognized the word *tempus*. In the post-Assembly archaic language, that meant "time." Beside it, a symbol that looked like a wheel. I rifled through the delicate pages of the green leather book, and there it was. The exact same wheel-like hieroglyph.

I grabbed a sheet of parchment and opened a bottle of ink. *Wheel shape: time.*

The translations came slowly, but I made good progress. My paper was soon full of knot-like patterns and pictures and their accompanying translations. *Birth. Mother. Cycle. Maid. Star. Bell. Sorrow. Joy. Death.*

I paused on the last one, ink dripping from the point of my pen and leaving blood-like black splatters on my parchment next to that word.

Death.

But the translation wasn't right, not quite. I looked from *Mane Magicas* back to the symbol book and struck through the word *death* with two dark lines. Then, beneath it, I wrote a more accurate interpretation.

Nothing.

Just then, the bells in the tower began to chime, filling the silent room with a discordant clangor that vibrated into my bones. I pushed the chair back, hurrying to fold the parchment, though the ink was not yet fully dry, and slide it between the pages. I gathered my books up and picked my way through the stacks to the wall to mimic Cesare's taps. When it swung open, I shoved the two books inside and then slammed the door shut just as the bells finished their hymn and fell silent.

The procession had arrived at the sanctorium's front door. It was time to crown a king.

T he pews on the first floor were all too exposed; I took the stairs past the hatch to the belfry and found a secluded place to stand on the balcony. Others began to fill in the spaces beside me, village folk and manor workers, mostly, but no one looked at me twice. I was just another celebrant, come to watch a new king take his throne. Through the pointed-arch windows, I could see the cerulean flag of Renalt waving above the maze.

When the common folk had filled the balcony and the aisles of the ambulatory, a herald began announcing the courtiers as they arrived and shuffled into the pews. *The Marquess of Hallet. Baron Henry Fonseca. Lord and Lady Leong. Duchess Amin and guest.*

I kept to my corner until every empty space was occupied, and then I realized that my view of the dais was completely obscured by the throng of buzzing people clamoring for a peek at my brother. Conrad's tour must have been a smashing success; there were far more in attendance than I ever dared hope.

I pushed through the milling crowd, trying to elbow my way to the balcony balustrade, where children were waving sticks tied with streamers over the edge and laughing joyfully.

"Lord Fredrick Greythorne," the herald called, "regent of Renalt, and his wife, Lady Elisa Greythorne."

Fredrick, his wife on his arm, gave thoughtful nods to the gathering as they both walked the length of the nave and came to stand in front of their chairs behind the altar.

"Captain Kellan Greythorne," the herald called, "head of the king's guard."

Kellan, white-gloved hand on the pommel of his sword, had his chin held high as he walked alone to the dais, stopping on the other side of the throne from Fredrick.

"And now, all rise for His Majesty, Conrad Costin Altenar, High Prince of Renalt."

Kellan and Fredrick both drew their swords—Kellan bearing the gold-hilted blade of the king's guard, and Fredrick bearing the Greythorne family's blade, its hilt forged to look like twisted hawthorn. They crossed them over the king's throne as my brother began the walk down the marble aisle of the nave, the final length of his journey toward the royal seat. Two ushers closed the doors behind him, and the hall settled into an expectant silence.

As he got closer, the curtains that covered the stained-glass window were parted, letting the image of the Empyrea look down upon our ascendant king. Light shone through and around her open arms, as if she were welcoming him into a heavenly embrace. At the end of his walk, Conrad bowed to Fredrick and Kellan, then turned. The glow from the window lit his golden hair like a halo; he didn't even need a crown.

At that moment, there came a heavy pounding on the other side of the crimson doors.

Thud. Thud. Thud.

Then the courtiers in the pews began to whisper, looking to one another in confusion. Who would dare interrupt this ceremony after it had begun?

The knocks came again.

Thud. Thud. Thud.

Hair prickling on the back of my neck, I looked back to the dais, where Kellan and Fredrick were leaning protectively over Conrad. Their swords were no longer crossed above him but were held in a wary stance on each of his sides, a cage of two blades.

From within the crowd, people began to move, separating themselves from the rest of the onlookers, doffing capes and cloaks to reveal black-collared Tribunal uniforms beneath. I stood frozen as they all gathered at the transept—there must have been two dozen at least— and stood in a line. Side by side, they looked like the avenging angels depicted in the frescoes of the Grand Basilica clad in flesh and dispatched by the Empyrea to rain retribution down upon the proceedings from which they had been wrongfully excluded. One of them took Father Cesare by the cowl of his robe and laid a blade to his neck while another went to the doors and threw them open.

There stood a woman all in white, her hands clasped in an exaggerated approximation of prayer to the Empyrea. Slowly and sedately, she walked down the nave, stopping at the foot of the dais before swiveling to look up at the balcony.

Her gaze fixed itself on the person at the center of it. Me.

"Ah, Princess Aurelia," she said. "So glad you're here."

My voice did not shake. "Magistrate Arceneaux," I replied. "I wish I could say the same."

6

sobel Arceneaux was beautiful. It was the first and easiest thing to assess about her, and the most deceiving.

She walked the dais with a dangerous grace, her hair pulled back from a high-cheekboned face, her eyes dark and flinty. As a magistrate, she'd always been one of the most stringent in her observations of the Founder's Book of Commands, the least merciful in her judgments. Toris himself had singled her out from the other clerics early on in her career. Had she been a man, I'd have put money on her to take his place in the Magisterial Council. But she had the misfortune of being a woman; while the reports from Syric had mentioned her name once or twice in passing, I never thought she could wrest any real power from the tight fists of the cretinous old men who made up the magisterial majority. Those goblins would rather die than let a woman lead them.

That she was here now meant that they'd likely gotten their wish.

"Join us, Princess," Arceneaux said. "Don't hide in the shadows. It's your brother's coronation day!"

The people parted for me, making a path to the stairs. I took them slowly; whatever game Arceneaux was playing, I was in no hurry to become a pawn in it.

"Magistrate Arceneaux," I said loudly, "how good of you to come. But the festivities started early this morning. You're late. And as I recall"—I cast her a withering stare—"uninvited."

A white cape hung from the stark line of her shoulders. Her high, stiff collar distinguished the strong line of her jaw and the severe sweep of her dark hair from her brow. She gave her cape a swish as she lifted her gaze to me. Her irises were a disconcerting, deep arctic blue—only a few shades darker than the cold, cornflower eyes that still sometimes troubled my dreams.

"My apologies," Magistrate Arceneaux said. "I did not mean to interrupt, but the Tribunal has been officiating the Renaltan coronation ceremony for the last five hundred years. We come to honor that tradition."

"The Tribunal's time is over. This is the beginning of a new day. For Renalt. For all of us. You can't stop this."

She held me in her cool gaze for a long moment. "Strong words from you, Princess, caught as you are—excuse me, were—between two callow kings: one without a country, the other without a crown."

At the mention of Zan, I stiffened. She motioned to one of her acolytes, and I noticed her gloves for the first time: blue-black and marbled with dark colors that shifted as she moved, like oil stains or beetles' wings, with satin laces crisscrossing up past her elbows and punctuated by silver buttons. They were a jarring contrast her to ice-white robes.

She said, "At least, with one of these problems, I can be of assistance. Lyall, if you please."

Bowing at her feet, an acolyte—tall, rail-thin, fair-haired—presented a satin-draped parcel. As the fabric fell away, the silent watchers in the pews let out a collective gasp.

It was my father's crown, a circle of white-gold tines studded with oval sapphires and diamond-encrusted stars. The homemade headpiece of sticks and twisted stems on the altar looked flimsy and fragile next to the weight of gold and the history of a hundred kings.

"I don't want to stop our king's ascension," Arceneaux said. "On the contrary, I wish to help prop him up, to assist him in his righteous rule. It is, as you say, a new day for Renalt. As the recently appointed leader of the Magisterial Council, I welcome the opportunity to work side by side with King Conrad and his regent. It is for this reason that I and my associates here will be setting up a permanent residency in Greythorne Village. So that we can be on hand to watch and guide him."

I felt my hackles rise.

Watch. Not watch over. Just *watch*.

Arceneaux lifted my father's crown and brought it over to me. "Generally, the king's closest relative is asked to present the crown. Whether we like it or not, that's you."

I raised my hands to accept the offering; I didn't know what else to do. As my fingers and hers touched, I felt a quick, sharp sting. I didn't see the implement she used—likely, it was some kind of needle hidden in her gloves—but I saw her smile twist as she stepped away. "There you go, now. Crown your brother. Name him king."

I mounted the first step toward the altar. Was there poison in the pinprick? Had she assassinated me in one single, subtle move? But I didn't feel any sudden frailty or faintness. Just the familiar spill of magic from the tiny droplet of released blood waiting for my command.

Stars above. *Magic.* Was she trying to draw out my magic?

I approached Conrad with caution, gauging his expression, but he didn't seem scared or even surprised. The only thing that betrayed his apprehension was how tightly he was clutching that silly wooden box. I gave a clumsy bow and situated the too-large crown atop his golden curls.

There was a long, laborious script meant to accompany this moment, but Father Cesare was immobile on the dais, a knife still pressed to his neck, eyes glazed with fear. I cast around in my memory for the words and found none. Instead, I put my hands on my brother's shoulders and said, "You are king now, Conrad. Be a good one."

From behind me, Arceneaux said, "All hail Conrad, king of Renalt. Long live the king."

The audience reluctantly repeated her words, and Conrad raised a hand in response to their listless cheer.

Arceneaux's voice rose again, filling every corner of the hall. "Now, for the first order of business, dear king. There is an enemy of your people here, even now, hiding in plain sight among you." She walked the length of the nave, her white cape swirling. "Our long-held laws state unequivocally that any invasion by a hostile foreign power must be met with our full military might, and all who aid and abet our enemies must face trial by fair tribunal for treason."

"No one has invaded our land, Magistrate," Kellan spoke up. "We have no quarrels with our neighbors."

"I do so wish that were true, Captain Greythorne," she said. "But we *have* been invaded, and if we don't do something about it now, the Renaltan way of life that we all cherish will be taken from us, little by little, until there's nothing left. How many of you here"—she lifted her arms to the watching nobility—"came today not simply for the privilege of watching a new king ascend, but also to ask the ascendant king to do his duty on your behalf?"

A wave of affirmative whispers and nods crossed the pews.

Arceneaux paused to let them steep into the atmosphere. Then she said, "We all want to know, King Conrad, what you plan to do about the Achlevan infestation."

I curled my pinpricked finger into a tight fist to muffle the urge to send magic lashing out against her. Wasn't that what she wanted? To provoke me into demonstrating my magic in front of this collective? To turn me and mine into something monstrous so that she and hers could justify murdering us? And despite all the hunts and trials and executions Renalt had performed over the generations, it was likely that none of these assembled courtiers had ever witnessed real witchcraft. I did not relish the idea of being the one to turn their amorphous anxieties into indisputable reality.

"Infestation?" I hissed.

"Lord Gaskin?" Arceneaux said, pointing to the reedy, pepper-haired man near the front. "Six days ago, an undocumented Achlevan vessel docked without permit in your port. Can you tell us what was on it?"

"Achlevan miscreants," he replied readily. "About a hundred of them. Dirty, squalid, riddled with disease. They wanted to sully my city with their filth. Of course, I did not allow them off the boat."

"Leopold, Marquess of Hallett? Your land is not far from the border of the Ebonwilde. What have these last weeks been like for you?"

"We were in the middle of my mother's funeral," the marquess stated nervously, eyes darting from me to Conrad and then back again. "And we saw them coming down one of the old army trails from the woods. A caravan of at least ten wagons, two dozen men and women and so many children I couldn't keep count. They looked like animals—wild and unkempt. I had my men herd them to a campsite outside our limits so the good folk in my town wouldn't have to see them."

My lip twitched. "These people you call animals, miscreants, vermin . . . they are *refugees*. Good people! Hard workers. Families . . . men and women who have lost everything and have faced unimaginable hardship looking to start a better life! What kind of devils must you be to see their suffering and still turn them away?"

"She calls you devils!" Arceneaux said, advancing on me. "She disparages you, the faithful, the beloved chosen of the Empyrea, in favor of the Achlevan invaders."

"No," I retorted steadily. "I am for the peaceful sharing of our resources with those in need, whether they be Renaltan, Achlevan, or any other country asking for our aid. What would *you* do, all of you, if the tables were turned? If *you* had lost everything, only to be spurned at the gate by the people who could save you?"

"Our resources are stretched thin as it is," Arceneaux said. "And if things carry on as they are, our economy, our traditions, our very lives will be threatened." She paused. "But that's what you want, isn't it?"

My nails were biting into the skin of my palms—if I wasn't careful, I'd draw more blood. I wondered how long I could maintain control of myself if that happened.

I joined her in the aisle, addressing the pews beseechingly, "My fellow citizens, I ask you to listen. I understand that you're afraid. Of me, of Achleva, of what you don't understand, of a future that can't be known." My soft entreaty was quickly taking on the hard edges of a demand. "But we *will* take in the refugees. We *will* give aid to the lost and needy. And we *will* become better for it!"

Arceneaux moved with a predatory grace. "Do you think to speak for the king, Aurelia?" My name without a title—she was artfully sabotaging my already flimsy authority.

"You are on dangerous ground," I said tightly. This close, her perfume was sickeningly sweet, a musky floral that made my head ache.

She said, "We'll see."

Dread was twisting into a dark funnel inside me. This was her crescendo, her big move. If it were a game of Betwixt and Between, this was her setup to play the Two-Faced Queen.

"I submit to all here," she declared, "that Aurelia Altenar, a blood witch known to have caused the destruction of the walled city of Achlev and thus Achleva's subsequent descent into civil war, has been conspiring with her lover, the former king of Achleva, to overtake Renalt and subjugate its citizens."

"I haven't! And that's impossible, anyway! Valentin is *dead*." My voice cracked. "Zan is dead. How dare you invoke his name—"

But Arceneaux continued over me, "When she speaks of a new age, mark it: she means an age bathed in blood and witchcraft. Where ordinary, innocent people like you and me are little more than servants and slaves to her wicked whims."

"Lies!" I declared furiously. "Every last ridiculous word. All lies." I pushed the words out through my bared teeth. "I want only peace! Equality! Equanimity! Tolerance—"

"I don't expect anyone to believe my word alone," Arceneaux said. "I've come with proof. Lyall"—she gave a decisive wave of her gloved hand—"and Golightly. Bring in our honored guest."

The two acolytes went out the crimson doors while the occupants of the church waited in uneasy silence. I traded a tense glance with Kellan, but when my gaze moved to Conrad, it found him sitting with his hands resting in his lap, quiet and composed.

The acolytes returned moments later, dragging a man between them. He had a sackcloth hood covering his head, and blood from his clothes left a crimson streak across the pristine marble floor. When they reached the head of the nave, the second acolyte, Golightly, yanked the man's head back and ripped off the hood as the audience gasped.

My world stopped.

I stared, as still as an insect in amber. Unable to move. Unable to think. Unable to breathe.

My bones were leaden, but my blood began to surge through the concourse of my veins, hot and heady, like the strongest of spirits set suddenly aflame.

Zan.

Zan.

Alive.

Beneath his coat, his linen shirt was torn and mottled with blood-stains, of both old rust and fresh ruby. He was gagged, but through the dark strands of his hair, his eyes, emerald green and glinting with golden fury, met mine.

The magic in my blood responded to the sight of Zan in danger by battering against my skull and the skin of my fingertips. To quiet it, I tried to employ the calming methods he'd once taught me. *Breathe in. One, in. Two, out. Three, in. Four, out* . . . But I might as well have been using a bellows to quench a fire; the flame of my anger fed on the air and grew.

"Release him," I said through clenched teeth. "He is a *king*."

"He's not *my* king," Arceneaux replied. "Or yours. Or even Achleva's, really, as they seem to have already found a replacement, and this one was supposed to be dead."

The pinprick in my finger burned as the magic, fueled by my wrath, demanded release and retribution.

But that was what Arceneaux wanted. I would not give in.

Golightly and Lyall dragged Zan up the nave and pushed him to his knees at the altar in front of Conrad.

"If I'm wrong about you, Aurelia," Arceneaux said carefully, "now is your chance to prove it."

Golightly stepped aside as Lyall pulled a Tribunal blade from the black scabbard at his hip and placed it against the back of Zan's bent neck.

Kellan and Conrad were silent as Zan tried not to shudder; one wrong move could permanently relieve him of his head.

"Give the order," Arceneaux whispered into my ear as I trembled. "Prove your loyalty. Say the word."

"May I speak, Magistrate?" It was Father Cesare.

Arceneaux's expression wrinkled just a little, but she gave a nod and a snap of her fingers, and the cleric released his grasp on the old priest. "Say what you need to say, Father."

"While I appreciate the good magistrate's desire to root out the disloyal, I wonder if perhaps there could be another time and place to conduct this kind of meeting. This is a holy house, a refuge from tribulation. It is not meant to hold trials."

Cesare came to stand beseechingly before Conrad. My brother's eyes flicked from Arceneaux to the priest. "There are many interpretations of our Book of Commands," Cesare continued shakily, "but I choose to believe that our divine Empyrea is a goddess of light and peace. She would not want this."

"Would she want us to believe the word of a drunken priest who spends more time cavorting with whores than ministering to his own flock?" Arceneaux's voice was flat. "We know about your dalliances, Father." Her eyes slid to mine. "We know everything. Including your allegiance to *her*. A known witch. We have here" — another acolyte scurried to thrust a bundle of papers into her hands — "letters between our late queen Genevieve and this priest acknowledging Aurelia's witchcraft and conspiring to smuggle her from the country to keep her from ever having to face fair trial." She shook the papers. "Dated eleven years ago. Locked away in her desk and discovered only when it was removed and dismantled."

I closed my eyes; they'd gone through my mother's effects. Destroyed her belongings. I wondered what, if anything, would be left of her in the castle that had once been our home.

"The priest is a witch lover!" someone shouted. "An enemy of the Empyrea!"

Father Cesare tried to reach for Conrad. "No, Majesty, I—"

"Stop him!" another voice cried. "He's going after the king!"

I screamed as two of the acolytes stepped forward and ran Father Cesare through with their weapons, both at once, with eerie precision and without pause.

The priest's body was suspended between them for several silent seconds, skewered by blades from both directions, until they withdrew their swords and it slid off, slumped backwards over the altar, and crushed the floral crown beneath its weight.

"May the Empyrea have mercy on your soul," I growled out to Arceneaux, "for what you have done!"

"Last chance," Arceneaux said, too quietly for anyone else to hear. "What are you going to do, little witch?"

Her blue eyes sparked as she waited for my answer.

There was no way to win this. If I used magic to stop her, she'd have the leverage she needed to continue to hunt and kill witches. Ordering Zan's death to prove my loyalty would only implicate me further; no one would believe I didn't just want him killed to save my own skin and cover my tracks—not to mention the additional charge of regicide that could be brought against me. And if Conrad tried at all to intervene, he'd look like a puppet, dancing to a witch's will. Arceneaux had played her hand beautifully.

There could never be a "fair tribunal" now. In the eyes of the watching court, I was already convicted.

"That's it?" Arceneaux said, almost disappointed. "Nothing to say? No magical powers to display? You're weak."

"Toris de Lena did not think so," I muttered under my breath, "when I killed him."

Her expression immediately hardened. "Take her!" she barked to Golightly, who grabbed my arms with surprising strength and hauled me up to the altar, forcing me to my knees beside Zan.

No one had bothered to remove Father Cesare's corpse from the altar, and his sightless, upside-down stare seemed to be fixed upon me as the blood from his split-open belly seeped across the white satin.

It had spattered across Conrad's shoes, too, and my heart twisted as I remembered noticing their newness in the maze. Straight-backed in his chair, my bloodstained brother met my eyes with a look of expectancy. As if he were asking, *What are you waiting for?*

The knife in my pocket. What had he said, not an hour ago?

Keep it with you.

You're going to need it.

Arceneaux's voice lifted once more. "Aurelia Altenar, princess of Renalt, and Valentin Alexander, former king of Achleva: You have been tried by fair tribunal and found guilty."

Conrad gave me a tiny, barely perceptible nod. *Do it.*

Beside him, Kellan's jaw had become a rigid line. I hoped my eyes conveyed my silent command: *Take care of my brother.*

Zan's gaze met mine as Golightly copied Lyall's stance, situating his sword at the back of my neck.

My hand slipped into my pocket.

"Have you any last words to say?" Arceneaux asked coldly.

"I do," I said, feeling sweat stand out on my skin as rage roiled in my belly. *"Nihil nunc salvet te."*

And before anyone could stop me, I ducked under Golightly's sword and slashed my sharp knife in an upward arc from his navel to his sternum, painting a bright line of red across the white vertical line of his Tribunal robes. His lifeblood poured into my hands, and I could feel the magic churning within it. The hate. The fury. The pain and shock. I let my own livid magic meet it, my control giving way like the breaking of a dam.

Then I turned and threw my bloodied arms around Zan.

"Ut salutem!" I cried.

To safety.

7

We hit the ground and rolled together, scraping over rocks and collecting twigs and bits of dry grass in our clothes. When we came to a stop, Zan clambered away from me, ripping the gag from his mouth with a loud gasp before collapsing back to his hands and knees.

"*What* in all the *holy stars* did you just *do?*" His voice was grating and guttural, as if it had been a while since he last used it.

I got to my feet, breathless and still burning with blood magic. I lashed back, "I saved your damn life; that's what I did!"

"You little *fool!* You could have killed yourself!"

"And what difference does that make to you? Up until a few minutes ago, you were supposed to be dead! Tell me, Zan, how's the afterlife treating you?"

"Oh, yes, these past months have been simply *wonderful* for me. Nothing but garden parties and pretty girls all day long, dawn till dusk. Thank you for asking."

"Stars save me, I'd kill you right now, were it not for the fact that it *never* seems to *stick*."

"Why don't you just cast a spell? That's the answer to everything, isn't it? Doesn't even matter that it might destroy you. Anytime a problem comes up, you think magic is the answer. Don't want to wait for water to boil? Cast a spell to heat it. A tree has fallen, blocking the road? Cast a spell to move it. Even the stupidest, most frivolous things . . . 'Oh, look, Zan, your shirt is missing a button! Better cast a spell to mend it!' Never mind that a needle and thread would work just fine!"

"You're right," I seethed. "Using magic to keep my not-dead fiancé's idiot head on his idiot shoulders is totally, completely frivolous. Next time, I won't bother."

"What about your brother? What about Conrad?"

"He's with Kellan and Fredrick," I said, "and Arceneaux is counting on controlling him, not killing him. Now *stand up,* you bastard, before they come to finish what they started."

We might have gotten a head start, but we were at a disadvantage; we had no horses, and they'd likely bring hounds. And now that the blood magic was burning off, I was beginning to feel the leaching effects of its use: the weak limbs, the spinning head, the sluggish heart.

And it wasn't any ordinary spell I'd cast, either: it was teleportation. The last time I'd tried to use it was just after Zan had embarked on his five-day sea voyage to visit Achleva's coastal provinces and convince their lords to re-pledge their allegiance. I had received an anonymous tip that Castillion's warship was waiting to ambush Zan's vessel in Stiria Bay. I was already sick and weak when I tried to spell myself to his ship and warn him; I didn't make it far. He never got the warning, and I spent the next days in and out of consciousness, knocking at death's door.

That was the first time I ever experienced the Drowning Dream.

When I finally woke up, my universe had been turned on its head. Zan was dead, Achleva was at war with itself, and all hopes of uniting our countries had crumbled to dust. There was nothing left to do but retreat to Greythorne and turn our attention to Conrad's ascension.

At least, that's what the rest of them did. I settled into life at the Quiet Canary, close enough to Greythorne to know what was happening to the others and far enough away to keep them untarnished by my reputation. Undamaged by the scourge of my black luck.

That I was able to stand now, after attempting teleportation again, was probably because I had used only a pinprick of my own blood to do it. The rest had come from Golightly.

I had bought our freedom by breaking the Assembly's cardinal rule: Never use unwilling blood.

My own accusatory voice sounded in my head. *If Simon knew . . .*

But if Simon knew . . . what could he do? Refuse to teach me anymore? Ban me from blood magic altogether? I'd earned the punishment before ever committing the crime.

And despite wanting to knock the teeth out of Zan's stupid face, I didn't regret the choice. He was here, alive, and more aggravating than ever, and I'd never be able to thank the stars enough.

If what I did to save our lives was a sin, then I was a sinner. It was a title I'd gladly bear.

Zan got to his feet, gingerly straightening his spine, hand to his chest. "They got me three days ago, pulled me off the boat in Gaskin after your illustrious Lord Rudolph refused to let us disembark and sent for the Tribunal to 'take care of the vermin.'"

I put his arm over my shoulders, but even though he was the one covered in bruises and old bloodstains, I was beginning to sag from the post-magic strain. As we hobbled forward together, I wasn't sure which of us was leaning more upon the other.

"You were on a refugee ship?" I asked. "All this time?"

He shook his head. "Just the last few weeks."

"And where were you before that?"

"Around."

"Around?" I scoffed.

"What do you want me to say?"

"I want to know what you were doing while I was here, *mourning* for you."

"I've been moving refugees. Freeing workers from Castillion's mines . . . anything I could do to help alleviate some of my people's suffering."

"And you found skulking around in the shadows more effective than working out in the open as Achleva's rightful monarch?" As soon as I said it, I bit my lip; Kellan had used a similar argument on me yesterday. But this was different . . . I was Renalt's unwanted witch princess. Zan was Achleva's *king.* "You'd rather be a vigilante? The horseman they're talking about. Is that you?"

"No," Zan said. "Not exactly."

"What does that mean?"

"The horseman is just a story. Something to make the bad men fearful and the good men brave. All I do"—he winced as we shuffled along—"is perpetuate the idea that someone, somewhere, is standing against Castillion. That the common folk haven't been forgotten.

Castillion can push his borders, force resistors into working his mines, dam the flow of outside news into his territory, but he can't ever fully eradicate a rumor."

"You're betting your problems can be fixed with a story?"

"No. I'm hoping the story will give people reason to survive another day. Things are bad in Achleva," he said. "You don't know how bad." He was quiet for a moment. Then he said, "I'm buying time."

"And what happens when time runs out?"

"For a while there, I thought it had."

"If we've gained a stay, it's not much of one."

A howl echoed across the hills. A hound, maybe. Or a wolf.

"Stars," I said. "That's too close. Can you hurry it up a bit?"

"I don't know if I mentioned this, but I just spent the last three days in the Tribunal's custody. Lyall appeared to harbor a bit of a grudge against me too, and he happens to be very fond of kicking. I'm not sure I have *any* ribs left that aren't broken."

"Yes, well, I'm sure you were a model obedient prisoner and never once made snide remarks about his torture techniques."

Zan's lip curled back just a little—a hint of a smile. "What was I supposed to do? His kicks were all force, no finesse."

When the steeply pitched eaves of the Quiet Canary finally came into view, my relief was tempered by another howl, closer than before. It was a thin, eerie ribbon of sound that rippled down and settled slowly around us.

"That doesn't sound like hounds," Zan observed.

"No," I said. "It sounds like wolves."

"We have to go faster," Zan said as the grass a few dozen feet away began to rustle.

"We won't make it." The Quiet Canary was less than a quarter mile off; if either of us could run, we might have had a chance. But we couldn't, which meant we didn't.

I went for my knife.

"Stop," Zan hissed, but it was too late. I'd made a slight incision in my forefinger, and the blood was already welling up, fresh and vivid red against the dried and cracking smudges of Golightly's lifeblood, which still coated my hands and arms.

"*Sunt invisibiles,*" I stammered, pressing my hand to Zan's, skin to skin. "We are unseen."

The effect was immediate, and just in time. The tall grass next to us parted, and a creature padded out, looking one way and then the other. It was black as night, nearly indistinguishable from the darkness from which it had materialized.

A wolf—or something close to it.

We held absolutely still as the creature grew closer, scratching at the dirt and making a strange huffing sound that was half growl, half gurgle. An overwhelming odor of putrid flesh was emanating from it in waves, causing my gorge to contract painfully. Even so, I kept the spell going, mouthing the words soundlessly even as it came closer and closer to where we stood.

That is, until I saw its face.

The snout was flayed open; all that was left now were strips of fur falling away from the bone and a swollen, dripping tongue that lolled out from behind gleaming teeth. One eye had rotted away; the one remaining glinted an unholy red. I trembled and clung to Zan's hand, desperately trying to keep the threads of the invisibility spell in place by repeating the words in my head, *Sunt invisibiles, we are unseen,* too scared to even breathe as its empty face peered into the grass where we stood.

My strength dwindled with each second the abomination waited there, bathing me in its nauseating breath, drops of acrid saliva sliding off its engorged tongue and onto the dirt at my feet.

Then another wolf howled. I looked up and saw a silver-gray outline in the far distance—a horse and rider, galloping at a clipping pace. I'd have thought I imagined it, except that the wolf's head whipped up toward it, as if it could see it too.

Then the creature made a whistling roar and started bounding away after the silvery shadow, turning only once to look back at the place where we still stood.

When I let the spell go, I sank to my knees, my strength expended. Zan had to yank me to my feet and hold me up as I dangled, doll-like, in his arms.

"What *was* that?" he asked.

I couldn't tell if he was talking about the wolf or the horse and rider, but either way, the answer was the same. Trembling, I said, "I don't know."

"Come on." For all his bruised ribs, Zan was astonishingly swift; we made it across the last stretch to the tavern in mere minutes.

Zan dragged me up to the back door, which he pounded three times. "Hello?" he called. "Help, please! Open the door!"

It took a few moments before Hicks managed to open it. "What's with all the racket?" he grumbled. "This is a private office. The door to the tavern is around the—" He looked down at Zan, who was propping me up on the stoop, his crinkled eyes taking in Zan's mottled linen shirt and my blood-coated arms. "Front. Merciful Empyrea."

"Sorry to trouble you, sir," Zan said. "But we need your help. Please, *please.* Help us."

"Oh, bother," Hicks said, and stepped aside to let us in.

"Finally overplayed your hand, did you, darling?" Rafaella asked as she helped me down the steep stairs to the cellar, Zan following. Upstairs, Lorelai was comforting the weeping Delphinia; she had a soft heart and had been very fond of Father Cesare. I spared her the details, but the bare facts were jarring enough.

"Perhaps a little," I managed in a weary whisper, looking at my hands. "But don't worry yourself. I'm just tired, that's all. None of this is my blood."

"Didn't think it was," Rafaella said.

Jessamine was waiting for us at the bottom of the landing. "This way."

Rafaella grimaced. "I *still* think we could hide you in one of the rooms upstairs . . . It's awfully cold and damp down here, and you two look like death. Maybe we can get you warmed up first, have some hot tea . . ."

Zan said, "The Tribunal is looking for us. I promise, you don't want them to find us with you. If we hide in the cellar and are caught, you'll have some deniability; say that we broke in and snuck down here without you knowing. You won't be able to do that if we're found in your rooms, drinking tea."

"Saint Urso," I said haltingly. "Cesare said that he built this place, and that he always made hiding places for witches. Is it true? Does the Canary have a secret room down here somewhere?"

"There is one like that, yes, down this way," Rafaella said. "I think Hicks uses it for extra storage now. It's very small."

Lorelai was coming down the stairs. "Better hurry, my dears. There are lights on the moor. Horses, carriages. Looks like they are on their way here, and coming fast."

"We'll have to take you up on your offer of tea later," Zan said to Rafaella.

"And who are you, exactly?" Lorelai asked, an eyebrow raised; she was always the most cautious and skeptical of the girls.

"My name is Valentin," Zan said. "But most call me Zan."

Rafaella's eyes widened. "As in . . . Valentin, the king of Achleva? Really?"

He nodded grimly. "Yes. But contrary to what is often said about me, I am not mad, murderous, or dead."

"You do look like you've spent some time on death's doorstep, however. Both of you." Jessamine put her hands on her emerald-silk-swathed hips.

My exhaustion was bone-deep now; I could hardly keep myself upright. But I made for the stairs, despite swaying precariously. "This was a mistake. It's too risky. There's no place in the tavern they won't find us. And even if they do believe we hid without your knowledge, they could punish you for *not* knowing just as well. We should go."

"You can barely stand!" Rafaella protested, blocking my half-hearted attempt to escape.

Jessamine clucked her tongue and went to the back of the cellar, where shelves were crowded with wine bottles and jugs of ale. "I didn't know that this closet was meant for hiding witches, but it makes sense; the Quiet Canary has long been a waystation for those on the wrong side of the law." She reached behind the shelving, flipped a latch, and then stood aside as the whole wall swung pendulously forward. Her lamp illuminated a small opening on the other side, a tiny closet jammed with two tables and no chairs. The ceiling was so low that Jessamine, at nearly six feet, could not quite stand at her full height.

"Is that my sombersweet wine?" I asked, eyeing a cluster of bottles on the table.

"Hicks thought it best to keep it apart from the rest of our supply," Jessamine said. "It's too valuable to end up being guzzled by our less-discriminating patrons. Some of them would drink cups of arsenic if someone poured it for them and told them it was ale."

Lorelai called again from the stairs. "Girls! Make haste!"

"All you have to do," Rafaella said, handing off a few blankets to Zan, "is sit still and stay quiet until we get rid of them. Can you do that?"

"Quiet as the grave," Zan said.

"Easy enough for you to say," I said, wearily lowering myself to the cold dirt floor. "You've had four months of practice."

Zan sighed as he situated a blanket over my shoulders before sinking beside me, arms draped over his knees. Softly, he said, "I had my reasons, Aurelia. I know how hard it must have been for you—"

"You don't," I said, shifting as far away from him as the tiny room would allow, just as Jessamine sealed up the door, taking the last light with her.

I was glad of the dark then; this way, Zan couldn't see the two foolish tears that had escaped my eyes and were now leaving salty trails on my cheeks.

It was easy to tell when the Tribunal arrived, because everything went silent.

There was always a low buzz in the tavern: quiet conversations, the clink of glasses, drunken laughter. I didn't realize that we could hear it, even from within the thick walls of our hiding place, until it stuttered to a stop.

The silence made the blackness seem blacker.

I felt my breath becoming shallower as time ticked past. Zan and I hadn't spoken since the door was closed, but after listening to my sharp huffing for several minutes, he finally whispered, "Are you all right?"

"Yes," I hissed. Then, "No. I have a dream like this sometimes, where I'm lost in the dark. But it isn't dark, not really. Because there *is* no light or dark. It's just . . . nothing. And I'm nothing. And there's no past or future, or up or down, or land or sky. Everything is just . . ." I swallowed hard. "Nothing."

"You're having a panic attack," he said. "I used to have them all the time. Steady your breathing. One, in. Two, out. Yes. Just like that." His tone was low and rhythmic. "You have to ground yourself. Put your hands to the floor. What do you feel?"

"Dirt. It's cold. Hard."

"Yes. Keep that in mind. The earth is beneath you. It's real. You can hear my voice. I'm real. You have to keep yourself tethered to something solid."

There was a slight scuffling sound and then a soft *pop!* to my left.

"What was that?" My breaths started to speed up again. "They might hear us . . ."

"They can't hear us from upstairs, I promise. I just opened a bottle of wine, that's all. At the very least, it will warm you up a little."

He passed it to me in the dark, and I clumsily accepted it with shaking hands. I put the bottle to my lips and let the rich liquid slide down my throat. Zan was right; I felt warmer immediately, as if a small candle had been lit in my core. I took a greedy second swallow before handing it back to him. "Jessamine said this stuff costs three times more than regular wine."

I heard the slosh of the liquid as he took a sip. "It is better," he said. "Not sure if it's three times better, but still . . ."

"I hope you like hallucinations," I said. At this point, I'd almost have welcomed them. Anything would have been a break from reality.

"It's the demand for it," he said. "If you can't have it, you want it more." I could hear him shift, leaning his head back against the table. "And then when you *do* have it, you realize you might not want it that much after all."

"Zan," I said, "I am not sufficiently drunk to have this conversation."

"Fair enough," he answered, and took another swig himself before passing it to me once again.

We were both quiet, but my wine-tinged feelings were spinning out wildly in all directions. I was nerving myself up to break the silence when there came a creak from one of the cellar stairs. Then another. Then another. And voices, though I could not yet make out what they were saying.

Panicked, I felt my breaths begin to quicken once more. Without a word, Zan crawled closer, pulling me into him so that my back was to his chest. He found my right hand with his and directed it to the floor so that I could feel the cool solidness of it. "Shhh," I heard his voice by my ear, just the barest whisper. Now that we could not use words, he was helping me breathe by letting me feel the rise and fall of his chest, the break of his breath on my neck. *One, in. Two, out. Three, in. Four, out.*

I closed my eyes. I was so tired.

The voices grew nearer. One was Hicks. "I told you," he said gruffly. "Nothin' down here but barrels o' ale and a few crates of vegetables and too many damned stairs to get to 'em. Not worth it, if you ask me."

"I did not ask you," a man's voice replied, soft and scornful. A thin thread of light was showing through the bottom of the distillery door; I could see shadows shifting across it as they moved around the cellar.

"I assure you, Mr. Lyall," Hicks said, "ain't nobody hiding in the radishes."

Lyall was moving bottles around on the shelf. "Is this *all* there is to the cellar?" he asked.

He was like the wolf we'd encountered on the moor, sensing somehow that we were nearby, but unsure of where. Instinctively, my left hand went to the pocket that held Conrad's knife. If he opened the door, I could already be reciting the invisibility spell . . .

But Zan's hand clamped on my arm and held it tight. I could feel the brush of his hair as he shook his head. *No, Aurelia.*

"No witches here," Hicks huffed. "Just honest drunks and whores."

As Lyall continued to stalk outside our hiding-place door, I closed my eyes helplessly, casting up an incoherent prayer to the Empyrea. *Please make him go away. Please get us through this.*

She didn't answer, of course. She never did.

"If you're all done inspectin' those turnips, we still have a few other places for you to check. The chimney. The cesspits out back. There's an old birdhouse, too, if you want to be really thorough, see if someone's hidin' in there . . ."

"Enough," Lyall said sharply. "I'd like to look at your stable once again, if you don't mind."

Hicks grumbled all the way back up the cellar stairs. As soon as we heard the door open and shut, we leaped apart from each other once more, so that when Jessamine and Lorelai came to spring us from our dungeon several long minutes later, we were exactly where they had left us.

"Hello, darlings!" Lorelai said. "Our visitors have finally gone, thank the stars. Wait, where are you going?"

I'd already stumbled past her and was heaving myself up the stairs and out the door. The air was cold and crisp; I gulped greedy lungfuls, back pressed against the faded planks of the Canary's wall, a single gas lantern flickering on the hook over my head.

I was not alone for long.

When Zan joined me on the back stoop, he waited a few seconds before finally venturing, "Lorelai said she's not going to let us sleep in the cellar. She's going to stay in Delphinia's room tonight, to keep her company, and insists I use her room. Jessamine said she'd let you take hers, but she knew you'd say no. She said, 'She actually *likes* that cramped little broom closet she sleeps in.'"

I nodded. I didn't suggest we keep the same room; I preferred to take my chances out here, with the Tribunal and their wolves. They hadn't left a sentry behind, but that didn't mean they weren't still nearby.

He rocked back on his feet. "Aurelia, about what happened, after Stiria—"

With a hard sigh, I left him at the door.

"Wait!" He chased me down the steps. "Aurelia. Just wait." When I ignored him, he threw his hands in the air. "You know what? Fine. Let's do this now. Go ahead and blame me for what happened at Stiria, but we both know there was a division between us long before that."

"You think that excuses you from letting me believe that you were dead?"

"I thought . . . I thought it would be easier for you."

"Easier?" My voice was shrill. "Easier than what?"

"Than making you finally say out loud what you had been

thinking for weeks. That every time you looked at me, you regretted saving me. Because if you hadn't, your mother would still be alive. That you *wanted* me gone."

I cast my gaze away. "I think, perhaps, I'm more tired than I thought . . ."

He gave a barking laugh, grabbing my arm and pulling me back to face him. "Don't do that. Don't just keep it all bottled inside."

I fumbled for words, something that would articulate the pain I felt every time I glanced his way, terrified I could lose him, guilty that saving him had cost my mother her life. My searing, all-consuming anguish and fury when I'd thought he'd died. At Castillion. At him, a little. But mostly at myself. "What do you want me to say?"

"Anything!" he said. "Just talk to me. Yell at me. *Something.*"

"You really want to know why I pushed you away?" My words crackled. "Because every single time I looked at you, you were dying on the tower. Again and again, over and over. Nothing but decay and loss."

"You know what *I* saw when I looked at *you?* A wall. I witnessed the collapse of one, only to be confronted by another."

"Everything that happened was *my* fault. Every single loss was my fault. Mother, Kate, Falada, Lisette, Father Cesare . . . I'm a . . . a . . . *plague* to everyone I come in contact with. An infection. A poison. And when I thought you'd drowned . . . it broke me, Zan." I felt tears pricking my eyes. "How could you do that?" I whispered. "How could you do that to me? After I *died* for you."

"And I died for you in return!" he burst. "By all the bloody stars, I would have gone into the afterworld, or death, or whatever miserable thing waits beyond, and dragged you back just like you did for me. But I am *not* you, Aurelia. I have no magic. No power. After Stiria, it became clear that Castillion would stop at *nothing* to see me dead. It didn't matter to him who was on that ship; he killed them all to get to me. Dozens of innocents . . . Everyone around me was a target, including you. There was only one thing I knew to do to keep you alive, and, Empyrea save me, I did it." His jaw tightened. "I 'died' so you could let me go and move on with your life. And as soon as I was gone, you gave up magic. You got well." He waved at the building behind us. "You made friends. Tell me I'm wrong."

"You're wrong!"

"Am I?" He moved in close. "Prove it. Let's find out what would happen if you finally stopped running and let me *find* you."

He glared down at me, mere inches from my face now, close enough that I could have kissed away the hard line of his lips if I wanted to. Which, of course, I didn't.

His eyes, on me, weren't green anymore; they were gold. A trick of the light, I thought, still trying and failing to catch my breath. But that wasn't true — they were definitely gold. Churning , molten pools of liquid gold.

That color. It reminded me of something . . .

My hand went to the charm at my neck. The firebird.

Twice now, Zan had risen from the dead.

I gently lifted the cord over my head. "Kellan sent soldiers to the wreck. They found this on the shore." I placed it into his hands. "It belongs to you."

"Aurelia . . ."

I pulled away, leaving the necklace behind in his grasp, and went inside without another word.

✳

I let the Canary girls coax me into a bath, mostly because I didn't have the energy to argue against it. Though the water was warm and soothing, my hands remained dirty, and even after I finally scrubbed them clean, I could feel the stain of Golightly's unwilling blood under my skin.

Jessamine came into the washroom to find me sitting in the basin of long-tepid water with my knees tucked under my chin.

"Hello, lovey," she said softly. "Are you all right?"

I shook my head mutely. My mind had me trapped in another endless loop of regret and worry, replaying everything I'd said and done, intensifying its blame and criticism with each go-round.

"Do you want to talk about it?"

I shook my head again.

"If you need anything . . ."

"No," I said. "You've done enough. I should never have come. I've put you all in danger—"

"You don't need to worry about us," Jessamine said.

"They'll come back, you know." I shivered.

"And we'll figure it out when they do. Look! I brought something." She took a bottle out from behind her back. "I saw you'd opened it—thought it would be a shame not to finish it. Shall we?"

I laughed a little and nodded. At the very least, it might help me fall asleep.

She took a long swig and then handed the bottle over. "Have you ever heard how the sombersweet flower came to be?"

I shook my head again, and she took the bottle from me. "When I was little, my grandmother would take me with her on herb-collecting ventures to the Ebonwilde, and she'd tell me old feral-magic stories to keep me from getting bored on the way."

"Have you ever attempted it?" I asked. "Feral magic?"

Jessamine shook her head. "No, not me. The only magic I know how to work is between the sheets." My cheeks blazed, and she gave a lovely, throaty laugh, handing me the bottle. "We all have our talents."

I took another long, slow draft; it felt like swallowing tiny, fizzing sparks of honey. "So, what was the story? How was sombersweet created?"

"Well, the story goes that Mother Earth and Father Time fell in love."

I froze, immediately thinking of Simon's book. Jessamine was taking a sip and didn't notice my stillness.

"And together, they created all the living things of the earth. But with each new creation, the Mother grew weaker, until she knew she had enough immortality—life, or spark, or divinity, whatever you want to call it—for one more creation. A flesh-and-blood daughter."

This *was* the same tale as the one in Simon's book now lying hidden behind a wall in Cesare's study; I hadn't gotten to finish it before the coronation began.

Had that been only that afternoon?

". . . And her tears became a jewel," Jessamine was saying, "and her joy became a flower, and she threaded them together to make a bell."

I felt as meek as a child. "And then what happened?"

"Well . . . the Mother died. And the last of her spark burst into a thousand bits of light that nestled into the ground and became seeds. When the seeds took root in the soil, they grew into flowers in the shape of the bell she left for her daughter. Sombersweet." Jessamine lifted the bottle. "Said to have many magical properties—but most of all, it is supposed to allow us to see, within each living being, the spark given to us by Mother Earth herself."

I took another deep drink, letting the story and the spirits settle into my soul.

"I've never seen any 'spark' myself," Jessamine admitted. "But, magical life light notwithstanding, wine does have *other* marvelous properties."

"Such as . . . ?"

Jessamine gave an impish smile. "It can help make us brave." She stood, leaving the not-quite-empty bottle on the floor beside the washbasin. Faux-innocently, before closing the door behind her, she added, "Lorelai left her room unlocked. Just in case."

9

I had to drink the rest of the wine before I felt even the littlest bit brave.

When the bottle and the last of my excuses were finally spent, I took a deep breath and stepped into the darkened hall. Two hours to midnight, and the Quiet Canary was terribly still; the Tribunal's visit had scared most of the tavern's customers onto the road or into bed. The only light was the soft glimmer coming from under the door of the last room on the right.

The door, of course, was unlocked.

Zan was sitting on the windowsill, drawing something on Lorelai's stationery. "Aurelia?" he asked, looking up in surprise.

Was that a glimmer of gold under his skin? Perhaps the somber-sweet story was true after all. Or perhaps I'd just drunk too much wine and had begun seeing things.

"Aurelia, about what I said—" he began, setting his sketch aside.

"Stop talking," I commanded. His eyes wandered over me, and I was suddenly aware of the flimsiness of my nightgown and how delicately it clung to my chest and hips, just translucent enough to hint at the shape of my body beneath it.

The shimmer on him seemed to grow brighter.

I came in closer, taking the pencil from him and setting it aside so I could place his freed hands on either side of my waist.

"I don't know if we should be . . ." He trailed off, nervous. Disarmed.

I brought my lips down to his and murmured against them. "I don't want to think anymore, Zan. I just want to let *go*." And then I kissed him. Slowly, carefully, thoroughly. Until the light coming off him became actual heat.

He pulled me closer, and our kiss deepened, punctuated by shallow breaths stolen between parted lips. I threaded my fingers through his thick, dark hair and let my kisses wander to his ear and then down his neck and back to his mouth again. Wherever we touched, I could feel the dispersion of my anxieties and inhibitions into his light, leaving me in a state of thrilled dizziness, drunk with the desire to let my entire soul dissolve into his.

Now that I was aware of it, I could see a glimmer in our every touch.

"Aurelia." He murmured my name against my lips like a double-edged entreaty — *Stop* and *Don't stop* together at once.

"I love you, Zan," I whispered, turning his face to mine so he could see the conviction in my eyes as I untied the ribbons of my nightgown and let it slowly slip to the ground. His gaze was a storm of green and shimmering gold, his eyes blazing bolder and brighter, scorching my skin as they raked across the bare expanse of it.

I whispered, "I *want* you. I want *this,*" and then I kissed him again with all the worshipful conviction of a pilgrim star kneeling at the Empyrea's feet. He sighed and relaxed into me as his apprehensions melted and fell away. This was right. *We* were right. And we had waited for far too long.

He said under his breath, "Are you sure you want this? Aren't you afraid that things could end badly for us?"

"I *am* afraid," I said. "But I am not unsure."

He rose to his feet and pulled me tight against him; his hands, finally free of their inhibitive fetters, roved the curve of my back as my clumsy fingers worked the last buttons of his linen shirt and eagerly sought the warm skin beneath it. Each touch felt like a revelation and a provocation in one; as if a long-locked book was falling open before me and every magic word I discovered inside made me want to devour the next and the next, until I had consumed its entirety and forever committed it to memory.

We stumbled together, tangled in each other, to the bed. He lay down first, bare-chested but still wearing his leather breeches, and I followed by placing a leg on each side of his hips and leaning over him, my still-damp hair enclosing us in a curtain as I traced curling patterns of glimmering gold across his chest. There was dried blood on his torso, but beneath it, his skin was pristine; there was not a mark or bruise left upon him. I could feel the intoxicating piper's call of his pulse under my fingertips, and my own spark went singing after it, across the muscle and sinew and into his bone and the blood in his veins. He could not see the light the way I could, but he must have felt it. With an agonized sigh, he hooked his arms around me and, in a twist and a roll, pulled me down on the bed while he stretched out above me. Our positions reversed, my hands were free to explore the chiseled planes of his jaw, his cheeks, his shoulders, and marvel at the beautiful, sharp bow of his mouth as he brought it down hard on mine . . . With every kiss, I could feel the craggy border of life and death coming into relief. Was this what it felt like to die? If so, I'd die again and again, willingly and without reservation.

But shadows began to fall all around me. Why was I suddenly so cold? And my eyelids were growing heavy. A ringing began in my ears, muffling Zan's voice. "Aurelia?" he asked, but he sounded so far away. "Aurelia!"

I could not answer. I could not move. My blood was slowing, slowing . . .

And then my heart gave a final shudder and gave out.

I dreamed I was back at Greythorne, standing in my red dress on the steps of the Stella Regina.

There was nobody around; no priests, no clerics, no noblemen. I cracked the double doors open, and a shaft of thin moonlight fell across the marble nave and up to the altar, whereupon a single person was kneeling in prayer as bells clanged overhead.

But—I was wrong; this was not the Stella Regina. There was no stained-glass depiction of the Empyrea overlooking the altar. Rather, the entire chapel was a work of intricate carvings and dark reliefs, murals of monsters and mythic beasts, angry angels and fallen kings.

They peeked through shrouds of cobwebs and glared at me from beneath layers of dust.

And as I got closer, I could see that the altar wasn't an altar at all; it was a long, elegant box of thick glass and spun gold.

A coffin of crystal, with someone lying inside it. Silent, still, face obscured by the darkness.

The sound of my footfalls against the black marble alerted the worshipper to my presence. He reluctantly rose to his feet, still staring at the glass casket. "So it begins and ends," he said. "Just as you said it would."

"Simon?" I asked hesitantly, squinting to see him through the darkness. "Where are we? Is this . . . real?"

He turned slowly, his face finding the light like a waxing moon. "This," he said, waving his hand at the bleak chapel, "is the Great Sanctorium of the Assembly. And it is real enough, if not real in the way you currently understand it. This is the spectral plane. The in-between place. A borderland between the Now and the After. Some people call it the Gray."

I lifted my hand in front of my face, trepidation growing. "I'm a . . . ghost?"

"You're a shade of yourself, in a way, yes. I know it's a lot to take in, but we are both here for the exchange," he said. "My life for yours. Bound by blood, by blood undone." Watching me, his face softened. "Ah, don't fret, child. I knew the risks when I facilitated the spell."

The blood spell that had killed my mother was now taking Simon, too. "I'm not dead!" I cried. "I can't be dead! This is just another dream. Like the Screaming Dream and the Drowning Dream. I just have to wake up, that's all, and everything will be fine . . . You will be fine!"

"Aurelia," Simon said gently, "you know what I say is true."

My bare feet on the stone weren't cold, I suddenly realized.

My breath quickened, though I had no lungs. My heart raced, though I had no heart. I was merely a collection of thoughts and moments that remembered how to do those things. My body—my physical body—was somewhere else. The realization hit me like a frigid gust of air that would have sent shivers across my skin if I'd had skin that could shiver.

"But I was *fine*. I used a little blood magic, but not much. Not enough to . . . to . . ."

"No, child," Simon said. "We were wrong about your magic. *I* was wrong about it. It was never blood magic that was killing you. It was Zan."

"No. No. I don't believe you. Zan would never hurt me," I said with conviction.

"He wouldn't mean to," Simon replied. "He'd never want to hurt anyone. But he *is*. And he doesn't even know it. Look."

The scene shifted. Simon and I were no longer at the abandoned sanctorium but standing on the balcony by the window of Lorelai's room. On the bed, there were two people frozen in a single moment. A girl and a boy, locked in a passionate embrace.

I should have felt embarrassed seeing myself that way, but I was moved instead. This girl, wearing naught a stitch of clothing, was equally vulnerable and invincible with her skin and soul laid bare. And the boy in whose arms she lay wore an expression that was bashful and brash and disbelieving all at once.

This was love, in all its frailty and fervor.

"Do you see it?" Simon said, coming up behind me. "Do you see the connection?"

I'd thought the glimmer was just the effects of the sombersweet wine, but while Zan was burning brightly, my light was faint and flickering, trickling from me to him like water from a drying creek toward an insatiable lake.

"It is your vitality," Simon said. "Your life. Your Goddess-given spark."

Zan was glowing everywhere, but our interlocked hands were nearly white as the sun. He was stealing life from me, killing me with his touch, and he had no idea.

"When he died on the tower . . . I couldn't let it stand." I was trying to put the pieces together, to understand.

"You went to the other side. This place, here."

"Yes," I said distantly. "I used my life force to awaken his. I took his wounds as mine. And then I crossed the borderline into death and tried to take his place on the other side."

"But the transfer was never completed," Simon said. "The connection was never closed. Because . . ."

"Because of the bloodcloth ritual," I said, realizing. "My mother died instead of me."

"There are two grave consequences of that event that you must now face, Aurelia. The first is the reality that when neither you nor he died, the tower spell was left unfinished. If you had died, the conduit between planes would have been closed forever. If *he* had died, it would have been torn wide open, and the Malefica, the entity that has forever been exiled to the darkness of the After, would have been free to roam the material world at last."

"One or the other," I whispered. The rhyme recited to me by my reflection was not so nonsensical after all. I was descended from Aren, the sister. Zan was descended from Achlev, the brother. And we were the key to keeping the Malefica locked up or setting her free.

One or the other. One or the other. Daughter of the sister, or son of the brother.

At the red moonrise, one of two dies.

"Aurelia," Simon said, "you have to listen. We don't have much time left, and I still have a lot to tell you. You cannot touch Zan again. His life recognizes yours as its own. It will take and take from you until there's nothing left."

"But I *have* to die. Isn't that what you just said? If I die, the portal is closed for good."

"There were three drops on that bloodcloth, Aurelia. Mine was only the second."

"Stars," I breathed. "Kellan. Can the bloodcloth binding be broken? Please, Simon," I begged, "what do I have to do?"

"It can be broken only by death or something like unto it. I can't give you answers, child. I don't have them. What details I have are few. All I can do is set your feet on the right path: If there is a way to break your bond, you'll have to do it here—in the Gray. It isn't a border you can cross on your own, but there is one person to whom you can go for guidance: a feral mage who lives in the Ebonwilde. Powerful. Dangerous. And very, very old. You must go to her. If you're going to stop the Malefica from entering the world without taking Kellan with you, you're going to need her help."

"But how?" I asked. "How do I find her?"

"Onal can show you the way."

"Onal? But—"

The edges of Lorelai's room began to darken just a little. Simon looked up and around. "My time to cross to the After is at hand."

"No, wait, Simon—" I stopped, helpless. "Don't go. I'm so sorry!"

His eyes fell on me, full of sympathy and sadness. "Take heart, child. You'll see me again. This may be my end, but it is your beginning." He cocked his ear to the side. "Did you hear that? Wings."

"You sent me a book," I said hurriedly. "What is it? What does it mean?"

"It's feral magic," he said. " Hundreds of years old, and full of ancient knowledge. It is supposed to help you with what's to come."

"But *what* is to come?" Wrenchingly, I said, "I don't understand any of this!"

"You will." Simon had a far-off look on his face. "Soon." His eyes, reflecting a light I could not see, turned back to me. "You have a difficult path ahead," he said. "But you'll rise to meet it." His voice was growing distant. "Do you see it? Do you see the raven?"

"I don't see anything. Simon—"

"I think it's come to guide me," he said, smiling at empty air. He held out his hand, and for a second, I thought I could glimpse the shadow of a bird alight upon it, gleaming a strange, incandescent silver.

Then Simon started to fade. And as he faded, so did the scene. I was being overtaken by what felt like a rushing current of nothing. Of Gray.

"Just don't forget, child . . ." The last echo of his voice surrounded me. ". . . Bound by blood, by blood undone."

And he was gone.

✳

I awoke with a gasp.

Zan was staring at me, mouth agape. "Aurelia!" he said. "Are you all right? I think you stopped breathing for a second. I didn't know what to do . . ." He reached to put his hand against my cheek, but I recoiled from him, slamming my body back against the bed. My head was still spinning, my thoughts muddled with wine and the remnants of a terrifying waking dream that wasn't a dream at all.

"Stop," I wheezed as I clamored to cover myself with blankets —anything to put a barrier between his skin and mine.

"What?" Zan stuttered, stunned. "What just happened? I'm so sorry, Aurelia. Let me—"

"Don't *touch* me," I cried breathlessly. "Please. Don't come any closer."

"I don't know what I did," he said, voice breaking, "but I'm so sorry. What do you need? What can I do? I knew I shouldn't—Oh, Empyrea." He put his hands in his hair.

"This was a mistake," I said tremulously. "I made a mistake, and I . . . Stars, I can't *think*." I cast around for reassurance to give him, some explanation that might lessen the damage to us both, but came up with nothing. Instead, I snatched up my fallen nightgown and struggled drunkenly into it.

"Aurelia, what—?"

"I can't believe myself. I let my guard down for one second and . . . I'm such a fool. Such a fool. I'd do it, too, you know? I want to . . . but I can't do this to him. To Kellan."

"Kellan?" Zan asked, stricken.

"No. It's not what you think. Not like that." Words were tumbling from my lips in a senseless stream. "My fault. Always my fault. Because . . . because I can't . . . I won't let you hurt me. I won't let myself hurt Kellan."

"I won't hurt you," Zan said. "I would never want to hurt you."

"But you have. And you will. And so will I. I hurt everyone." Tears were flowing freely now, blurring my already distorted vision. "Because I'm cursed. I am a curse." My head was spinning with a chanting singsong. *One or the other. One or the other. Daughter of the sister, or son of the brother.*

I fumbled toward the door, tripping over the hem of my nightgown and then cringing away from Zan as he tried to help me back up again.

My memories of that night would be troubled and tangled, but that last image of Zan before I fled etched itself onto my consciousness with crystal clarity: his hand outstretched, his hair askew, his expression confused, heart bruised. But it was his eyes that affected me the most.

They were bright and bewildered, and gleaming vivid gold.

10

I closed my bedroom door and sank against it, only to find myself being watched from the mirror by the me-that-was-not-me. Her cheeks were flushed, nightgown rumpled, arms wrapped tight around herself. Her dark hair took on ruddy glints from the lamplight, her blue eyes bright with tears. But she wasn't me—on *her* lips, there was a hint of a smile.

I turned and slammed my hands onto the wall on either side of the mirror. "Tell me what it means," I demanded. "Tell me what to do."

Instead of answering, she spoke in sync with me, almost mockingly.

Angrily, I reeled my hand back and drove my fist into her face. The glass split into a dozen radiating shards before falling from the frame onto the desk below and shattering into a thousand silver pieces.

I slowly pulled my fist back, staring at my bloody knuckles. Despite everything, there was one thing that had changed for the better in the last hours:

I no longer had to be afraid to use magic.

My blood seemed to sing in response to the thought, begging me to do it. To use it. To unleash the power within it.

With Simon gone, the only place I knew to find answers was in the book he'd sent me, and that was back at the Stella Regina. My blood surged as I closed my eyes and whispered, *"Urso fons est scriptor."* *To Urso's fountain.*

The spell I'd used to transport Zan and me away from the coronation was an incredibly taxing one; I hadn't really felt the effects then, because most of the blood I'd used had belonged to the Tribunal cleric Golightly, and I was fueled by rage and the imminence of our demises. My second attempt did not go so smoothly. I meant to transport myself to the statue of Saint Urso, too drunk to worry that it might still be occupied by the Tribunal; I ended up in the River Urso instead.

The water was shockingly cold, and I sputtered as it dragged me toward the lights of Greythorne Village downstream. The river rocks were jagged enough to bruise and scrape me as I tumbled past but too slick to catch hold of.

There! The mill loomed up in the dark. I threw a hand out and caught the water wheel by its edge. My fingertips scrabbled for purchase against the splintery wood, and the whole contraption creaked and sagged precariously beneath my weight, but I kept my head above water long enough to catch my breath and secure my hold. From there, I was able to move across to the river's edge and haul myself up into the reeds at the shore, shaking in my thin, waterlogged nightgown.

On the other side of the mill, I could hear voices. Harsh, angry. I hunkered lower into the cover of the rushes and crept to the corner of the mill. From there, I peered out at the scene on the other side.

The place was crawling with Tribunal clerics, each with a spinning wheel hoisted over his shoulders, marching imperviously past the anguished cries of the women to whom the wheels belonged and into the village square, where they tossed them into a pile. The wheels sat in an akimbo stack, cracking and groaning each time another was added to the top.

Arceneaux was standing like a steel rod by the door of the mill, her features a mask of cold calm, unmoved by the pleas of the Achlevan spinners. Prudence Lister was standing beside her, nodding her approval as her clerics worked. "Every last one of them," the old woman said. "We can't let them weave anymore witchcraft."

"Thank you for your help, Lister," Arceneaux said, her eyes sliding over the woman with a toleration that seemed to border on disdain. "You've done your country a great service."

The icy river had shocked me into sobriety, and with it came full understanding of my predicament. I was cold, unclothed, shaking, and surrounded by Arceneaux and her collar-wearing cohorts. Even if I used a blood spell to render myself invisible, I'd leave wet and muddy footprints in my wake, and that was if my chattering teeth didn't alert anybody first. But I had to move, and soon, or risk death of cold.

I had no choice; I had to use magic. And despite the poor outcome of my transportation attempt, the invisibility spell was one I knew well. As luck would have it—if you can call being scraped across serrated river rocks luck—I was already bleeding.

"*Ego Invisibilia,*" I whispered. "I am unseen." I took a tentative step from my hiding place.

I ducked behind one of the Tribunal clerics carrying the last of the spinning wheels on his back, mostly to keep out of Arceneaux's line of sight. Spell or no spell, I felt quite certain that Arceneaux would see right through it if I got too close to her.

I had to scramble out from underfoot as the cleric hoisted the wheel onto the mountain and then stepped back to admire his work, as if he'd just added the finishing flourish to a painting. I slid from foot to foot to keep up with him as he moved to make room for Arceneaux.

"My brothers and sisters!" She raised her voice to the townsfolk, who'd come out of their houses to watch the midnight spectacle. "Today is an auspicious day! We have crowned a king, yes, but more importantly—we have exposed his traitorous sister and freed him of her influence. Make no mistake, we have a lot of work ahead of us. It will take months, perhaps even years, for us to fully recover and rid ourselves of the vermin that have infested our communities. Our homes and businesses. But we are strong!"

There was a murmured assent rising up from the townsfolk. Arceneaux smiled. "We are transcendent! And tonight, we are the first spark of a wildfire. Together, *we will take our country back!*"

With that, she struck a match and tossed it into the towering collection of wheels. I watched in helpless horror as the flames took hold, slowly growing larger and more ravenous while people clapped and cheered.

Today, it was spinning wheels. Tomorrow, it would be witches. Cael was dead, but his legacy lived on.

I'd been wrong to believe that things were changing. This animosity was an infection of the heart, but it lived in the blood and bones—nearly impossible to eradicate, because it could lie dormant for years, just waiting for the right set of conditions to come roaring back. First as fear, then as fury, and finally a full-scale epidemic of hatred.

Despite the surging heat from the bonfire, I still felt cold.

✳

After escaping the tumult in the village, I was lucky my cloaking spell held until I made it all the way to Kellan's chambers inside the manor. Even with my clumsy, ice-cold fingers, I was able to start a fire in his bedroom grate. When enough warmth had returned to my numb extremities, I stripped off my wet nightgown and tossed it into the fire, which hissed and spat angrily but slowly accepted the offering.

My satchel hadn't been moved since I'd left it next to Kellan's bed along with my discarded clothes. I had dressed with a fervent prayer of thanks to the Empyrea that I'd left them behind yesterday; I was never more grateful for the worn-in comfort of breeches and blouse than in that moment.

Then I waited.

Kellan's shoulders were stooped when he entered removing his cloak with the weary slowness of a man thrice his age. He jumped when he saw me appear from the shadowed corner by the window, but his shock was immediately replaced by relief.

"Aurelia," he said, pulling me into a tight hug. "Thank the Empyrea you're all right." Then his excitement evaporated, and he held me at arm's length to ask sternly, "What in all the blessed stars would compel you to come back here? After you gutted that cleric, the whole place went into an uproar. Arceneaux put a reward on your head and ordered all the refugees to be rounded up and arrested, their property burned—"

"I saw," I said, casting my eyes toward the fireplace, remembering the spinning wheels as they were slowly eaten away by the flames.

"Fredrick forced them off the manor's grounds, invoking an old law that maintains lords have judicial rights on their own property, and Conrad—" He stopped, face falling.

"What? What is it? Is Conrad all right?"

"He's fine. He's perfectly fine. But you should know . . . he has released me from his service. He told me that I'd fulfilled my duty to him, and that he'd find someone else to head his king's guard. He said he wanted me to return to my former post, effective immediately. He dismissed me. And then he told me to go to my room, like a disobedient child." He sighed heavily. "All I've ever wanted was to be a soldier, to serve the royal family faithfully, and now . . ." He trailed off.

"Your former post?" I almost laughed. "He didn't dismiss you; he's assigned you to go back to protecting *me*. And he did it in such a way no one listening would think twice about it." Clever little rabbit, my brother.

"You think he knew you would be here, waiting for me?"

"He gave me the knife this afternoon. Said I'd need it, and I did." I turned to the chamber window. "I wish I could thank him for it. Without it, Zan and I would be dead."

"Where *is* Zan?" Kellan asked carefully.

"Safe," I said. "I hope. I left rather quickly."

"*Why?* You should have gone with him as far away as you could get. Across the isles, if you had to. To Halderia, maybe. Or Marcone. Started a new life together."

I closed my eyes. "He and I . . . we can't be together. Not ever again."

There was a long stretch of silence before Kellan said, "So, what now? We can't stay here. If you are caught, Conrad will have no choice but to order your death." His eyes narrowed at me. "Did you just *shrug off* potential execution?"

"I'm afraid we've got bigger problems now."

"Bigger than dying?"

"I'm not afraid of dying, Kellan. I *have* to die." I knew the truth of it as I said it. There was no other outcome. It was me or Zan, and if Zan died, the Malefica would be let loose into the world.

Stomach tightening, I pulled the bloodcloth from the satchel and handed it to Kellan.

His eyes flicked to mine.

Where there were once three drops of blood, there was now just one: his.

I said, "The only question that remains is whether or not I take you with me."

After I told Kellan all that had happened—carefully omitting the part where Zan and I ended up in bed together—and though he wanted to leave for the Ebonwilde immediately, there were two things we had to do first. Simon had said we'd need Onal to help us find the Ebonwilde witch, so I sent Kellan to fetch her while I went back to the Stella Regina to retrieve Simon's book.

I knew Greythorne well enough that I didn't need the invisibility spell to walk its halls, slipping from shadow to shadow. It helped that the manor was all but abandoned; most of the visiting courtiers had hitched up their fancy carriages and taken their leave of the location the first minute they could, putting the coronation's unpleasantness behind them as quickly as they were able. I was able to reach the kitchen servant's door and dart out into the maze without encountering a single soul.

The hedges were high, and the night was quiet. Any members of the Tribunal not currently burning Achlevan heirlooms in the village were most likely spread across the province looking for me.

The blue guide ribbons were, thankfully, still tied into the hawthorn. I followed their zigzagging course to the center plaza, glaring up at Urso's statue as I passed. It was my own fault I ended up in Urso's river instead of at Urso's fountain, but I felt resentful toward him all the same.

I stole to the rectory entrance on the south transept side, creeping through the unlocked door and into the darkened hallway of the priests' living quarters. Through the iron-grate door ahead, I could see the gentle gutter of the mourning candles from the chapel.

The study was empty, but in the darkness, the stacks of books became a gauntlet of obstacles; one wrong move, and I could send them all toppling, one into the other. At least the maze had the ribbons to guide me through it.

I made it to the hidden closet and opened it with soft taps, feeling around blindly until my hand fell upon the softened leather of the green book's cover. I was stuffing it into my satchel when someone cleared his throat behind me.

One of the Stella's priests was standing in the doorway, candle aloft in his hand. He was as slight as Cesare had been large, and he blinked at me, birdlike, from behind bottle-thick glasses.

"I'm sorry," I stammered. "I'm just retrieving something I left here. I don't mean you any harm . . ."

The priest gave a sad, faint smile. "No, no. I know you don't. Cesare spoke often of you, and very highly. You're welcome to take whatever you need."

I closed the closet door softly and then, head bowed, said, "I'm very sorry for what happened to him. I never wanted . . ."

"We know, child. Would you like to come see him? To say goodbye?"

I followed the priest and his bobbing candle down the transept hall and into the chapel. My departure from the coronation proceedings had brought chaos to the Stella: broken relics sat in darkened corners; pews were overturned and left at odd angles; abandoned ribbons littered the floor. Only the first row had been reset into its original position. It was now occupied by two more of Cesare's brethren priests, heads down as they paid last respects to the fallen Father, whose body had been dressed and laid out for viewing on the same altar upon which he had died. There had been no time to fully eradicate the bloodstains; in the low light, they looked black.

Seeing him there made it all real.

I quickly blinked away tears as the priest took my hand, gently guiding me to the altar.

"It is a sad thing to have to say goodbye to our beloved mentor, Father Cesare, but take heart, child. He would have been glad to know he died in service of the Stella's true purpose."

I sniffed and tried to wipe my eyes on my sleeve. "Which is?"

"To keep the innocent from the hands of those who would hurt and destroy them. Everything here was built to thwart the Tribunal. They may be the judicial faction of the faith, but they do not impart justice anymore—if they ever did. No. They serve only themselves and their most vicious prejudices, questing for unmitigated power, all under the guise of serving the Empyrea." He sighed. "Who can argue with a person who claims they're acting under divine mandate? The greatest evils are perpetrated by those who forsake their humanity in the name of deity."

A lump had formed in my throat. "I'm so sorry, Father, to have brought that evil here."

He turned to one of the brass candelabras and removed a tallow candle. "Would you like to leave a light in remembrance of our mutual friend?"

I accepted the candle and approached the dais where Father Cesare lay in repose. I held the wick to the flame of another and, when it sputtered to life, settled it into the sconce, adding my tiny light to the dozens already burning.

"Empyrea keep you, Father Cesare," I murmured, trying to look at his peaceful face and not at the dark spots of the altar and dais floor.

When I returned to the others, still waiting in the nave, I took the priest's hand. "Thank you, Father," I said. "For letting me say goodbye."

"We'll be interring him in the crypt tonight, among our most revered leaders since Urso himself. It is an honor to be put to rest there and, for him, well deserved. Will you join us?"

"I'm afraid I can't, Father. I'm due on the outskirts of Greythorne within the hour. I've got people waiting for me."

"Call me Edgar, child. And these are my fellows, Father Brandt and Father Harkness. Please, come down with us. I promise you will not be late for your rendezvous." And he went to the side of the altar, tapping it in a similar fashion to the study closet.

To my shock, the four sides of the altar rose several inches and broke apart with a mechanical groan. The altar at the royal sanctorium in Syric had been empty; I'd used it to hide my books on witchcraft. This one was not empty at all; it seemed to house a network of gears and pulleys.

There were two bobbin-like fixtures, one on each side of the altar platform. Harkness and Brandt each took a handle and began cranking. As they did so, Cesare's body began to slowly lower into the floor. When they finally stopped, I peered down into the altar cavity. Cesare was resting serenely, hands clasped, face bathed in a rectangle of soft candlelight from above.

"Come along, now," Edgar said, motioning for me to follow him. "We've got to take the long way down."

The crypt was accessible through the base of the bell tower, where the winding staircase continued down past the floor through another hidden door. The stairs were incredibly steep and narrow. "Thank goodness we didn't have to bring Cesare down this way," Brandt said. "I might have considered giving him a sky burial instead, like I've heard they do in the highlands on the continent."

"Cesare would have enjoyed the prospect of vultures feeding on his spleen, to be sure," Edgar replied fondly, "but I imagine hoisting him up on a platform in the mountains would have been a feat of engineering too much for the likes of Urso himself."

"What creature do you think came to ferry him into the after?" Harkness asked. "My guess would be a coon cat, one of those with great tufts of hair and a ponderous tail that looks intimidating, but who mostly likes to sleep in the sun."

"A black-and-white bear, like they have on the continent," Brandt replied.

"No," Edgar said. "One of the northern dogs, with a coat of white and massive paws. He had one of those when he was growing up; the more connection you have with an animal on this side of the border-land, the more likely you'll be greeted by it on the other."

"I've never heard this part of Empyrean canon," I ventured.

"It's not," Edgar replied. "It's Ursonian canon. He believed that when we die, the part of our makeup that tethers our souls to our physical body takes the shape of a guide to help us through the bor-derland to the After. He saw it himself once, in his youth, when he almost crossed to the other side."

"I died once," I said. "Mostly. I never saw anything like that."

"Then your quicksilver binds were never fully severed," Brandt said.

"Quicksilver?" I asked.

"What blood is to your flesh, quicksilver is to your soul," Hark-ness replied, "and the divine spark is to your consciousness."

"We all have two bodies," Edgar said. "One is material; that is our flesh and blood. The other is subtle, able to traverse the spectral and astral planes. When we live, the two exist together. When we die, we leave our material self behind on the material plane and move on to the next world, our consciousness and soul together as one."

"What you might call a ghost," Harkness said. "If you believe in that kind of thing."

When we came to the bottom of the stairs, we stepped out onto a floor of packed dirt and gravel. Edgar removed a torch from a sconce on the wall and lit it with his candle. The other two priests followed, lighting the low ceilings of the crypt cavern with a flickering orange glow. Along the passages sat small stone boxes, stacked at least four high, each scratched with old runes.

"The Stella Regina was built on a network of catacombs," Brandt explained. "Ossuaries housing bones from many centuries before writing was developed. But those earliest of ancestors were not without their ways of record keeping. Look." We moved past a column to a catacomb wall, where several symbols were scratched into the stone. The first I recognized. A wheel, representing time. Then two shapes, each overlapping the other. Beyond that, pictures of animals: birds, bears, crows, cats, foxes, horses, bats . . . They looked like oversize paper-and-plaster heads.

"The Day of Shades," I said.

"Yes," Edgar replied. "A celebration of the natural passage of one's subtle self, comprising the soul and the consciousness, through the borderland and into the beyond on the night when the curtain between the planes is the thinnest. It was a tradition to this area long before Renalt claimed it, and it will likely remain long after Renalt is gone."

"It's a wonder the Tribunal never put a stop to it," I said. "They do so dislike anything that can't be explained by their Book of Commands."

"Until recently," Harkness said, "they had no reason to bother. Just the harmless traditions of backward country folk, too far from the capital to make the effort of eradication worth it. Not when Syric was still so full of sinners to persecute."

"And now . . ."

"We'll adapt," Edgar said reassuringly. "We always do."

Cesare's body was resting in an open, central room, around which several smaller alcoves held stone coffins in radiating spokes like a clock. The first recess, at one o'clock, held the most ostentatious sarcophagus, decorated by intricate floral carvings and bearing the likeness of the person held within it. This version was much younger than the statue in the fountain in the plaza above, but even without the lines of age, Urso was immediately recognizable. He was dressed in the simple robes of a monk, but clasped in his stone hands was a sprig of bell-shaped flowers. Sombersweet.

I jumped when Edgar laid a soft hand on my shoulder. "Cesare's coffin is ready to receive him, but we need your help to move him there."

"Yes," I said. "Of course."

The pulley system had laid Cesare's body onto a litter. The three priests put their torches aside, and each of us took a corner and lifted him onto our shoulders, quietly shuffling to the open casket in the eleventh alcove. Only one stone casket would remain empty after this, the one sitting at the highest point of the circle, number twelve.

"Empyrea keep you, my brother," Edgar whispered as he unfastened the stretched cloth from the litter's frame.

"May you find safe crossing across the gray river," said Brandt.

Harkness murmured, *"Ligat sanguinem, sanguinem facere."* *Bound by blood, by blood undone.* The same words that Simon had used at the making of the bloodcloth. But on Father Harkness's lips, it sounded more like an invocation than an incantation. I wanted to ask him what he meant by it, but Edgar and Brandt were already lifting the stone lid over the casket, and I felt panic rise up inside me.

"No, don't!" I cried. "Not yet. Please. I can't bear the idea of him being trapped in there forever. Just alone and confined in the dark."

Father Edgar gave me a knowing smile. "Don't worry, child. *He* is not going to be trapped in this box. This is just a place to house his material remnants, no different than laying an old cloak away in a drawer." He nodded to Brandt, and they finished settling the lid over the coffin. And despite Edgar's reassurances, I still shuddered as Cesare's face disappeared behind the slab of stone.

12

Edgar made good on his promise to get me to my rendezvous on time, but not by leaving the crypt; instead, he led me through it. The main section, where Cesare was laid to rest, was a hub for many interconnected tunnels branching out in all directions. While the other two priests retired to their cots, Edgar led me down a dry, dusty passage.

The way narrowed as we went and was made even more uncomfortable by the fact that, after a few hundred feet, there were no more neatly arranged ossuary boxes. Rather, the deepest catacombs were lined with layers of bones and stacked skulls.

I tried to keep myself calm in the cramped, dark space by rehearsing Zan's breathing techniques. *One, in. Two, out. Three, in. Four, out. This isn't the Nothing Dream,* I told myself. *This isn't the Nothing Dream.*

Thankfully, we ended our march before the tunnel ceiling became too low for me to stand; I didn't relish the idea of crawling on my hands and knees in the dark, skulls staring at me from either side.

I coughed as Edgar pushed against the ceiling and dirt poured down into my face and eyes. Once I'd blinked the dust away, a square of midnight star-studded sky shone down on us.

"Where are we?" I asked.

"This arm of the catacombs ends where the wild hawthorn thatches begin," he said. "There's another arm that comes up in the floor of the old mill, but if you ever come back this way, you won't be able to find them—they are impossible to detect from the outside. The catacombs were still more scattered throughout the flax fields and the sheep pastures on the south side of the Stella, but many of them have caved in over the years, as they were never used as much by the brethren. A boat taken from the mill could get an accused witch down to the Calidi Bay, where the fugitive could buy passage to the isles or even to the continent. Heading north from here, escapees would have the cover of the hawthorns most of the way to the Ebonwilde, where an old road—rough, it was, but travelable—led right up to Achlev's Forest Gate. Now, listen. I don't know where you're going, or what you intend to do next. But if you head a half mile straight north from here, there's a rock marked with the seven stars of the great bear constellation. Beneath it, we keep a cache of food and supplies always ready. You're welcome to it, should you head that way."

"Thank you, Father," I said. "Empyrea keep you."

"And you." He hunkered down, putting his hands together. "Are you ready?"

I let him boost me up over the edge of the opening, and no sooner had I rolled away than I heard the scrape of the door sliding back into place.

I closed my eyes and breathed in the cold night air, thankful to be back in the open once again. But my relief didn't last; it wasn't more than a few minutes before an irritated voice came from above me, and I opened my eyes to find an irritated face to match.

"There she is," Onal said testily. "Lying spread-eagle in a field like she hasn't a care in the world while her brute of a bodyguard drags me from my bed in the middle of the night." She was wearing her best blouse, the one with the silver button at the collar, and her most vicious scowl.

Kellan was only a few paces away, wearily leading two stout Greythorne horses and Madrona. "She complained every step of the way, Aurelia. Every single step. It's a wonder, when we passed the village, we weren't immediately apprehended by Tribunal clerics. Please, for the love of all the holy stars, tell her where we're going and why she needs to come with us. She won't hear it from me."

Onal growled. "I think I got the gist of what he was trying to tell me: Zan touched you, you died, then Simon died, but before he went off into the hereafter, he said *I* have to go hightailing it who-knows-where to do who-knows-what, at the risk of my own life. For an *outlaw*. That's right; you're an outlaw, Aurelia. Which means that if I go with you, or cooperate with you at all, then *I* will be an outlaw. At *my* age? It's far too late for me to be considering a career change at this stage in my life."

I shot Kellan an apologetic look before addressing Onal, who had crossed her bony arms in front of her. "I have to find a way to break my bond with Kellan before I die," I said. "Simon said that the only person who can help me do this is the witch of the Ebonwilde woods, and that you are the only person who can help me find her."

Onal's mouth screwed to one side. "You've got a long time yet before you have to worry about dying, girl. Decades. And he's a soldier. Worse, he's one of those sickening *noble* and *dedicated* soldiers, and they always die the quickest. Odds are, he'll beat you to the grave anyway." She turned on her heel as if to head back the way she came.

"I don't have decades," I called to her retreating form. "That's what Simon told me."

She froze. "How long do you have, then?"

"Until the next blood moon. I have to die, or the Malefica will be let loose in the living world. And I refuse to take Kellan with me. Just like you said, he's noble. Dedicated. And he's exactly the person I want watching over my brother when I'm gone." I swallowed the hard lump forming in my throat. "Please, Onal. If you know how to reach the witch of the Ebonwilde, help me find her."

Finally, Onal said, "All right. Yes. I'll do it. But be warned: She doesn't like strangers. Or visitors." Onal paused. "Or people in general."

"*You* think *she's* not good with people?" I asked.

Unsmiling, Onal replied, "She lacks my effervescent charm. As you will see."

We stayed off the roads, riding through thorny hawthorn thickets for most of the night in hopes that any of the Tribunal's fearsome hounds would be less likely to follow us if they happened to catch our scent. We stopped only once, to locate the supply cache Edgar had told me about. It was a good thing we did, too; we left Greythorne with little more than the clothes on our backs. The waterskin, tin cups, dried meat, and half dozen potatoes were a great boon.

We made a hasty camp among the hawthorns a few hours before sunrise. I took first watch. When I was sure the other two were asleep, I filled one of the cups with water from the skin and then took out my knife.

I pricked my finger, hissing at the momentary pain, and let a tiny drop of blood break the water's surface. I was out of practice; I could feel the magic, but I resented the hurt it required. It made it hard to concentrate, but I conjured Zan's face in my mind and did my best to hold it there.

"Ibi mihi et ipse est," I whispered. *Show me.*

The blood bloomed in the water, tiny red threads that spread and swirled into an image of Zan riding away from the Quiet Canary on the back of a piebald mare I felt certain belonged to Hicks. But the image was fleeting, gone before I could even determine how fast he was going, or in which direction.

"No, no, *no,*" I said, frustration finally spilling over. "Show me what I need to *see.*"

At that demand, and in the very last second, a single image did form in the reflection: another horse and rider—but not Zan. This one was hooded and hulking, his steed rearing on its back legs, striking at the air.

When the second vision was gone, the only image left in the water was my dark-haired reflection.

One or the other, she whispered.

I gave a start, knocking the cup over as I jumped away from it. The pink-tinged water spilled into the dirt, and the cup spun like a silver top in the moonlight.

Defeated, I drew my knees up under my chin, pulling my wool cloak tight around my shoulders. When Kellan woke to take his turn on watch, I was ready to relinquish the responsibility.

I didn't expect to sleep, but I did. And surprisingly, my slumber was unburdened by dreams of blood, or drowning, or darkness, and though the dawn came too soon, it came softly.

Until we were out of the Greythorne province, we rode at night and slept during the day, stopping only occasionally to eat and rest the horses. It was the same route Kellan and I had taken to the Ebonwilde less than a year earlier, but it felt as if a lifetime had passed. It was a strange experience to travel this way again, albeit a much more pleasant one without Toris's incessant whistling. Still, the folk tune managed to worm its way into my head: *Don't go, my child, to the Ebonwilde, / For there a witch resides . . .*

I'd always thought it a bit of legend made into a song to frighten children, but we were now following this path with the specific goal of finding the song's reclusive subject.

> *You'll know her by her teeth so white,*
> *Eyes so red, and heart so black,*
> *But if you see her, child, in the Ebonwilde,*
> *You won't be coming back.*

I knew I should have been more nervous to meet such a ferocious figure, but I did not care if the Ebonwilde witch *did* eat wayward travelers; if she could help me break my blood tie with Kellan, I'd bathe in butter and crawl into her oven myself.

I didn't realize I'd been humming it to myself when Kellan said, "Conrad made me teach him the second verse to that song while we were on the tour. Against my will, I might add."

"I didn't know there was a second verse," I said.

"There are three. But the second one is the one we Greythornes try hardest to forget, since it is about one of our most disgraceful members."

"Oh?" I asked. "I didn't think the Greythornes had *anything* disgraceful in their past."

He grimaced. "A hundred or so years ago, one of the Greythorne sons—name of Mathuin—deserted his post in the king's cavalry. Abandoned everything and just disappeared into the woods. Most think he just became a hermit, but others say he got entangled with the Witch of the Woods and became slave to her . . . ahem, *other* hungers . . . until she got bored of him and cut off his head, forcing him to ride around as a headless ghost for all of eternity."

"And you taught my brother that story?"

"It's much more benign in verse," he said.

"Honestly, I'm more surprised you'd dare perpetuate a tale that references a failure in the Greythorne line."

"It never mentions him by name. The Greythorne pride remains fully intact."

On the fifth day of travel, we came at last to the forest's edge. On the sixth, Onal told us she was going to go ahead alone.

"The witch is a sly one, she is. And powerful enough to tangle the roads and paths if she so chooses. No one can find her house unless she wants them to, or unless they already know where it is."

"Which one is it for you?" Kellan asked.

Onal grinned just a little, but she never did answer. Nor did she seem at all afraid of going forth into the dense woods on her own.

Alone together for the first time, Kellan and I set up camp that night quietly. Our fire was small, just enough to keep the autumn chill at our backs and to warm the night's potatoes.

Kellan poked at his potato in the fire's embers. "What I wouldn't have given for this bounty the last time we were here."

I smiled. "Not hard to beat rock cress and field grouse." I paused. "Though, at the time, *that* felt like a bounty."

"Well, when the alternative is starvation . . ."

We settled into a comfortable silence, watching the fire crack and pop.

"Aurelia," Kellan finally ventured, "have you given any thought to what you'll do if we can't find the child-eating witch?"

"I'm sure that part is just a story." I put my chin on my knees. "And we will."

"All right," he said. "Say that we do—what if she can't help us?"

"I haven't thought that far ahead," I replied, hedging.

"No?" He sat back, regarding me with those pensive brown eyes. "Because I have."

"What do you think we should do if we can't break the blood

bond? Just let Zan die, and take our chances with the Malefica?" I shivered. "You know I can't do that."

"No," he said. "I was going to suggest that . . . well. We go together."

"What does that mean?" I asked suspiciously.

"For most of both our lives, I've been responsible for protecting you. If you're going to save the world, I want to save the world with you." His voice dropped. "I can't think of a more honorable death."

"Death isn't honorable, Kellan," I said, touched. "It's just . . . death. The world would be worse for your sacrifice."

"You don't understand," he replied. "*This* is my life's purpose. To fight, and die, for the Renaltan crown. For the common good. For *you*." He cleared his throat. "I just want you to know that now. That no matter what happens here, I will remain by your side. Even if the witch bakes us into a cake. At least you'll have company." He paused. "Though if we can figure out a way for us both to survive . . . that might be preferable."

I could hear my reflection's whisper in my ear. *At the red moonrise, one of two dies.* There was no escape from this fate. Not for me. But I could see his earnestness, and I sighed. I didn't want his company heading into death. It was hard enough letting him be here now. "Kellan," I said, "I—"

But his eyes had slowly moved past my face to the forest beyond.

"What is it—?" I asked, turning, but he pressed his fingers to his lips to quiet me.

We were being held in the incisive gaze of a watchful fox. Against the charcoal tones of the forest, she stood out like a bright brushstroke of color—rich red-orange fur, white-stained feet, and yellow eyes that shone like the moon at midnight.

I threw out an arm and caught a handful of Kellan's cloak. "It's her," I breathed. I had seen those eyes in this forest before, just after Toris's betrayal. I'd cried to a fox about Kellan, and he had ended up on Greythorne's doorstep days later, a fox sighted nearby. It was too uncanny to be mere coincidence. "It has to be her."

The fox turned tail and bolted into the wood.

I crashed through the trees after her, with Kellan close behind. "Wait!" I yelled. "Wait, I need to talk to you!"

And then, without warning, she reversed her course and launched herself right at me, transforming mid-leap, her bones shifting with a snap and crack, flesh re-forming over elongated limbs, shimmering silver in between. In less than a second, the fox was gone and a fierce, feral girl with flaming hair lunged in its place, her hand coming around my mouth to stifle the scream about to escape it.

"Quiet," she whispered, her voice dark and drifting, like autumn woodsmoke. In her other hand, she held a knife of leather and bone.

Kellan had been right on our heels, but when he saw her knife, he skidded to a stop. "Don't hurt her," he said, dropping his sword. "Just let her go."

"What in the Ilithiya's name are you doing?" she hissed. "Pick up your sword, you idiot!"

That's when I saw them—lurching shadows between the tree

trunks all around us. The girl muttered a string of creative expletives under her breath.

"Too late. They heard us. Do *you* have a sword? A dagger?" she asked me, releasing me to brandish her bone blade at the advancing silhouettes. "Anything?"

I procured my luneocite knife from my boot. As the shadows began tightening their circle, we heard a single soft growl.

The growl came again, deeper and closer. Unease rose inside me like a tide; I could see the wolf's eyes now, glowing a preternatural color of red. Its jaw was hanging slack, unhinged on one side and with a swollen, rotting tongue lolling out of it. It stalked around us, even more pieces missing from its decomposing hide than the last time I'd crossed its path.

"It's the Tribunal's," I whispered.

Beside me, Kellan strained away from it and its putrid smell.

"Don't run," the girl said. "And no matter what, *don't* turn your back to it. Protect yourself first, your horses second."

As if in response, the wolf grinned a half grin and lunged.

I held up my knife to fend it off, but not high or fast enough to get a good slice of it. It clawed at me as it fell back, shredding my sleeve and my arm underneath it. Blinded by pain, I lashed out instinctively. *"Uro!"* I shouted, and sent a blast of fire across its rotting flesh.

"Are you mad?" the girl yelled, sliding her knife down the belly of another wolf. "You'll burn down the whole forest!"

Another beast leaped at Kellan, and his sword slid like butter through its hide and out the other side as the creature snapped and growled and slavered on the skewer. Kellan shook it off, and it landed on four feet, entrails spooling out from the new wound, its patchy fur raised in a ridge along its back as it pawed the ground.

I breathed through the pain in my arm and prepared myself for another onslaught. The wolf had retreated ten paces back and was shrinking in on itself, compressing like a coil ready to spring. Then it let loose, catapulting forward with a howl, jagged teeth ready to rend my throat.

A flash of red-orange bolted across the darkness. Clamping her own jaws around the animal's neck, the girl—now a fox again—tumbled with it into the litter of leaves on the forest floor. Kellan jolted toward the wolf, slicing at its back as the fox wriggled out from beneath it. In another bound, the fox became a girl again, so smoothly and fluidly that there was no pause between one shape and the other.

"Help him hold it down!" she snapped at me.

Kellan had lost his sword and was rolling with the quivering mongrel, his arms locked around it to keep the thing from scouring his face. I threw myself beside him and we wrestled with the creature, gagging as the cold skin began to slop away from the muscle in ragged, sticky strips. The girl raised her hands and drew an intricate pattern in the air, leaving little sparks of bluish light in her fingers' wake with each swoop and swirl. Then she put her hands to the ground and closed her eyes, and the pattern wrote itself into the earth beneath her palms, streaking out like lightning across the ground and into the wolf, darting in crisscrossing lines around it.

As the blue-white lines flew faster and faster, binding the animal tighter and tighter, an oily smoke began leaking between the glowing binds. The dog whimpered as it was consumed by the light, and as the smoke dissipated, the red light in its eyes faded, leaving behind open, empty eye sockets, and the magic zagged to the other two, repeating the process until they were all husks.

"You can't kill what's already dead," the girl said. "You have to exorcise it. Now get up," she said, wrinkling her nose. "No need to keep hugging that maggot-ridden carcass now that the thing infesting it has been sent back to the afterworld where it belongs."

Kellan trudged to his feet, sloughing putrid, black sludge from his pants and sleeves. He looked at me apologetically. Then he ran to the first nearby bush, retching uncontrollably.

"You saved us," I said to the girl. "We didn't see them. We didn't even know they were there."

"Well, you're lucky that's all you attracted." She stomped out our little fire.

I approached her, but she sidestepped, swiping Kellan's fallen sword from the ground. "If you so much as breathe on me while you smell like that, I'll run you through."

I put my hands up. "All we want to do is talk. Ask you a few questions, and be on our way."

"And here I thought I was going to get me a birthday cake out of you," she said. "Though honestly, you don't look like very good eating, bony as you are. Him, though . . ." She tilted her head toward Kellan, considering. "Maybe."

He had pulled himself together and was watching her, too, forehead wrinkled in consternation. "Do I *know* you?"

"You *should* know me. I know you both well enough. This

is the second time I've saved both of your sorry lives." She eyed the wolf corpses. "Though, right now, I'm having some very deep regrets."

Lifting her yellow eyes to us, she said, "I'm Rosetta. Better known as the child-eating cannibal witch of the Ebonwilde Woods."

PART TWO

ISOBEL ARCENEAUX HATED MIRRORS.

It wasn't that she didn't like her reflection; if forced to look at it, she would admit that there was a pleasing quality to her face, a symmetrical group of features that balanced well with the bright color of her eyes and the dark contrast of her hair. She had an ageless beauty. But that was also the problem.

Now fifty-three years of age, she did not look a day over twenty-seven. At twenty, she'd looked fifteen. At thirty, nineteen. She'd aged normally until she reached womanhood; this curse came upon her at the same time as her monthly courses.

"A gift," her father had called it. Irving Arceneaux was a merchant of sorts, a man with an eye for opportunity, who could turn crumbs into capital with a wave of his hand. To him, she was a commodity; when his "friends"—mostly musty old men with sour breath and sagging skin—bought time with her, Irving always shaved several years off her true age to gain a few extra coins. She couldn't keep track of how many times her virginity had been auctioned away—a dozen at least.

Isobel's agelessness was no gift to *her,* however; it was a punishment. A curse. The work of wickedness or witchcraft. There was no other plausible explanation.

The only thing that eclipsed her loathing of her father was her hatred of magic and of all the starsforsaken practitioners of its arcane arts. When she finally killed the former, shortly after her twenty-ninth birthday, his blood was not yet dry before she retrieved all her hard-earned coins from his safe and set off to destroy, one by one, the latter.

She never regretted ridding herself of her only family. Irving Arceneaux wasn't her real father anyway. She'd heard him bragging to his friends about the foundling he'd acquired after coming upon the site of a stagecoach crash on an icy winter night in 1567. The driver and the lone adult passenger were both deceased; Irving Arceneaux had made a cursory search of the bodies and the interior of the cab, but there was nothing to identify the men. He had considered it a great bounty and helped himself to their valuables: coin, pocket watches, lapel pins, even the silver-plated handles from the cab. He'd already set fire to the coach when he finally heard the cries from the snowy roadside rushes and found the baby still bundled in her basket. She must have been thrown when the carriage rolled—lucky not to have been killed on impact, luckier still that she had not frozen to death afterward. But he was mostly glad he found her because the homespun dressing gown she was wearing featured four flower-shaped buttons of pure platinum gold. He snipped the buttons and warmed the baby by the burning coach, wondering if she might be worth something too. Barren wives would be eager to part with their riches for a pretty baby like this, he felt sure.

It turned out that many barren wives preferred to purchase boy babies; the offers for the little girl were laughably soft, and in the end, he decided to keep her. After all, a baby could be sold only once, but a young woman could be sold again and again. It would be Irving's greatest investment.

But even the best investments sometimes go sour. Isobel killed him slowly, to give him enough time to fully realize his miscalculation before he died.

The buttons were never sold; Irving never dared put them into the marketplace because he thought they were too distinguishable and someone might recognize them. Isobel found them in the same lockbox where he kept his collection of gold teeth.

Either way, the buttons were the only memento of her birth, and from then on, she wore them always. When she first entered Tribunal clerical training, she sewed them into her black robes. When she moved up in rank to officer, arbiter, and then justice, she always found a way to work the buttons into her uniform: the collar, the sleeves, the pockets . . . anywhere they would fit.

She was wearing them the day she first met Magistrate Toris de Lena. He'd been watching her conduct an interrogation, and when he came up to compliment her performance afterward, the silvery buttons did not escape his notice. "What a perfect representation of Queen Iresine's favorite earrings! She was such a beautiful woman, was she not?"

Later, as he began to take Isobel under his wing and helped sponsor her own ascension to magistrate, he walked her down the Hall of Kings in the royal palace and showed her the portrait of Iresine and her husband, King Costin. The queen, who was by then dead thirty years, wore earrings that were exact copies of Arceneaux's buttons.

The next portrait in line was that of King Regus, Iresine and Costin's only son. The face that stared back at Isobel from that frame was so like her own that she audibly gasped. His hair was blond and hers was dark, his skin was tawny while hers was more pale, and his eyes were a deep brown while hers were blue . . . but the structure of their faces, the shape of their noses, the set of their lips . . . they were all the same.

"Ah, yes," Toris said thoughtfully, watching her. "The late king Regus in his youth. He was twenty-five when that was painted, not yet married to Genevieve. He was considered quite dashing in his day."

Isobel stepped closer to peer at the brass plate beneath the portrait.

King Regus Costin Altenar
15 Primus 1567–27 Tertius 1612

King Regus had been born in midwinter, the year 1567, just a day before she was found.

That's when she finally knew who she really was. An unwanted princess, sent away at birth to keep Renalt from having to make good on its treaty to Achleva. And this face—this familiar stranger's face —was that of her brother. Her twin. A man who'd lived a prince and died a king.

They were on their way out of the hall when a small, unkempt slip of a girl crashed by them, running with wide eyes as if she had some-one behind her, though there was no one else in the hall. Her feet got tangled up under her skinny legs and she careened into the portrait of Iresine and Costin, knocking it from its nail to the floor.

Isobel's eye had twitched at the sight. She had heard the whis-pers about the princess—that there were things about her that just seemed off—witchlike, even—and had never given it much thought.

But knowing what she now knew, Isobel felt rankled by Aurelia's very existence. What was it about this unnatural little imp that had encouraged her royal parents to keep her, when Isobel had been abandoned and erased by hers? How was it fair that *Aurelia* had been raised in these glittering halls, while Isobel had been Irving's little moneymaker?

Isobel instantly hated her.

Onal, the spindly old spinster Queen Genevieve called an adviser, appeared at the other end of the hall, rushing to replace the fallen portrait while scolding the devil who'd toppled it. Her words to the little girl were sharp, but in Isobel's opinion, a whip would have been sharper and far more effective.

Toris had had to tug her away. He'd been observing Isobel with the acuity of a hawk, and when they were out of earshot, he said, "I think it's time we have a talk, Warden Arceneaux."

She told him everything. About her curious origins, the denigrator who'd passed himself off as her father, and even—with reluctance—about her inability to properly age. Toris had listened with interest, and when she finished, she raised up her hands for him to arrest her.

He did not bind her wrists. Rather, he put both his hands over hers.

"You bear a burden, yes. Your condition is most certainly caused by magic . . . Some might even go so far as to call you a witch. But I've seen the vigor with which you work, the deep devotion you carry to our cause . . . and I believe there is a great change coming soon. The Empyrea has charged me with preparing this world for the reckoning that must come before her return, in human form, to our world. It is now my belief that she has sent you—*saved* you—to be my partner in this divine purpose. Will you join me, Isobel?"

She had already agreed in her heart long before she was able to release the words from her mouth.

And after eight years of effort, they'd come *so close* to the fulfillment of their mission. The night of the black moon, she'd felt the change happening. It had been right there in her hands.

And then, just as quickly, it had been taken away.

Because of that *girl*.

At first, she'd just wanted revenge. She wanted to make Aurelia suffer the same way she had. She thought finding Valentin alive, so close to the infant king's coronation, was a gift from the Empyrea herself. She would kill Aurelia's lover in front of her, provoke her into demonstrating magic, and then arrest her for witchcraft.

It was the best way to punish her without damaging her body. No matter how much Arceneaux hated the girl, she was still too shrewd to waste such a valuable resource. If the magic inside her blood was strong enough to kill Toris, imagine what it could be used for when given to someone more deserving?

Arceneaux could think of at least four or five loyal vassals to whom she could entrust such a powerful vehicle. Aurelia's body, occupied by one of Arceneaux's entourage, would become the greatest tool the Tribunal ever had.

She'd gotten too careless, though. Let herself feed too much on the thrill of triumph. Until, once again, Aurelia had slipped from her grasp. And now she was here, in a damp and dirty old mill, out on the starsforsaken edge of civilization, trying to figure out her next steps.

There was a knock at the door of her cramped sleeping space. "Come in," she said curtly.

"Pardon me, Magistrate," Lyall said. "The priest is here for you."

Arceneaux stood and straightened her white dress. "Good."

She followed Lyall through the lab he'd set up on the second story of the mill, past the unsettling contents of his worktables, trying to ignore the sour stench that always accompanied his experiments. The purpling body of the murdered acolyte Golightly was laid out at the end of the room surrounded by a half-empty vial of blood and Lyall's iron implements: a pair of tongs, shears, and an awl with a wicked point, still hot from the fire. Golightly was one of the first of the Tribunal to support her claim to power within their ranks. He'd embraced her leadership and served her with devotion, always dog-gedly loyal; he would be the first of her followers to earn the honor of becoming a Celestine at his death. But if anyone deserved to be reborn on the day of the Empyrea's descent to earth, he did.

Lyall had become quite good at harvesting spirits in the last months, his collection of luneocite acting as lodestones for the newly untethered before they could move to the afterworld. Somewhere within the clear stones, Golightly's spirit awaited its promised rebirth. And not just any body would be suitable; no, he deserved something grander than a canine or common cottager, and Arceneaux would make sure he got it.

Father Edgar of the Stella Regina was waiting just inside the doorway on the first floor. If he could smell the decaying body from downstairs, he was too polite to say so. "Hello, Magistrate," he said, his eyes cautious and disturbingly large behind his thick spectacles. "I was surprised to receive your message."

"Not as surprised as I am that you actually answered it," Arceneaux replied.

"It is my duty as an Ursonian monk to offer knowledge and assistance to the Empyrea's servants wherever I can."

Arceneaux gave a small *hmph* at that. Then, "As lovely as it is to be in your company, Father, it is your archive I wish to spend some quality time with. I've heard many accounts of Saint Urso's predictions. Indeed, King Theobald heralded the monk as a true high mage. A seer chosen by the Empyrea herself."

"Urso had keen foresight; that is true enough."

"I'm looking for one prediction in particular," Arceneaux said. "I've encountered several references to it in my own studies of King Theobald's Empyrean visitation at the Stella Regina. One that has to do with the timing of the Goddess's return to the earth. The writings I came across mentioned a 'red moonrise.' I would like to spend some time in your library to see if I can't find that passage and study it in its entirety."

"I'm sorry, Magistrate, but the Stella Regina sits on Greythorne land, and now that Lord Fredrick has claimed seclusive rights to his property, there is no way to arrange such an appointment, even if I wanted to."

Arceneaux's eyes narrowed. "Well, if I am not allowed on

Greythorne land, perhaps you can bring whatever records you have on the matter to me instead."

"Can't do that, either, mistress. What remains of Urso's writings are very precious and cannot be moved from the safety of the Stella's archives."

"Not even by order of a magistrate?"

"Not even then."

Arceneaux's lip curled. This little country priest was so small and mousy, she hadn't expected this kind of insolence. "That's very disappointing," she said. "But I'm not the type to be so easily dissuaded. I will just have to find another way."

Father Edgar turned to go, but Arceneaux had motioned to Lyall, who was now blocking the door. "Pardon me," Edgar said. "I really should be getting back."

"Oh, there's no hurry," Arceneaux said smoothly. "Lyall, take him upstairs, won't you? Father Edgar is a scholar. I'm sure he'd love to see some of your work. Perhaps even participate in the research." She smiled as Father Edgar fidgeted. "In fact," she added, "I insist."

13

We waited out the night next to the ashes of our stomped-out fire, and in the morning, Rosetta went about skinning one of the wolves with well-practiced proficiency. She would not carry the freed hide afterward, however, claiming that Kellan or I, in our squalid states, were better suited to the task. But Kellan retched again the moment he tried to heft it, so the responsibility fell to me by default.

We'd already gone most of another mile through the tightly packed trees before I had the sense to ask why she needed the thing. No one in her right mind would want to wear it or sleep beneath it.

Rosetta did not answer the question. Her only response was "Keep walking."

To be fair, there was no *real* indication that Rosetta was in her right mind.

Kellan also tried to initiate conversation with her. "We had another friend who went ahead to find you. She was supposed to let you know we were coming. Have you seen her?"

Rosetta said, "No," with a note of finality that silenced us both.

She may have been taciturn to us, but her interaction with our horses was friendly and familial, as if she'd known them for a long time and was pleased to be finally catching up with them. Madrona's reluctant fondness for me had been hard-won, but she was immediately enamored with Rosetta; she trotted alongside her like a carefree puppy. As I labored under the smelly wolfskin, I mentally vowed to sneak Madrona more apples. I was not above winning favor with bribery.

"How much longer?" I wheezed after another mile—I thought. It was hard to know how far we'd gone. Everything looked the same so far off the known paths and in the endless twilight of the forest. Rosetta could have just been walking us in circles for her own amusement, and we'd never know.

"We'll go until we stop," she said, leaning over to whisper in Madrona's ear, which flicked back and forward in response.

"What do you think those two gossips are talking about?" Kellan asked. He walked several feet to my left to avoid my smell.

"Probably something about my hair. Or clothes."

"In all honesty, it is not your best look," he said. "Even before it got all covered in . . . wolf sludge."

"That's funny," I said. "I was just telling myself how much your wolf sludge suited you. I think you should wear it more often." I tried to hand the wolfskin off to him, but he jumped away, laughing.

Rosetta stopped abruptly, hand up in the air. "Shhh," she said, and we fell silent, suddenly wary.

After a moment, she began to move forward again, and we tiptoed to follow. "Did you hear anything?" Kellan asked nervously.

"No," she said. "I just wanted you to be quiet."

We settled into an annoyed silence, following her deeper and deeper into the woods.

It gave me an opportunity to examine her closer. I'd expected a woman to match the witch of the song—wrinkled and sallow, with red eyes and a wealth of oversize teeth—but this girl appeared to be my own age, if not younger, wearing a simple homespun dress in a long out-of-fashion style. Her hair was a tangled, wild cloud of deep sienna, with strips of leather and gold-dipped leaves braided into the plentiful waves. Her skin was tawny, with freckles sprinkled across her cheeks like stars. But it was her eyes that were the most stunning: a vivid array of ochres and umbers that gleamed like discs of polished tiger-eye.

She was fresh-turned earth and autumn leaves and caustic wind. I liked her.

"We're here," she announced.

"We're . . . where?" Kellan asked. Our surroundings were exactly the same now as they had been the entire time we'd been walking.

She waved us forward, and we took a few steps farther into the clearing. As we did, there began to be a ripple across the darkness. Colors started to bleed out from the forest's unending palette of blacks, blues, and grays, and shapes became visible: a red tile roof on a yellow-painted cottage, with tall sunflower stalks clustered under the second-story windows. A tract of garden was laid out beneath the late-morning sky, overflowing with harvest vegetables in rich jewel tones—vermilion pumpkins, purple-black eggplant, peppers of emerald and citrine, tiny tomatoes dangling from curling vines like rubies from a delicate necklace. Smoke trickled from the chimney as if to welcome us, promising a cozy fire inside.

"Welcome to the homestead," Rosetta said. "Don't touch anything."

"You live here alone?" Kellan asked.

"You make it sound like that's a bad thing." She unlatched the gate, which screeched mightily as it swung open.

"So," Kellan said, "if you're the only one who lives here, you're also the only one responsible for upkeep on the gate?" He leaned down to eye the rusty hinges. "Because this is unacceptable."

"Spoken like a true Greythorne," she said. "I liked it better the last time you were here, when you were quiet."

"You mean, that time when I was stabbed and dropped off a cliff? That time?"

"You're welcome," she retorted.

"For what? When I was delivered to my brother at Greythorne, I was all but dead."

"All but dead is not dead. And it was not exactly easy carrying your sorry self all the way there. And if *I* hadn't done it, who would have? Not Miss Princess over there. Didn't see her doing anything useful to help you. She just sat there in the forest, crying like a helpless baby."

I blushed.

As she led us past the gate, Kellan whispered to me, "When Onal said the witch wasn't good with people, I assumed it was because she liked to eat them. *This* might actually be worse."

But as we approached the cottage, I was no longer listening to him. I dropped the wolfskin and stared.

"I know this house," I said. "I've dreamed about this house."

Rosetta watched as I began to make a circle around the cottage.

Her chin lifted. "What happened in this dream?"

I was suddenly hesitant to tell her, but she stared me down, waiting. She seemed the type that, having asked a question, expected an answer.

Reluctantly, I said, "There was screaming coming from the inside. I'd try to get in to see what was happening, to see if I could help, but couldn't open any of the doors or windows. Eventually . . ." I trailed off and shrugged. "The screaming would stop and the dream would end."

As if on cue, the cottage door opened and Onal stepped out.

"Rosetta," she said. "Took you long enough to get home. I regret to inform you that I have eaten all the blackberries you had in your cupboard." She sniffed the air. "Dear me, what is that *smell?*"

"Rotting wolf guts," Kellan said.

Rosetta regarded the older woman with her arms folded. She said, "I should have known it was you who brought these two *wits* into my forest again. They caused me quite a lot of trouble the last time."

"They *are* both very irritating," Onal agreed. "But it can't be helped. They're young and stupid."

"So why, exactly, have you brought them to me?"

Onal's gaze moved to me. "I'm still a little foggy on the details, but it seems as if the fate of the world is at stake."

"I wondered what it would take to get you to come back here.

Now I know: the end of the world." Rosetta gave a mirthless smile. "Welcome home, little sister."

✶

The water they doused me with was frigid; it didn't help that I was standing in naught but my underclothes in the windiest part of the clearing.

"You're . . . sisters?" I asked, teeth chattering as Onal handed Rosetta another bucket and went to the well to refill the first.

"You don't see the resemblance?" Rosetta asked, emptying another bucket over my head without warning.

I gasped as the icy splash of water hit me. When I recovered enough to speak, I said through gritted teeth, "No. I can see it."

Rosetta handed me a homemade cake of soap. "Scrub," she ordered, and I obeyed, barely getting a good lather up before she soaked me again. I shrieked.

Kellan, waiting nearby with his back turned, was chuckling.

"I don't know what you think is so funny," Onal said. "You're next."

Rosetta put down her bucket and waved me forward, handing me an old blanket to wrap around my shoulders. "That will have to do. There's a trunk of old clothing under the stairs. You can wear what-ever you find."

Behind me, Kellan's peals of laughter were cut off by the sound of a splash as Onal tossed her first bucket over him.

✶

The interior of the cottage was warm and snug and smelled of sage and cedar. The trunk Rosetta had mentioned was filled with clothes of meticulous construction but of long-outdated style. I found a dress that looked as if it would fit well enough, a simple shift of pale green with long, loose sleeves and that tightened at the bodice with ties down each side of the waist.

When the task of dressing was over, I turned my attention to my hair, running my fingers through the wet tangles as I wandered around the cottage. The main parlor contained an odd collection of rough-hewn furniture and homespun fabrics that were woven into intricate designs. *Spells, probably,* I thought, wincing as I tugged a knot from my hair.

In one corner was a spinning wheel—a large, lumbering device made of old well-oiled oak. In the other corner, a cradle sat under a thick layer of dust. A rag doll was nestled within, and the teardrop flowers painted on the sides bloomed in faded red-violet.

My eyes drifted up from the cradle to an oval portrait frame hung above it. For a minute, it looked as if the frame was empty, but closer inspection revealed that it was, in fact, a mirror that had been turned to face the wall.

I cataloged the bric-a-brac over the mantel: strings of herbs hung to dry in the fire's heat, a dusty clock that seemed to have been robbed of its gears, and a line of a half dozen carved figurines of varying sizes. The first was a young maiden made of white pine with tresses almost to her feet and a look of wondering innocence on her face. The second figurine was another young woman, this time carved from plush mahogany. She was warm and lovely, endowed with comely curves and a cloud of curling locks. The third was much younger—just a child, really, carved out of deep walnut. Her back was straight, chin defiantly aloft, with a sleek fall of hair that gleamed in the light. In her arms, she held a baby, or a tiny doll.

The next few were animals: A fox, a bear, a snowy owl . . .

Kellan entered the room behind me, muttering curses through his chattering teeth. He made a beeline to the fire, clothed in nothing but his dripping braies and an abundance of goose bumps. "I asked Rosetta if she had anything I could change into, and she laughed and said none of her dresses would fit me." He sighed in relief as he turned his backside to the warmth of the fire.

"Shame," I said. "You'd look ravishing in a dress."

"I know it," he said. "But she doesn't want my arms tearing any of the seams."

"A valid concern," I said, eyeing his swordsman's shoulders. Then I said, "Kellan, look here. What do you see?"

He turned toward the mantel. Then his eyebrows shot up. "They look like . . ."

". . . the statues from the hedge maze," I finished for him. I picked up the carving of the littlest girl. "They are almost exactly alike."

"Come away from there." Rosetta had come in with a section she'd cut away from the wolf pelt, Onal following on her heels.

"This one looks like you, Rosetta," I said, undaunted. I pointed to the mahogany maiden.

"The first one is Galantha, our sister who passed away," Rosetta said, more focused on spreading out the piece of wolfskin on the table. She glanced at Onal. "The little one is Begonia."

I stifled a snort. "Your name is Begonia?"

Onal crossed her arms. "Do you find that amusing?"

Rosetta had begun to scrape fur from the skin with her bone knife. She said, "*Begonia* has always hated her name—"

"It's a stupid name," Onal cut in.

"—so she decided she was going to change it to Nola, after the first warden. But she used to always get her letters switched around when she was trying to write, so instead of spelling it *N-O-L-A* she wrote *O-N-A-L*. I teased her about it mercilessly."

"No! You?" Kellan said.

"So she kept it just to spite me."

"Not just to spite you," Onal said. "*Any* name was better than Begonia."

"I used to call her Beggie. And Goney," Rosetta continued. "She had a lot of nicknames, my little sister."

"And you wonder why I left and never came back." Onal's thin eyebrows were arched dangerously.

"Maybe if you'd stayed, you'd have aged a little better," Rosetta said with a shrug. "Grandmother lived over four hundred years, and you look just like her now, at a mere one hundred and twenty."

Kellan and I both gaped. I'd never been foolish enough to ask Onal her age, but if I'd had to guess, I would have put her at seventy —at the most.

"You're one hundred and twenty years old?" Kellan asked incredulously.

"In another two months." Onal's lips pinched together. "It's not something I typically advertise."

"Onal ages slowly, like any daughter of the woods," Rosetta said, "even if she was born lowly and talentless and left home in shame."

Onal folded her long fingers under her chin. "You make it so hard to like you."

I looked at Onal with new eyes. "Now I know where you come by all your herb knowledge. But never in my lifetime would I ever have guessed—"

"That's the folly of the young," Onal replied. "Seeing all the years lining a person's face without fathoming all the life that was lived to gain them."

"Did Mother know any of this? Your family, your ties to feral magic, your slow aging?"

"No. Nor did your father. I never told anybody; it was dangerous enough to be so adept at the healing arts. Why bring any more scrutiny upon myself than was necessary?" She looked down her nose at me. "A question I wished you'd asked yourself more regularly over the years."

"Simon knew, didn't he?" I thought aloud. "How else would he have known you could help us find Rosetta?"

"I don't see how he could have guessed it," Onal said. "I had planned to take the secret to my grave."

"You got awfully close, sister," Rosetta said. "You should feel proud."

Onal tipped her head. "What secrets did you take to yours?"

They both glared at each other with an animosity so sharp, it could have been honed only by sisterhood.

"Are all feral mages like this?" I asked. "Slow to age, quick to anger?"

"I'm not a feral mage, and she's not *just* one," Onal replied. "She's the warden of these woods."

"What does that mean?"

"Once every age, one of the female descendants of the Mother goddess is chosen to maintain balance among her creations, to ensure that the patterns and cycles she created continue on through the generations."

"The Ilithiya," Rosetta said, holding up the strip of wolf pelt, now sheared close enough for the gray skin to show through. "Call her by her name, if you please." She examined the piece of skin for a second before saying, "There! I found it." Crowing triumphantly, she slapped the pelt down on the kitchen table. We all eyed it uncomfortably.

Onal cleared her throat. "What, exactly, did you find?"

"The answer to where these creatures are coming from," she said. "There have been more than just wolves. I've seen broken-necked crows, and red-eyed weasels . . . It seems that someone has been experimenting with whatever creatures they could get their hands on. Usually, by the time I get to them, their bodies are too rotted to find the seal. But this specimen was more recently dead, and . . . well, just look."

She passed her hand over the piece of hide, and a faint, blue-white light began to take shape in the form of an intricate, five-pointed knot. "This is how they're doing it—fastening human souls in the bodies of animals."

My stomach turned. *"Human souls?"*

"It wouldn't be impossible to do, if one had enough knowledge of the spectral plane and a complete lack of empathy."

"The first time I saw a creature like this, it was when the Tribunal was looking for us," I said, remembering Zan and my encounter. "But while the Tribunal is certainly lacking in empathy, it would be less likely that they'd be using witchcraft against witches." I sighed.

"Would you put it past them?" Rosetta asked. "Because I wouldn't. Collecting spirits and binding them into mismatched bodies sounds exactly like the type of thing the Tribunal would look into."

"What purpose could there be," Kellan asked in disgust, "in putting departed souls into animals?"

"Plenty," Rosetta said, leveling her yellow eyes at him. "If your goal is to someday do it with human bodies."

We fell absolutely silent, shocked.

"You could live forever that way," she continued, "jumping from body to body until the end of time. But souls are meant to inhabit only the vessels into which they are born. Someone has devised a way around that. See? This symbol is an amalgamation of two magics: blood magic embedded into a feral knot. But the spell isn't right yet. The magics clash. And the mismatched spirit cankers while the body rots."

Rosetta tossed the pelt into the fireplace, where it began to curl and blacken. "Stars save us if they ever make it work."

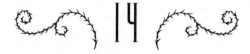

W hen the pelt had burned to ash, I broke the silence by clearing my throat. "As troubling as the creature is, it's not why we've come."

"No," Rosetta said, prodding the fire with a long, thin branch stripped of leaves and twigs and crudely sharpened. "You've come to tell me about the end of the world."

"You're going to burn that stick up," Kellan said, looking around. "Don't you have any iron tools lying around this place?"

"No iron," Rosetta said flatly.

Onal sighed and tried to explain. "Women of the woods and feral mages are not particularly fond of iron. They don't like anything made of it either, even in the smallest amounts. Like steel . . ."

"Or blood," Rosetta said, turning her yellow eyes on me. "Or magic that requires blood."

"How did you know——" I began.

"I could smell it on you the first moment I saw you," she said. "Worse than the wolf pelt, that smell. Like anger and iron and brimstone."

I snapped, "I don't care if you don't like my magic. I don't care if you don't like *me*. I can't say I'm particularly fond of you at the moment, either. But the wisest man I know told me to find you, so here I am. Asking—begging—for your help."

"And what, exactly, do you think I can help you with, girl?"

"He said that you could show me how to go into the world between the Now and the After. He called it the Gray."

Rosetta burst into hoots of laughter. "How wise can your friend be that he sent you to the one person in all the world who *can't* go into the Gray?" She turned to face us. "I will let you stay the night, but you must be gone in the morning. I don't have time for any more of this nonsense."

"On the contrary," Onal muttered, "you've got all the time in the world."

I was burning with frustration and disappointment, but I hadn't slept more than a few hours in the past three days, and I knew that arguing with Rosetta would serve only to get myself removed from the homestead faster.

Rosetta gave me Galantha's old room. It was a snug little space near the attic, with most of the furniture covered in white sheets to keep the dust off. I removed each sheet in turn and marveled at every discovery: a pine-bough bed, an old wardrobe carved with dainty spring flowers, and a chair painted a sweet, summery yellow.

There was a dresser, too, with a mirror edged in colorful bits of river stone. Despite its prettiness, it was the only piece I left covered; one glance at my wan reflection was more than enough.

A single, west-facing window let in the forest-filtered light, and the room was scattered with souvenirs of her short life: a wreath of twigs, paper flowers, stacks of old books. Garlands of found objects —bronze keys, seashells, acorns, gold-dipped leaves, and oddly shaped glass beads—crisscrossed the steeply angled eaves of the ceiling.

I would have liked her, too, I decided, if I'd had the chance to know her.

I crawled into the bed and fell asleep quickly. It was like being swept away on a swift river; as soon as I began to slip into slumber, I was helpless to crawl back out of it.

I dreamed of Galantha.

She was sitting on the side of her bed, watching me sleep. She had long waves of blond hair with just a touch of Rosetta's red that shone when the moonlight hit it just right, but her eyes were buttery brown like Onal's.

"What happened to you?" I asked.

She said, "I made a choice."

"Are you a spirit?"

"In a way. I'm more like . . . a memory."

"Yours or mine?"

"Both," she said. And then I saw that she wasn't Galantha at all. She was me. Not the me who'd appeared when I was drunk with sombersweet; that girl was someone I didn't know. This one was well and truly *me*. Older, maybe. Wearier, certainly . . . but definitely me.

She turned to leave.

I stood up too. "No, wait—" But the white sheet had slid from the dresser mirror, and I caught sight of us in the reflection: one girl with fair hair, the other with dark, facing each other. Two sides of the same coin. The Two-Faced Queen.

I bolted awake, but the room was still and quiet. The only movements were mine, reflected back at me from the uncovered mirror.

I heard a sound outside the window and flew to it, just to see Rosetta's outline stealing across the homestead garden. I wrapped the blanket from Galantha's bed around my shoulders and raced down the stairs and out the cottage door before I could lose Rosetta to the forest.

It was near midnight now, and the forest was fully settled into its second state, a world of purpling shadows and silvery strands of moonlight. I followed Rosetta past a border of twine knot spells gently waving in the chill night wind. Apprehension skittered along my spine as I hurried to keep up with her. I had not forgotten what it was like to be lost in the Ebonwilde at night.

When she stopped, it was at another clearing. This one was smaller, and the air within it felt dense and heavy and unnaturally warm, like the interior of a sanctorium on a humid summer day.

Rosetta walked to the center of the expanse, where long, curling flower stalks were in full bloom, dangling lines of blossoms consisting of two heart-shaped violet-red petals that enclosed two droplet-shaped white petals.

"You can come out now," she said to the air. After a moment, I realized she was addressing me.

I timidly stepped from the trees to join her in the glade.

"I thought sombersweet was a spring flower," I said, bending to run my finger along a line of the dangling blossoms, which bounced and quivered on their vine. "How are they blooming here in the fall, so close to winter?"

"They never stop blooming in the Cradle," Rosetta said. "This is their place of origin."

"The place where Mother Earth gave birth to her child with Father Time?"

"The Ilithiya."

"Pardon?"

"The Ilithiya. That was her name. And his was Temporis."

The clearing of the Cradle was a near-unbroken sea of the dangling, gemlike buds. Rosetta plucked a sprig and twirled it between her fingers. "These little flowers are facsimiles of the Ilithiya's Bell, comprising her Joy"—she touched the red-violet petals—"and her Sorrow." She touched the white petals. Then she gave the sprig a little shake, and the flowers sprang back and forth, just like tiny bells. "This is where the first warden, Nola, was born. And this is where her mother, the Ilithiya, died. The Cradle is a sacred place. It is not meant for the eyes of outsiders."

"Then why did you let me follow you?"

"I figured it was only fair, after I stole this out of your pack." She lifted Simon's book in the air, its rose-gold branches glinting.

I tried to make a grab for it. "You went through my things? That is a gross invasion of privacy."

She pulled it out of reach and said, "You are all grossly invading *my* privacy, are you not? Entering my woods, overtaking my home? And besides, this doesn't belong to you. Where did you get it?"

"It was given to me."

"What for?" She cracked it open and removed my hastily scribbled list of translations. "You obviously can't read it."

Sourly, I replied, "I don't have any idea. Which is the same answer I'd give to you if you asked me why, in the name of all the stars and the Most Holy Empyrea, he wanted to send me to *you*."

"So it was this Simon, then? The blood mage you killed."

I took a deep breath, reaching for the last scraps of my serenity. "Yes. Simon sent it to me. And then, when he died, he told me to find you."

"And you never showed this to Onal?"

I shook my head. "No."

"I'm not sure she'd have recognized it, even if you had. She was young when Galantha died."

"What do you mean?"

"This"—she held the book up—"is Galantha's grimoire. I'd know it anywhere; she began compiling it the year after our mother died birthing Begonia and she moved up as next in line to serve as Warden of the Woods."

"You mean . . . it's a book of spells?"

Rosetta said, "What did you think it was? A bunch of fairy tales?"

"I hadn't ruled it out," I huffed.

"Every warden keeps one, and then they pass their knowledge on to their successor, who then writes her own."

"You have one of your own, then?"

"Of a sort," she said. "But my inheritance of the warden's mantle came with no warning or training. Everything I know, I've had to figure out on my own."

"Simon said it was hundreds of years old—"

"One hundred and sixteen years, give or take."

"Maybe Simon knew you'd want it and sent it to me as . . . a payment, or something . . . to convince you to help me." She looked skeptical, so I continued. "Maybe there's a spell in there you can use to break the blood bond between Kellan and me."

"There's only one way I know of to break the bond," Rosetta said, "and that is by using the Ilithiya's Bell. Unfortunately for us both, that relic was lost at the same time as the grimoire. There's no way of knowing where it went, or how to get it back, without going into the Gray. And there's no way to go into the Gray without the Ilithiya's Bell." She brushed a few strands of her red hair out of her eyes. "Do you see the conundrum?"

"But I've been to the Gray," I said. "Twice now. That's where I was when Simon told me to find you."

She gave me a skeptical look. "And you *died* to get there. Is that something you're willing to risk again? No? I didn't think so."

"Simon told me you could help me. Why would he think that?"

"Wardens have been responsible for maintaining the balance between the planes. To fulfill this purpose, they had the Ilithiya's Bell, which gave them the ability to cross the lines between planes without leaving an anchoring part of themselves behind."

"What if a person *does* leave an anchoring part of herself behind? What then?"

She looked at me thoughtfully. "You said you had a dream about the homestead."

"I did."

"Have you had other dreams like that one?"

I hesitated. "A few."

"I have heard of Assembly mages traveling the Gray while sleeping. Projecting, they called it. Your consciousness leaves your material body behind and occupies your subtle body instead. You are able to observe, but not *be* observed. Able to influence, but not physically affect. You are, essentially, a ghost."

"If that was what I was doing, I didn't know it. I didn't do it purposefully."

"But if you did . . ."

"I've never had any control of where I go or what I see," I said. "Up until this moment, I thought they were just dreams. Or that I was dead. At least, I was supposed to be." It was warm, but I still pulled the blanket tighter, finally bringing up the distressing subject that never left the back of my mind. "Looks like I'll get another crack at dying pretty soon."

"Death is part of nature, part of life. The true feral mage honors that process. We do not seek to thwart it. We do not interfere."

With my tongue behind my teeth, I said, "That doesn't mean you wouldn't. It just means that you haven't lost anyone you loved enough to try."

"Or maybe," she said, yellow eyes narrowing, "I loved them too much to try."

"Why, then, did you help Kellan five months ago, if you didn't have to? He's alive because you interfered."

"He was stabbed. That's hardly 'natural.'" She went quiet for a moment. "But, honestly? He looks like Mathuin."

She looked down at her feet, her red mane ruffling in the night wind. I moved in closer, curious to see what she was looking at, and gave a start.

Her feet were planted on the edge of a bloodleaf island in the middle of the sombersweet ocean. A reminder of death amid this sacred monument to new life.

"How did this happen?" I asked, staring at the bloodleaf.

"Things are out of balance," she said obliquely. "They have been for a very long time. I always believed that if I could just keep the forest at peace, the civilizations of man would ebb and flow the same way they always have, and the world would right itself again over time. But time, I'm afraid, is not on our side." Rosetta crouched down among the flowers, pulling her knees up under her chin. After a moment, she spoke again, and I listened intently, unable to shake the sense that all of this was important. That I was supposed to be here, in this place, listening to this story at this moment.

I was no believer in fate, but if it was real, I imagined it would feel something like this.

A small breath of wind suddenly gusted across the blossoms of the sombersweet, and they bowed and swayed in response, as if to say yes.

"I was never meant to be warden," Rosetta said quickly. "Galantha was the one who was chosen to inherit the mantle from Grandmother after our mother died. She was born for the task—bright, beautiful, loved by everyone and everything. When Begonia was little, I told her that crocuses would sprout wherever Galantha walked, and she used to watch Galantha's footprints, waiting to see the flowers come up. Not because she believed *me,* but because Galantha was exactly the type of person for whom flowers would spring to life to follow.

"Galantha took on the mantle at sixteen. Warden of the Seventh Age—the Maiden Age. Grandmother's stewardship had lasted four hundred years. Galantha could have had at least that long, maybe longer. Grandmother used to say that Galantha was going to be the strongest warden since Nola, and *she* was said to have lived for thousands of years."

"What happened?" I asked quietly.

"Mathuin," she said. "Mathuin Greythorne." She reached into her pocket and removed the figurine of the second sister, the one of Rosetta's own likeness.

"I know that name. Kellan told me about him. Greythorne's family shame. The deserter who was lured into the Ebonwilde by a witch and lost his head."

"Not his head," Rosetta said. "Just his heart. Mathuin was an artist; he was never meant to be a soldier. So when he abandoned his military post, the Tribunal went after him. He narrowly escaped with his life and tried to make a break for safety in Achlev, but he never made it that far. Galantha and I found him wandering the woods, mortally wounded and near death. We brought him back home to heal, and then he just . . . stayed."

She smiled a little at the memories. "He'd carve his figurines and tell us beautiful stories about his life in this faraway oasis of magic and mazes called Greythorne. He made himself busy, fixing little things, working alongside us in the garden, taking us for rides through the woods on his beautiful horse. Argentus, the horse's name was—a silver Empyrean. Grandmother was very frail by then, and she didn't like strangers much, but she appreciated that he worked hard and kept us laughing. When Grandmother got ill, he helped us care for her. When she died, he helped us bury her in the family plot, helped us carve her a headstone."

She heaved a deep sigh. "We all grew to care for him like a brother. Even Begonia, and she never cared much for anybody."

I said nervously, "Onal once told me that she collected bloodleaf petals as a child, when her sister was murdered in the woods." I looked down at the bloodleaf patch. "Is this where it happened?"

Rosetta nodded.

"Did Mathuin do it?" I whispered.

She gave a slight shake of her head. "I've never wanted to believe that, but what other answer could there be? She died, and he disappeared forever. And the worst part? I have no recollection of any of it, and I was *there*."

"What do you mean?"

"There was supposed to be a comet that night, one that passes only every few decades. We'd been carefully planning where it would be in our sky, and I remember waking up that morning, but after that . . . nothing. The next thing I knew, the comet had passed and Begonia was shaking me awake in the sombersweet. Galantha was dead, and the world was white with bloodleaf petals. Mathuin was just . . . gone. And I . . . I was the warden. Sometime during the comet and before she died, Galantha had rung the Ilithiya's Bell and passed on her mantle to me."

I was silent, digesting.

"Each of the wardens watches over an age in the history of mankind. Galantha's was the Seventh, the Maiden Age. Supposed to be like spring: full of beginnings and new life and hope. It should have lasted centuries, but she got only a year. I am the Warden of the Eighth, the Mother Age. A time of nurturing and growth, like summer." Her jaw tightened. "Ironic, considering I cannot have children."

"How do you know you—"

"Trust me," Rosetta snapped. "I've tried. Where do you think the stories came from? A witch in the wood, tempting travelers from the road? No, Mathuin Greythorne was the first, but he wasn't the last. I've gained a reputation over the years. Renaltan mothers began to warn their impressionable sons and daughters early, lest they wander and fall prey to my enticements." There was a wicked, self-mocking curve to her mouth. "But to no avail. It is kind of funny, isn't it? A barren Warden of the Mother Age.

"The Ninth Age is next," Rosetta continued, "the Crone Age. Sure to bring all kinds of devastation and darkness. It will need a new warden to greet it. One who has the specific traits necessary to see the earth through it. But between Onal and me, there are no inheritors of Nola's direct line left to whom I could pass the mantle. It may be that I could select someone else, but without the bell, I can't even try. Which means I will have to carry the burden forever. I'll never get to die."

"How do you know you'll never die?"

Grimly, she said, "Trust me, I've tried that, too."

I went quiet for a minute. Then I said, "Would it be so bad, an eternal age of the Mother? Most people would be happy for the chance to live forever. Isn't that what the Tribunal is attempting, with their experimental wolves?"

"Alone?" Rosetta shivered, though it was not cold in the Cradle. "Only someone who has never known true loneliness would say such a thing. The Mother Age can't last forever; I can already feel it stretching too tightly. Sooner or later, the balance will break. And when it does, if there's no warden to tend to it . . . it will be catastrophic. Everything . . . every*one* . . . could die. Trust me when I say the only thing more terrifying than death is the prospect of an endless life in an empty world."

She paused then, considering Galantha's grimoire for a moment before turning her piercing eyes on me. "But . . . there may be a single solution for both our problems."

"Oh?" I cocked my head to the side as that strange sense returned —not of rightness, exactly. More like . . . inevitability. It tugged at me like a waning tide, a soft demand for me to follow. I didn't fight it. It was probably useless to try. I'd waded this far in; I might as well let the current take me a little farther. "I'm listening."

She said, "You'd have to go into the Gray."

15

"houldn't we tell Kellan and Onal that we're doing this?"

Rosetta, who had produced a wad of strange, silvery string from some hidden pocket within the ragged layers of her skirts, was laying it out in a wide, weblike arrangement, knotting and twisting it and tracing tiny patterns in the air over it, all according to the incomprehensible notes within Galantha's grimoire. Her work lacked the boldness and immediacy of my blood magic, but there was definite power in the delicate intricacy of her art. Feral magic had, to me, always sounded wild and uncontrolled, when in fact, I observed, it was the opposite: it was rhythmic and methodical, a natural extension of the cycle of life, death, and rebirth.

Without looking up, she said, "Do you think either one of them will be excited to have you go wandering alone in the spectral plane?"

I pursed my lips, imagining Kellan's concerned, furrowed brow and Onal's disdainful scowl. "You're right. We can't tell them."

"If my hunch is right, walking the Gray will be easy for you; you may have already been doing it on your own, in your sleep. This way, you'll be fully conscious in your spectral body, and better able to control what you see."

"Is there any danger?"

Rosetta's hands went still on her string, halfway through making another tie in the web. "If I said yes, would you be dissuaded from going in?"

I thought of Kellan and the bloodcloth. "No."

"Then, yes. There is. According to Galantha's writings, the initial entrance into the Gray should be quite painless. It'll be like stepping into a mirror; everything is backwards, which might be a little disorienting. But she said it is also like wading into a river; the farther you go, the more powerful the currents, and the more likely you are to be swept away."

"And what happens if I don't make it back?"

She checked the green-bound book. "Your consciousness would be adrift in a dimension Galantha calls 'the all-at-once.' My best guess is that your subtle self would go mad while your material body wasted away and died. So try not to get too lost."

I cringed, thinking of the Bleeding Dream. "I'll do my best."

"Now, here. You have to lie in the center of the spell." She helped me step into the starry silver oval. With the green of the sombersweet leaves behind it, it resembled the facets in a vivid emerald. As I lay down in the center and settled myself into place, Rosetta took out a bundle of dried sombersweet and used it to draw another pattern in the air. It started to burn, giving off a rich, sweet-scented smoke that made my head swim.

"Keep in mind: What happens in the Gray *is* really happening. Or has happened. Or will. *You* are insubstantial, but what you're seeing is not." She forced herself into a soothing monotone. "Breathe the sombersweet in and concentrate. Separate your thoughts from the weight of the body that contains them. You are the *you* you see in a mirror. You are your reflection."

"This isn't working," I said after a while, but Rosetta didn't appear to be listening. Above me, the sky had changed color. No longer was it a star-sprinkled midnight blue; it was now a bright sapphire color that shifted to a deep oceanic green and back again. The lightning buzz of the ley lines began to hum along the silver strings and, without warning, the silver melted into liquid that spread and pooled around me. Soon, I was no longer lying among sombersweet blossoms: my back was flat against a silver, mirrorlike disc.

I began to sink into it, trying not to cry out in fright as I realized that I was no longer one Aurelia but two. One was lying on the silver plane of the melted thread, and the other was . . . here.

The same but not the same. I was a different version of myself. Looking down, I could see that my hair here was not my own ashy blond but a deep mahogany brown.

The Cradle melted away into an indiscernible fog of muddy color. I was adrift within it, weightless because there was no force pulling me to earth. There was no earth. No sky. No here or now.

This was the Nothing Dream. I'd willingly walked into the Nothing Dream.

I tried to remember what Zan had told me when we were hiding in the Canary's cellar. *Find something solid to hold on to. Tether yourself to something real.*

Zan.

I held his face in my mind and took a step forward into the awful emptiness.

But of course, it wasn't empty. It wasn't nothing. It was the exact opposite of that. It was, as Galantha said, the all-at-once. And my self —my real self—was lying in the middle of a quiet meadow. Real. Just not awake.

I took a step forward into the amorphous smoke of the Nothing Dream and was surprised to feel something solid form beneath my feet. I took another step and saw that it was a wooden floor I was walking upon, with thin planks laid tightly together in a crosshatch pattern.

I was in Rosetta's parlor. Recognizing it caused the fog to roll back further. There were four people in the room, three girls and a boy, all sprawled out on the braided rug. One was Rosetta. Another was a tall girl with a bright, happy face and light waves of hair. The third girl was much younger, maybe nine years old, and was busily rocking a baby doll in the corner cradle, back facing me. The boy was dressed in an old-fashioned Renaltan uniform that had been stripped of all identifying insignia. He had a chunk of wood in one hand that had a rosy tone to it, and a knife in his other hand that was slowly whittling away the sharp corners as Rosetta laughed and posed. I tiptoed around to get a better look at his face, and gasped.

"Kellan?" I asked.

Kellan's name had a destabilizing effect on the Gray, swirling across the scene and dispersing it into the atmosphere as a new Kellan emerged. This was the one I knew, but he was slightly older here, wearing his black hair longer and plaited into thin braids that were gathered into a high knot on the crown of his head. He was approaching someone who appeared to be shrinking back into the shadows.

"Wait!" he said, holding out his hand. "Don't go! I just want to talk." The extended hand was sheathed in some kind of armored glove or gauntlet that shone the same liquid silver as the portal into the Gray.

Gloves. It seemed as if my thoughts—even stray ones—affected what I saw. Now it was Isobel Arceneaux, twisting her hands in her beetle-wing gloves. Her acolyte Lyall bowed to her and spoke. "I'm very pleased with these last results," he said, motioning to the shriveled corpse of a man, his skin mottled a greenish gray, stretched out across a lab table. "The soul we used was one of our preserved Celestines from the thirteenth century, and it lasted a full five hours before disintegration and body rejection, our best trial yet. But I'm afraid to say that I'm running out of subjects—"

"And we're running out of time," she said, pacing by a filmy window. I recognized the building; they had set up some kind of base in the old mill from which they'd hauled the spindles. "The lunar eclipse happens on the Day of Shades—mere weeks away. We can't risk a repeat of last time. This vessel *must* be fully prepared. The seal *must* be perfect. We'll not get another chance. We have to get into th

We need Urso's writings to make this work."

"Well, I think it's safe to say that Father Edgar won't be of any help to us now. It was a sound idea, letting one of our souls into his body so that we could use him to get into Greythorne, but we couldn't have known that the time the souls spent in the luneocite would have such a negative effect on their consciousnesses. The Celestine we used was one of the oldest, and he couldn't talk. He could barely stand."

No. *No.* Father Edgar—I hadn't recognized him at first. Not like this. Not without his gentle smile and his thick glasses. But there he was. And there were his glasses, too, folded up on the table beside him.

Empyrea keep you, Father. I sent the thought out into the Gray, hoping that if Edgar was still in the spectral plane somewhere, he might hear it.

"We need more subjects—*live* subjects. That's all there is to it. And the refugees have all but abandoned their camp; our pickings are growing slim."

Arceneaux glared. "I'll take care of it. And the princess? Any news of her and her consort?"

"No," Lyall answered reluctantly, "but several of my emissaries have not returned from their scouting trips; they must be dead. The only people capable of killing them are mages. And as we both know, true mages are hard to come by these days. We'll find her. I'll go myself. While suitable human bodies have grown scarce, the most recent spectral harvest has proved to be fruitful, and we still have many canine subjects with which to make new emissaries."

"Do what you have to do," Arceneaux said. "We're running out of time."

Time. The Stella Regina's bells were tolling. I was standing in front of Urso's statue, where blood was trickling from his outstretched hand and into the fountain. At Urso's feet, a man was on his knees, a bloody sword bearing the hawthorn seal of the Greythorne family lying on the ground beside him.

This was the Bleeding Dream.

"No."

I lashed out with both hands and felt the Gray recoil from the force of my rejection, sending my consciousness skidding back into the Nothing.

I tried to conjure Zan's face again, and the Gray parted in response, but it did not take me to solidity or safety. I went from the red-lit Bleeding Dream directly into the icy Drowning Dream. Only this time, I wasn't watching Zan sink into the depths; I was leaning over him on the shore while, nearby, a cloaked rider mounted a spectral silver horse.

And just as the scene was about to change again, I saw it: the red-violet metal flower and white stone droplet clapper of the Ilithiya's Bell, hanging from a chain around the horseman's neck.

Si vivis, tu pugnas. The voice was little more than a whisper, but the words were unmistakable.

While you live, you fight.

I had barely enough time to register the meaning of those words before I found myself in the middle of a bustling midnight dock that smelled of fish and sweat and sulfur. A man in a dark jacket, hood pulled over his head, was leaning against the side of a squalid tavern. Splashed onto the wall next to him was a two-foot depiction of a horse and rider, painted in those bold black strokes I knew so well.

Underneath the painting, Zan had scrawled,

SI VIVIS, TU PUGNAS

The words blurred momentarily, and I could feel the tug of my material body calling me back into it. But I wasn't ready yet. A horseman had pulled Zan from the bay and told him to fight, but who was he? I remembered Rosetta's description of Argentus, Mathuin Greythorne's silver Empyrean horse. Was Mathuin still alive, a century after he left his family home and never returned? If so, why would he choose to show himself *now?*

Mathuin Greythorne. I hefted his name into the formless void like an anchor, and the smoke parted for it. I was back in Greythorne now, but not the one I knew. In this version, the house was a smoldering ruin, gray-white flames scavenging the skeletal timber remains. The balconies were caved in, the balustrades scorched black. I turned on my heel, slowly taking in the apocalyptic panorama as hot ash blew in my face.

Sputtering and coughing, I tried to wade through the smoke. The caustic air scoured my lungs, but I pressed forward, fixing my gaze on the Stella Regina as the clock in the bell tower struck midnight.

The sound crashed into me like a wave, and I fell back into a stone parapet draped in curling red-shot vines. From beneath the beatific statue of an ancient queen, I saw myself stretched out onto a spiderweb of silver threads across the bloodleaf.

No, not bloodleaf—sombersweet. I was not at Aren's tower but at Nola's Cradle.

I surged up from the liquid silver plane, and it instantly contracted into thread, taking the mirror portal with it. I tried to stand, but my legs buckled beneath the weight; my body felt like it was made of solid stone and not flesh and bone.

"I saw it," I panted, trying to catch my breath. "I saw the bell. It was around the neck of the horseman. If I'd just had a few more minutes. You woke me up so soon . . ." I felt exhausted. I looked around, surprised to find myself sitting beneath a dusky sky. During my sojourn into the Gray, it appeared that night had become day and was marching toward evening time once again.

And I was being watched. By not one face but three. Kellan and Onai had joined Rosetta in the Cradle, and they were wearing the exact expressions that had kept me from telling them of my plans in the first place.

Rosetta stood. "How long do you think you were in there, Aurelia?"

I scrunched my eyes shut, trying to reorganize my encounters into a sensible timeline. Sheepishly, I said, "I don't know. It felt like twenty minutes, maybe thirty. But judging from the sky, perhaps it was longer?"

Kellan, Onal, and Rosetta exchanged glances.

I asked, "How long was it, then?"

Kellan helped me to my feet. My knees were wobbly, my stomach empty and aching. "Aurelia," he said quietly, "you were out almost a full day."

16

have to go into the Gray again."

We were back at the homestead, where I was drinking warm tea by the fire as feeling crept back into my extremities in hot prickles, like a swarm of biting fire ants.

"Out of the question," Kellan said. He hadn't left my side since I'd reawakened. "Would you look at yourself?" To Rosetta, he said, "Do you have a mirror so she can see what she's done to herself?"

Rosetta's eyes flicked to the turned-back mirror on the wall, and then she answered, "No."

"I saw the bell," I said insistently, "and I think I can track it down. Things were so hazy and changing so quickly . . . I was just getting the hang of *how* to see what I needed to see. But maybe, if we found another place to use. One with more power . . ."

"There's not a—" Rosetta stopped as it dawned on her. "You don't mean . . ."

"Aren's tower," I said with certainty.

"The last time we were in Achlev," Kellan said to me, "it was on *fire*."

"I saw the tower while I was in the Gray," I answered. "I *know* that's where I need to go."

"'I'?" Kellan questioned. "Not 'we'?"

"I want you and Onal to go back to Greythorne," I said. "I saw Arceneaux in the Gray. She's set herself up in the village, and she is doing . . . awful things. Arcane things. And she's planning to infiltrate Greythorne. You're needed there. You should go as soon as—"

"I'm not leaving you," Kellan said determinedly, eyes flinty. "So stop asking me to."

"As much as I'd love to leave you all to this nonsense, I don't think any of us will be greatly benefited by returning to Greythorne," Onal said.

Rosetta said, "The bell. Focus on the *bell*."

"It was around the neck of a horseman I saw at the edge of Stiria Bay. I didn't get a good look at his face. But the bell was unmistakable." More vehemently, I said again, "I *have* to go back in."

Kellan grimaced. "How long will it take for us to get to Achlev from here, Rosetta?"

"I can bend the roads a little," she said, "and give your horses a spell for fleet-footedness." She shrugged. "Maybe two days? For you, that is. *I* can get there in one." She smiled a foxy smile.

"We can't all just transform into whatever creature suits us on a whim," Kellan said irritably.

"That's too bad for you," Rosetta said. "You're missing out."

"Tomorrow morning," I said, standing.

"But you're not yet—" Kellan protested.

I turned and repeated with all the conviction I could muster, "We are leaving for Achleva first thing tomorrow. Understood?"

I'd made a demand, and no matter how much the part of him that was my friend wanted to protest, it was the soldier in him that replied, "Yes, Princess."

★

I woke near midnight to the sound of a soft, whirring clatter coming from the first floor of the cottage.

Trying to be quiet, I tiptoed down the stairs to investigate, but the very first step let out a creaking groan in protest of my weight. From the room below, Rosetta's voice said, "Come down if you're going to come down."

She was seated beside her spinning wheel, feeding fibrous filament into it as she pumped the pedal, the spokes of the wheel blurring together as it turned.

I curled up in a chair and watched her work, mesmerized by the rhythm of her movements. Some sort of alchemy was taking place, transforming the waxy fibers between her fingers into the silver string on the bobbin.

"How are you doing that?" I finally asked. "Spinning flax into silver?"

"This definitely isn't flax." She stopped spinning for a moment so she could remove the bobbin and let me take a closer look. "This is made from the fibers in sombersweet stalks."

She watched me inspect the thread.

"It's beautiful. Why don't more people use it?"

Amused, she said, "Most people don't have spelled spinning wheels." The wheel had slowed to a stop, and I could see the patterns etched into the wood.

"Ah," I said, handing the bobbin back to her.

"Sombersweet was created from the very last of the Ilithiya's immortal essence. It is a very special plant. And this is very special thread. I call it quicksilver." She snipped off a piece and held it in one palm while her other hand drew a pattern in the air above it. "Named after the subtle filament that connects our souls to our bodies."

The silver melted together, and where there once was a string, there now sat a small bead. She let it roll from her hand into mine, where it changed shape again, returning to the form of the string. She plucked it up and turned back toward the wheel, but she was standing too close to the spindle, and the pointed end made a wicked slice across her arm. She let out a hissing breath, clamping her hand over the wound.

"Oh, no," I said. "Are you all right? Are there bandages I can fetch? Here, let me see —"

She yanked her arm away. "No. Don't bother. It's not deep. See? No blood."

The skin around her eyes was stretched taut, and her smile was stiff and forced, but she was right; there was no blood. I would have felt it if there were.

Rosetta seemed to have tired of my company. "If we're really leaving tomorrow morning, you'd better go back to bed," she said dismissively. "You'll need all the rest you can get."

"And when will you sleep?"

"When my work is done," she said, turning back to the spinning wheel once more.

The following morning, we got up at the crack of dawn to gather what we might need for a trek into the ruins of Achlev. Kellan gathered tools from Rosetta's shed—a shovel, a scythe, anything that might be useful for navigating the ruins—while Onal and I collected food. In silence, however—she had been quieter since I'd decided to go into the Gray and had grown quieter still after the decision was made to return to the tower in Achlev.

It was noon before we were finally able to take our leave of the homestead.

Kellan's pack, full of tools, clinked as we rode, and after only a mile's progress, Rosetta began to complain loudly.

"What is that racket?" she asked. "Every creature within a hundred miles knows we're here."

"We'll need these," Kellan said stubbornly. "What if we need to dig up food? Or chop down something? Or rake the forest floor . . . you know, in case of a fire?"

"Only an idiot would feel the need to rake the forest," Rosetta said.

"Oh, let him keep his little toys if it makes him feel better," Onal said. "He'd rather die than give them up now. Look at him. He's going to carry that shovel until he has to dig his own grave with it."

"If I'm digging a grave," Kellan said puckishly, "it won't be mine."

We rode in silence after that, and my mind was free to wander places I did not usually allow it to go. Seeing Zan, even if it was just for a moment in the Gray, had woken me up again. I knew I shouldn't think of him, that my time was already waning, and being near him would serve only to shorten it . . . but we had Rosetta now, didn't we? And if she could help separate my life from Kellan's, could she not do the same for me and Zan?

And, just like that, I was flooded with images of things I wanted and never dared hope for.

Waking up to a kiss from Zan every morning. Holding his hand and putting our heads together to make decisions for our kingdom, sitting on matching thrones in the Achlevan castle, which stood as tall and grandiose as it had for centuries, before the wall came down. I imagined what it would be like to tell him that he would be a father, or laying our child in his arms for the first time. I even allowed myself to imagine sending that child off to play with Ella in the old cottage by the pond, while Kate—still alive and as lovely as ever—watched their games with Nathaniel smiling by her side.

All equally foolish and equally impossible.

Rosetta glanced over her shoulder at me and dropped back behind Kellan to match my pace. "Thinking about your prince?" she asked. "Do you love him?"

I shifted my pack on my shoulders. "What does it matter? We'll never get a happily-ever-after."

"But here you are anyway, thinking about what it would be like if you did."

"Yes," I said. "I'm stupid that way."

"*He* loves you too, you know." Her eyes were on Kellan, ahead of us on the trail. "Even if you don't love him back."

"He's my oldest, dearest friend. Of course I love him back."

"But you didn't follow his voice. While you were in the Gray, he sat by your side and called you. But you didn't listen. If it was Valentin calling you back, would it have been different?"

When I didn't answer, she said quietly, "I hope you never have to know what a terribly painful thing it is to be left behind." She paused. "Or to know you are loved . . . just loved *less*."

Then she hurried to catch up with Kellan, leaving me to my troubled thoughts.

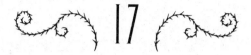

The city of Achlev was no more.

I knew that, of course. My last look at the fallen fortress as we sailed away from it was etched into my memory, remaining as vivid as the day I experienced it. But while my mind had suspended the city in that moment forever, the city's descent into ruin had continued well after we were no longer around to witness it. The elements were determined to reclaim what had been denied them for five hundred years, and they were successful in their endeavor. To such an extent that when we came upon the city, it was so overtaken by briar and thorn, I didn't recognize it.

The trees gave way to hawthorn and blackberry brambles, along with wild roses that hung in curling ropes from iron spokes that seemed to have been driven in a sheer outcrop of rock that loomed ahead. But it wasn't a natural edifice, and as we drew closer, it became increasingly familiar: stone set on stone set on stone, too tightly and symmetrically laid to be anything but manmade.

"Why are we stopping?" Kellan asked.

"Because we're here," Rosetta replied, lifting her arms. "Welcome to Forest Gate."

The iron spokes from which now dangled rose vines were once hangers for Domhnall's gibbet cages. There—something glinted from behind an ivy curtain. I pulled the plants aside, dusted off the object hidden beneath, and found my own face staring back at me, reflected in the glossy copper of Forest Gate's bell.

I gave it a tap, and it gave a low, rolling vibration.

"How do we get in?" Kellan asked, pointing to the rubble where once had stood a grand doorway, watched over by three magnificent statues of a maid, a mother, and a crone.

"Looks like someone else has already figured it out," I said, pointing to a hollow in the thatch that had been recently cut into the shape of a door.

Kellan drew his sword, looking around warily.

"I'll go first," he said. "Just in case the person who cut this pathway for us is still around somewhere."

The opening behind the cut brambles was tight—just a narrow, triangular space created when two large chunks of the gate fell against each other. We had to go single file, flattening our bodies against the wall to slide through. In some places, I had to hold my breath to do it; I wondered a few times if broad-shouldered Kellan would be able to make it at all. When we finally came out the other side, I rewarded myself by taking a deep and generous breath, marveling at how good it felt to fully inflate my lungs again.

"Hey!" Kellan called from ahead. "I think we go this way."

I caught up to him. "How do you know?"

"Because it's the only direction that isn't overgrown or covered with broken timbers and crumbled stone."

"King's Highway," I said, recognizing its bones. It had once been the main thoroughfare from the gate to the castle steps, wide enough to admit three side-by-side carriages down it at once. It was now covered in dirt, with broken beams and buckled buildings rising up on each side. But down the center of the ruin was a narrow ravine, and at the bottom of it a single strip of uncovered cobble pavement.

We walked slowly—there were still places where Kellan had to hack aside thorny branches—while I tried to pick out places with which I was once familiar. There—there was an alleyway down that direction. If you turned at the end and turned again, you'd find yourself at Sahlma's apothecary. And there—that towering wall of shrub was once a simple hedge. The same hedge I'd pulled Zan into with me when trying to hide from Lisette and Cael as they came down the highway.

And if I turned left at that juncture ahead and followed the lane toward the trees, I'd eventually come to the little cottage with bright yellow flowers in the front and a hut by the pond in the back. I could still picture Kate coming to the door of her house, welcoming me in with a bright smile. Nathaniel would be inside, quietly helping Kate make dinner. Zan too. He'd be lounging in the corner, an acerbic quip on his tongue and a glint in his eyes.

I was no longer literally haunted, but everywhere I looked, I saw memories of people I loved just as vividly as I once could see ghosts.

"Something wrong?" Kellan asked after I stopped to stare at the eastern trees for a little too long. Somewhere among them was the quiet makeshift memorial Zan called the Tomb of the Lost.

"No," I said. "Just . . . remembering."

"I would think you'd want to forget what happened here, traumatic as it was."

"I wish it hurt a little less," I admitted, "but I would never want to forget."

We reached the foot of the castle just as a hawk began to screech high above.

"Someone's here," Kellan said warily. "Stay behind me."

"Stay behind you?" I asked incredulously, drawing my knife. "I'm a blood mage. *You* stay behind *me*."

"Yes, but if you die, I also die. So *you* need to stay behind *me*."

Onal pushed past us both, rolling her eyes to the sky. "Such nonsense."

Rosetta, who'd shifted into her fox form to beat us through the tunnel and search the road ahead of us, came bounding down the lane, shifting back into her human self in one leap.

"I think someone's still here up ahead," she said breathlessly. "Stay behind me."

Kellan and I looked at each other, then glowered at her, but we did as she said.

Rosetta took the lead, followed closely by Onal and Kellan, and I brought up the rear. We were still a quarter mile away from the castle when I spied something peeking out from beneath a fall of vine to my left. It was an old public-decree board with several layers of the late king Domhnall's proclamations still waving slightly in the wind. But there was something that had been drawn over the top of them. Something in black strokes . . .

Unable to help myself, I pulled the draping curtain of vines aside and found myself staring at another depiction of the horseman, this one taller than me.

Beside it was a doorway with a side path leading out the other direction. It had been purposely hidden: someone had arranged the vines to conceal it.

Four words were painted across the lintel:

SI VIVIS, TU PUGNAS.

I cast a quick glance over my shoulder and, seeing that the others hadn't noticed me falling behind, plunged through the opening into the welcoming shadows.

The alleyway had been mostly protected from the destruction by a sidewall that had tipped, unbroken, against the building beside it, leaving a triangular hole just tall enough to walk beneath, while other debris collected over the top. It was dank and dusty, as well as darker than I expected at this time of day, and the tightness of the space had my breath quickening and my heart beating faster. With each step, I tried to ground myself, inching with my back along the perpendicular wall to give me the most airspace possible, letting myself feel the solidness of it behind me and under my hands and concentrating on the feel of the ground beneath my feet, while breathing as steadily as I could. *One, in. Two, out. Three, in. Four, out . . .*

I could hear movement ahead of and behind me, but I couldn't be sure if it was real or just my swimming mind playing tricks on me.

It wasn't until I tumbled out into a patch of light at the end of the triangular passage and immediately felt someone grab me and put a knife to my neck that I realized the sounds hadn't been in my imagination.

Seconds later, Kellan flew out of the opening, his sword raised, ready to fight.

My attacker pulled his hood back. "Kellan?" His grip on me relaxed just a little. "Aurelia?"

Zan's cheek was barely brushing mine, but, knowing what I now knew, I felt it was already too much. My knees began to wobble; the effects of his draw on my vitality were immediate.

"Let her go, Zan," Kellan said dangerously. "Right. Now."

Zan put his hands up and then carefully put his knife down. "I didn't know it was her. I mean her no harm."

Kellan scoffed, "Not true."

"Stop, Kellan," I said, trying to keep my feet under me and longing to put my head between my knees. "He doesn't know."

"Did *you* know he was going to be here?" Kellan asked me accusingly.

"No!" I said honestly. At our last encounter, I'd died mid-embrace and then fled without a goodbye. If I had known he'd be here, I would not have come.

Still, finding him felt like a gift. A drop of cold water on a parched tongue.

"Stars save me." Kellan sheathed his sword, but his anger was still bright and sharp and on full display. "I don't particularly want to die because you two can't stay away from each other."

"I hate to interrupt this little argument," Zan said tightly, "but I, for one, would love to know *what* in all the *bleeding stars* you're talking about."

Kellan glared at him down his nose.

"We can start with your uncle," he said. "Simon's dead."

"What—?" Zan gave a start. I could have smacked Kellan. Simon was the closest thing Zan had ever had to a father. The only family he had left.

Coldly, Kellan added, "You killed him."

The castle library was where Zan had made his encampment. The bookshelves had fallen one after the other and now leaned in a diagonally angled stack like dominoes, books spilling out below. But otherwise, there was little wrong with the room. The fire that had wreaked havoc on the roof and upper levels of the structure must have been doused by the torrential rain before it could make it this deep into the castle, while the floods that had come up from the fjord below had receded before reaching the higher levels. The checkerboard tiles still gleamed, and the crystal stars of the celestial chandelier were still suspended from the ceiling, as impervious to the devastation below as the actual heavens to the earth. Even the windows were mostly intact; with two battlements jutting forward on either side, they had been protected from the wind that had circled right past, leaving minimal damage. It was like finding a lost treasure in the heart of a shipwreck.

A massive ornamental fireplace presided over the room, and Zan had a fire in the grate.

"If someone was watching," Onal said, "would that not alert them to your location?"

"Some of the ruins still smolder," Zan replied from over his shoulder. "No one would notice another little bit of smoke." He shrugged. "Besides, nobody knows the ways in and out of this castle better than I do. Even if they knew I was here, they'd have a hard time reaching me."

"But your drawings," I said, staying carefully away. "The horseman. And the saying. *Si vivis, tu pugnas.* Aren't they *meant* to help people find you?"

"They find me in the places I designate," he said. "That I control. The only other person who knows of this is Nathaniel. It's where we were supposed to meet if ever our plans went south."

"But he's not here?" I asked.

"No. Kate's mother was caring for Ella; I can only hope that he went to Morais instead. It's well protected. I think it will be the last of the provinces to fall to Castillion." He kept his gaze averted; he still would not look at me.

Not that I blamed him. What Kellan had so unceremoniously dumped on his shoulders . . . it was a lot to take in.

"Listen," Zan said. "I don't have any extra supplies. I—obviously —wasn't expecting company. If you want blankets, you're going to have to find them yourself. I've already taken everything I could find on this level. You'll have to look on the next floor down, or next one up. They're in worse shape. So be careful."

"What did you do with everything on this level?" Kellan asked sourly.

Zan looked up with a surly cock of his head. "Everything I have, I've given to the refugees," he said. "I'm sorry I didn't keep anything extra around for you."

We all scattered in separate directions; I tried to follow after Zan, but he slipped down some hidden back corridor before I had a chance to call to him without the others noticing. In a way, I was glad; I had no idea what I'd say if I did manage to catch up with him. *Sorry your uncle died because I tried to seduce you.* I shuddered at the thought.

I decided to pester Onal instead. She was headed down the east wing toward the bedchambers when she saw me following after her. "Onal," I called, but she ignored me.

I tried a different tack. "Begonia!"

She turned around in a huff. "I've been traveling all day, and I'm tired, Aurelia. Why don't you find someone else to bother?"

"I've never in my life left you alone when you told me to go away," I said. "Why should I start now?"

"Stars, you're insufferable." We'd come to a hall of what might have once been bedrooms. She went to the first door and gave the knob a wiggle. Locked.

"I learned from the best," I said brightly.

"You didn't learn that from me."

"You assume you're the best at being insufferable?" I asked.

That made her crack a smile.

"You don't have to be here, you know," I said. "You could be with Conrad and Fredrick in Greythorne right now."

"You want to get rid of me?" She tried the next door. The knob turned, but the door wouldn't budge from the frame.

"Not what I meant."

"You think I'm too old to help you?"

"Didn't say that, either. You just have to understand—"

"I *understand* that you're as ridiculous and impulsive as my sister. Dabbling in things that shouldn't be dabbled in."

"Rosetta?"

"Galantha." She leveled her gaze at me. "Rosetta makes it sound like Galantha was second only to the Ilithiya herself. And in a way, she was. But she was just as bullheaded as the rest of us, and when she got an idea . . . nothing could stop her."

"You knew Mathuin Greythorne, too," I said, getting to the point. "When I went into the Gray, I saw you at the homestead with them. You, Galantha, Rosetta, and Mathuin. Do you believe he killed her for the bell? So he could disappear into the Gray?"

"I was very young when it happened, Aurelia. I'm old and jaded now; logic says that *of course* he did. Evil likes to hide behind benevolent faces. But if you'd asked me at the time, I would have said there was not a chance. He loved her. But more than that . . . he was kind. Caring. *Good.* All he wanted to do was run around in the woods and carve sculptures. He had no motivation to kill my sister *or* steal the bell."

A thought occurred to me. "Do you think . . . Rosetta did it? That she wanted to be warden so much, she forced Galantha to pass the mantle to her?"

Onal sighed. "That's not what happened."

"How much do *you* know about what happened?" I asked.

"Not enough," Onal said. Then, "Too much." The knob she was jiggling gave way. "Ah, success!" she declared, throwing open the door.

There was nothing on the other side but open air—and a long drop down two more stories. She promptly closed it and said, "We'll try the next one."

We had better luck on the other side of the hall; the first door we tried opened into an airy bedroom that was mostly untouched save for the broken-out windowpanes and the wind and water damage near that jagged portal to the outside. In a smaller, closed-off antechamber, however, we found what might once have been a nursery. There was a large bassinet adorned with a canopy of green silks and lined with yellowing satin.

"Those canopy curtains might work," I said. "Can you get them? I'm going to try this closet."

Onal wasn't listening. She'd gone to the edge of the bassinet and was looking wistfully into it, her hand resting on the mattress where a baby might once have lain. It was the first time I saw the echo of the doll-loving little girl in the prickly old woman. I closed my mouth and quietly turned back to the closet, letting her have that moment alone, lost somewhere in her long memory.

18

Rosetta passed around some of the rations we'd brought with us and a bottle of wine she'd dug up from the muddy sludge that had overtaken the wine cellar. The nursery closet had yielded enough blankets for everyone to have one, and we all huddled together around the fireplace, listening to the storm howl outside as we tried to get some sleep. One by one, the others seemed to drift off, but I remained awake long into the night, watching the celestial chandelier gently dip and sway.

I wasn't the only one with insomnia. While everyone else slept, Zan crawled out from under his blankets and shuffled quietly from the library.

I sat up. "Zan?" I asked in a whisper. But he didn't hear me.

I went out into the hall. "Zan, wait!"

I turned in just enough time to see him disappear in the direction of the kitchens below. He'd brought me to the library this way before, and I knew at once he was headed to the canal passages. I pulled my boots on and followed.

After the floodwater receded, the canal tunnels were left in much the same condition as they were before, but with an extra six inches of silt and sludge coating the bottom. I waded through it, hoping that up ahead, Zan could not hear my squelching steps. A couple of times, his bobbing candle paused, and I prepared myself for imminent discovery, only to have him carry on a few moments later.

I followed his light out of the castle as it flickered in the darkness of Achlev's eastern groves. Of all the city's landmarks, the woods were the only part that had absolutely flourished since the wall came down. No longer divided from the Ebonwilde, the trees seemed to have gained a new vigor, like lost children being re-welcomed into the fold. Even the large swaths of forest that had been burned were already showing new and not-entirely-natural growth.

I fully expected Zan to head toward Kate and Nathaniel's old house, once a haven to us both. But he did not turn west at the pond. Instead, he headed deeper and deeper into the woods until he and his light disappeared altogether.

He'd come to a ridge, seemingly impenetrable but hiding a secret: before the earthquakes began, there'd been an entranceway here that led into a hidden hollow. I ran my hands alongside the stone until I felt the gap. The doorway was still here, even after the earthquake. Holding a breath and hoping for the best, I ducked into it.

Zan was waiting for me on the other side, arms crossed over his chest.

"You heard me call your name," I said accusingly. "You knew I was following you."

"I was hoping you'd see the mud and turn around."

"I don't give up all that easily."

"No?" His eyes flashed green. Only a few flecks of gold remained from our encounter in the city, and I wondered if the effects of my vitality wore off slowly, over time, or if they were permanent and stayed with him long after the gold had disappeared from his eyes.

"Why are we here, Zan?" I looked around the tomb. The stone he'd erected for his mother as a child was lying in pieces. The drawing of Kate we'd left beside it was gone, probably long disintegrated into the earth upon which it rested.

"This is a place for goodbyes, and I just learned I've got one more to say." He had something in his hand, but when I leaned in to see it closer, he gave a hard sigh and raised his arm like a barrier, trying to keep me at bay. "If you stay," he said, "I'll ask you to keep your distance."

I nodded and gave him a wider berth. The object in his hand was a familiar one: a vial of blood.

"Simon gave this to me after my mother died. He said it was tradition for blood mages to give some of their blood to the people they love best. So that even after they die, some of their spirit—and their magic—remains." He held it up on the cord, more so that he could look at it closely than to show it to me. "It meant a lot to me. I had to hide it, of course, so my father wouldn't find it—he hated Simon —but it comforted me, knowing a little of Simon's spirit was always nearby."

"That's where you were earlier today, while the rest of us were looking for blankets," I said. "You went for Simon's blood vial."

He nodded, lips in a thin line. "But, stars save me, I am done with blood magic."

I watched, stunned, as he popped the cork and emptied Simon's blood onto the soil.

"Zan, what are you *doing?* Are you all right?"

"Am I all right?" He whirled around, eyes full of emotion. "I just found out that Simon is *dead* because of me. That *you* almost died because of me." He shook out the last of Simon's blood and then threw the empty vial down too. "No. I am not all right."

I dashed to retrieve the empty vial from the dirt—leaving it there felt like sacrilege—but I didn't know what to do with it. Any comfort I tried to offer would have sounded dismissive and remorseless at best, ruthless at worst. But the silence was no better; it hung between us, an indictment all its own.

Finally, I said, "I'm the one who killed Simon, not you. He died because I dared to *want* what I knew I couldn't have. To touch what I never deserved. And I'm going to pay for it. Have no doubt."

"Ah, yes. The lunar eclipse on the Day of Shades: the day you're going to die and save us all." He gave a short bark of a laugh. "Why? Why do you always get to be the martyr, Aurelia? Why do you get to save the day and all the rest of us have to just sit back and watch?"

"That's not—"

"Admit it. You were *relieved* when you found out that it had to be you to die to keep the Malefica out of the world, weren't you? And admit that if it weren't for Kellan, you might have already just gotten it over with." He smiled—a bitter, mirthless smile. "I never thought I'd be glad to have him around."

"If someone has to go," I demanded, "why *not* me? I have done terrible things. I *deserve* the consequences."

"No, no, no, no, no." He was shaking his head, scoffing. "This isn't about accepting the consequences! This is about *escaping* them. Because that's what you do, Aurelia. You push everyone out. You turn everyone away. When things get hard, you run."

Through gritted teeth, I said, "I do what is necessary to keep the people I care about *safe*. Even if it means keeping you safe from me."

He came as close as he dared, a hairsbreadth away from my lips. "That's not something you get to decide."

"Oh, I see now. You've got your *own* death wish! And here I thought you lived by the horseman's motto. What was that again? *Si vivis, tu pugnas.*"

"You think I want to die? I don't! I want to wake up every damned day to the sun. I want to fall asleep with you beside me. I want days of hard work and sore muscles and arguments and nights spent reading together by the fire. And, Dear Goddess on High, I want to be everything that my father was not. I want to live a life, a real life, and I *hate* that someone else had to die for it, but I do. And *damn* this curse and *damn* the Empyrea and *damn you* most of all, Aurelia, for wanting to leave me in this starsforsaken world without you."

I could feel my chest moving, I could hear air moving in and out of my mouth, but it felt like I was drowning again—not in a dream, but on dry land.

After a long minute, he turned back to the place where he'd scattered Simon's blood and gave a haggard salute. "Empyrea keep you, Uncle," he said.

And then he left me alone in the darkness, Simon's empty blood vial warm in my hands as Zan's words settled into my heart.

★

Eventually I returned to the castle, slipping beneath my blanket without waking the others. I slept but woke just after sunrise. Only Rosetta was awake before me; she was sitting in one of the window benches, next to the rattling panes, Galantha's grimoire in her lap and a candle sputtering on the table at her side.

"Anything interesting?"

She sighed and closed the book. "Nothing you'd understand."

I shook my head. "You think that just because I'm a blood mage, I won't understand the mere fundamentals of feral magic?"

"Yes. That's exactly what I'm saying. Feral magic and blood magic are diametrically opposed. You can't force them together any more than you can force the wrong sides of two magnets together."

"And yet the Tribunal is doing it, with success."

She snorted. "If you can call rotting-corpse wolves a success." Then she looked at me. "What is that?"

I had begun to absently fidget with Simon's empty blood vial, now around my neck. I tucked it away. "Nothing you'd understand." I sighed.

"Mathuin wasn't a blood mage," she blurted. "But he knew their traditions. He gave a vial like that to Galantha. A terrible gift for a feral mage, really. Iron weakens us."

I watched her thoughtfully. "You loved him," I said. "But not like a brother."

She gave a self-mocking smile. "There was a little fox I was especially fond of. A vixen who had made her home not far from the Cradle. She used to follow me whenever I walked the forest. I have always been good with animals, but she was the closest thing I had to a pet. Saffron, I called her. And then, one day, a group of Renaltan soldiers came into the forest to hunt. They didn't need meat; it was all for sport. They left a trail of carcasses all across the Ebonwilde.

"I was with Mathuin when I found Saffron. He helped me bury her, and he held me quietly while I cried. For hours and hours I cried." She sniffed. "And then he and I went to the soldiers' camp and destroyed everything in it. Everything. If they'd been there, I'd have destroyed them, too. And afterward, I gave Mathuin a vial of my blood. It was the only way I could think of to tell him how I felt. I didn't know then he'd already pledged himself to Galantha."

"Were you angry with them?" I asked.

"Not angry enough to kill either of them, if that's what you want to know. But the night of the comet—the night I lost both of them and somehow became warden—I dreamed I saw Saffron again. But she was not orange anymore. She was silver."

"Saint Urso believed that when we die, we're guided into the afterworld by a familiar spirit. Maybe that's what you saw."

"I didn't die that night," Rosetta said. "But, stars save me, I've often I wished I had."

I looked at Kellan, who was stretched out across the floor, snoring softly into his rolled-up cloak, which was stuffed under his head like a pillow. I said, "After we find the bell, and break the bond, and I finally fulfill my mission . . . I'll be glad to go knowing you're still around to look after him."

Slowly, Rosetta asked, "What happens if we don't find it? Or we don't in time?"

I swallowed and looked down at my hands. "I've dreamed about it many times. I'm back at Greythorne, in the maze, and Kellan is kneeling at my feet. And I've got a sword, and I . . ." I bit my lip. "I think I kill him. And then I say the words of the bloodcloth ritual: 'Bound by blood, by blood undone.'" I shuddered. The Bleeding Dream was never pleasant to relive, even awake. "Thank you, Rosetta, for what you're doing; for helping me. Because of you, that terrible dream will stay just a dream."

"Yes," she said. "Certainly." Abruptly, she snapped her book shut and stood. "We should get them up. We're wasting the day."

Outside, the rain was slowing and the pink threads of morning were beginning to show through the clouds. We ate a light breakfast of dried apples and raspberries brought from Rosetta's pantry. Then we set out for the tower. This was perhaps the most arduous portion of our trek, as the terrace gardens had been overtaken by the same thorny growth we'd encountered at Forest Gate; only here, it was wilder, stronger, with shoots of vines nearly as thick as my arm, bearing daggerlike thorns that would not prick you so much as impale you. It was as if the power intersecting in the ley lines beneath the tower was feeding the flora as well, turning it into something otherworldly.

Zan and Kellan took out their swords, while I brandished a scythe and Rosetta a shovel. Onal remained in the back of our slow procession, hiking with her arms crossed. "I'm too old to help you," she said with a look that dared anyone to argue otherwise. "Let me know when you're finished."

"You should have made a tunnel through this already," Kellan said to Zan, wiping his brow.

"We did," Zan said. "It grew back."

We hacked and hammered our way into the thatch, but it was slow going. And we had to be especially careful not to get nicked by the thorns; after fifty feet of tunneling, we realized that the bloodleaf that had once covered the tower had spread out and interwoven itself into the thorns. Here, to be pricked was to be poisoned.

The intensive work took the better part of the morning and most of the afternoon, but shortly after the sun reached its apex and began its trek to the horizon, we managed to break through to Aren's tower. I went in first, stepping into the lowest floor. It was dimly lit by the collected light from the dozens of small windows that circled up in a spiral to the top. The spire had been the epicenter of Achlev's destruction, a needle around which the terrible storms had pivoted. Even now, when all was quiet, I could hear the ravaging wails of wind and the booming rumble of thunder in my memory as I, once more, climbed up the staircase to the top.

The months of being open to the elements had not treated the tower or its matron statue kindly. Aren's visage was worn away and crumbling, rendered nearly unrecognizable in a few short months after standing untouched for the previous five hundred years. Still, as I looked upon her again, I was struck by a pang of loss, as if she were not the eerie wraith that had dogged my steps for the better part of my existence, but an old and fondly remembered friend.

The weather had not erased all the remnants of the ordeal Zan and I had endured before the storm. There was still a black scorch mark where Cael had been rendered to dust, his blood still ingrained in the space between the stones. And the bloodleaf that had cradled

Zan while he died was still there, surrounding the spot as if it were memorializing what had taken place there, leaving a perfectly shaped depression where he'd breathed what had seemed his last. It was as if the vines were preparing themselves for his inevitable return and creating a welcoming resting place for him to lie upon.

"Can you feel it?" Rosetta said in awe. "It's amplified through the tower."

"Yes," I said. The knot of ley lines thrummed like a beating heart somewhere far below, resonating up the ancient stone.

"No wonder King Achlev wanted so much to protect this place," she said. "The forest has taken up the job now, I suppose."

"We got here easy enough," I said.

"You thought that was easy?" Kellan asked, staring over the edge at the sea of thorns through which we'd so painstakingly tunneled.

"If the forest hadn't wanted us to get here, it wouldn't have let us through," Rosetta said.

Onal was standing over the scrubbed-out remains of my triquetra, drawn in blood in the center of the platform. "If it wasn't the forest drawing us here, it was something else," she said. "And we should be wary of the intrigues of immortal beings."

"You're almost immortal yourself," Kellan said.

"Exactly," Onal replied.

Rosetta coughed to smother a laugh. "Beware her intrigues."

"Please," Zan said, staring down at the—his—bloodleaf. "Let's get this over with."

Rosetta knelt down and began preparing the portal pattern with her quicksilver string, laying it as wide as the tower would allow, a wealth of purposeful loops and whorls and zigzags. Then came the sombersweet smoke. I breathed it in deeply.

"Now," Rosetta said, "things should work better this time around. But it's very important that you listen for the call to return and answer it immediately."

"I will," I said sincerely. "Trust me."

But, looking from face to face, I could tell that they didn't.

19

I lay down across the pattern and settled my hands against my stomach. Above me, Aren's statue seemed to be hovering like a fretting mother while the late-afternoon sky stretched across the expanse behind her. I closed my eyes as Rosetta began her monotone monologue, easing my consciousness across the border into the spectral world, and I felt myself leaving my light-haired material body behind and taking up my dark-haired subtle body instead. Soon the world was dropping away, replaced by currents of smoke and silence.

Concentrate, I told myself. *Think of the bell. Think of the horseman. Is he Mathuin Greythorne?*

I found myself again at the center of Greythorne's maze, face-down in front of Urso's feet. There was no blood dripping from his hands this time; the fountain below was still dry, but a water droplet ran down his cheek.

Then another, then another. Raindrops that looked like tears.

Tears, I thought, and the stray image caused the whole scene to dissolve and be remade in crimson-red tones. A girl was raising a sword. A man was bent at her feet, a single tear rolling down his cheek as she sliced . . .

Stars above, telling Rosetta about the Bleeding Dream had made it stick in my mind, and the Gray had somehow caught my thoughts and dragged me back to face them. My revulsion caused the Gray to spasm and contract, my thoughts and my subtle body both spinning out of control.

Lightning flashed, and the maze was gone. Instead, I was standing on a narrow strip of cobble laid in a careful design at the basin of a sweeping valley. It was raining heavily, but I could see a man not far from me, on his hands and knees in the storm, laying each piece with a bent back and a weariness so tangible, I felt it in my own bones.

That sense of loss and longing . . . reminded me of Onal standing beside the empty bassinet. The Gray, in response, pulled me into another nursery. Not any nursery, though—this one was the royal nursery back home in Syric. I'd spent many evenings in it as a little girl, helping my mother rock baby Conrad to sleep. A different woman was bending over another bassinet, smiling blissfully down at the child inside it. I knew her face from the castle portraits; this was Queen Iresine, my grandmother. The baby had to be her only son: my father.

I leaned back into the shadows as another man entered the room. He bowed before straightening his waistcoat.

"How is she?" Iresine asked, forehead furrowed.

"The delivery was very difficult," the man answered, "but she should survive."

"Thank the Empyrea for that," Iresine replied devoutly. "Will you let me know when she wakes?"

"I have another task to attend to," the man demurred. "Family business, if you don't mind my taking a short amount of leave? I'll be back in a day or two, But I'll make sure Carlisle keeps you apprised of her condition."

"Thank you, Henry," she said, smiling. "Take all the time you need. Your devotion to our family has been beyond all expectation. I don't know how to express my thanks."

Henry nodded gravely. "It is my pleasure, Majesty. Serving you is, and has always been, the greatest honor of my life."

Iresine picked up the baby carefully, cooing at him as she wandered over to look out the window.

"Oh, and Henry? Do be careful out there; it looks like snow."

He gave a deep bow. "I will."

The scene shifted suddenly, violently. It was the same nursery, just as before, but evening time. A woman burst through the door, hair matted to her forehead, eyes wild. She was wearing a dressing gown that hung loosely off her frame.

Onal. *My* Onal.

"Where is she?"

Iresine had been rocking the baby, but she stood up at the sight of Onal. A man scurried in behind her, flustered. "I'm sorry, Majesty. I tried to keep her in bed, but she wouldn't stay."

"It's fine, Carlisle," Iresine said. "Onal, my dear, you should be in bed."

"Where is she?"

"Not a she. A he. Look! A son. You gave us a son. Costin and I have named him Regus."

Iresine held the baby out to Onal, who came nearer and touched the infant's face with reverent, shaking fingers.

Iresine's eyes shone as she looked at Onal. "He's beautiful. He's got Costin's hair, definitely, but I think he's going to have your golden skin. And your nose, too, I think."

Onal's face sent a crack across my heart as she traced the curve of his round cheek.

"Thank you," Iresine whispered, "my beautiful, wonderful friend."

Onal took a step back. "But where is the other one? Where is my daughter?"

Iresine gave her a look full of pity. "My dear, this is the child you bore. There was only one."

"No." Onal was shaking her head, hands twisted in her gown. "No. No. I saw her! I saw her. There were two."

"You look feverish," Iresine said, glancing at Carlisle. She laid baby Regus away in the bassinet and then put herself between him and Onal, as if she were afraid for his safety from the woman who'd just birthed him. "Carlisle! Make sure Mistress Onal gets back to her room. She's not feeling well and needs to rest."

"As you wish, Majesty," Carlisle said, trying to guide Onal but then, when she resisted, wrestling her arms behind her back.

"No! She was there. I held her. *Dressed* her. In a gown I made myself." She was sobbing now, brittle and broken. "My baby," she said, over and over. "My little girl. What have you done to her? What have you done?"

When the man pried her away, she screamed. The sound bled across the shifting mists and echoed into the next scene. I found myself back at Rosetta's homestead. A high-pitched shrieking was already coming from inside.

I was in the Screaming Dream.

It was different, though, this time. More vivid. Expanded. The sounds were sharper. More excruciating.

But soon, the house went quiet.

This was when the Screaming Dream always ended; I never saw what happened next, and I was always glad I didn't have to.

This time I was not so lucky.

I ducked out of the way as three men in soldiers' uniforms stormed out the door. "We did it," one said boastfully to the others. "We made the Empyrea proud."

"I hope She ropes her to one of her hottest stars so she can burn for all eternity," said another. "Witch."

Their bags were heavy with goods taken from inside, and they loaded up their horses with their plunder.

"You don't get to take from us without expecting retaliation!" one of the men shouted toward the house, spitting on the ground. Then, to his friends, he said, "She won't be bothering us again, that's certain."

They laughed as they mounted their horses and were still laughing as they rode away, leaving the house quiet and the door swinging lazily on its hinges. I approached with dread. A slow-moving tide of viscous red liquid began to flow across the threshold and drip lazily down the stoop.

Hand to my mouth, I slipped inside and followed the source of the blood into the parlor. The blood was everywhere—spread in great arcs across the floral-painted walls, the furniture, the floor. A single, sightless body had fallen against the fireplace, hair matted with blood, hands hanging limp to her sides, head lolling.

Rosetta. I wrapped my hands around my stomach, but the only thing that came from my mouth was a strangled keening sound, audible only to me.

Did you hear that? She cried out!

Let her be.

Was this the future or the past?

On the mantel above her body, the clocked rhythmically ticked.

It had not yet been robbed of its gears. This was the past.

It was also impossible.

I heard voices outside. At first I thought it was the Renaltan soldiers coming back, but I quickly realized there were only two voices, and one was a boy, the other a girl.

"Something's wrong," the girl was saying. "I can feel when life ends and tethers break; it happens all the time. It's gentle, soft. I don't even notice it anymore, really. But this—I felt death. Ugly death. And so suddenly—"

"Wait, Galantha," the boy warned, his voice suddenly grim. "Don't—"

My surroundings blurred, streaking across my vision; the Gray was pulling me away. "No!" I said. "No! I can't go! I need to know what's going to happen! Her sister just—"

Sister. The Gray responded by showing me Conrad. He was with a pack of kids, huddled in the dark. Several of them were crying. "It's all right," he was telling them. "I know where we can go. A safe place, where my sister has friends who can help us."

"They took my daddy." One little girl sobbed.

He shifted his lamp, and I saw that he was sitting at the base of a stone sarcophagus. He and these children—there were twenty at least —were hiding in the crypt beneath the Stella Regina with the coffins and cobwebs.

Everything tilted for a split second, and I found myself looking at a web of knotted string. Galantha was bent over a body that had been laid in the web's center. Her grimoire was lying open beside her while hex knots twirled on the boughs of the perimeter trees.

"I'm going to do it," she was saying. "I'm going to bring her back."

"Are you certain about this? You know the risks." Mathuin was standing nearby, the reins of his horse in his hands. His face—so like Kellan's—was a mask of pain. He was grieving Rosetta, but he was also grieving *for* Galantha, who'd lost her sister. "This is dangerous," he said. "We don't know what might happen, tampering with time like this. And Begonia . . . what will she say if she sees this?"

"I sent Begonia to pick mushrooms," Galantha said. "And then I put her to sleep. It'll last until the comet has passed. She won't remember this, thank the Ilithiya." She wiped a tear from her eye and then lifted a chain upon which swung a lovely pendant. It was small enough to fit fully into her palm and made of velvety red-violet-stained silver in the shape of a flower blossom, a teardrop jewel dangling from inside. This was the Ilithiya's Bell. *This* was what I was looking for.

Galantha's hands trembled as she raised the bell and rocked it in her hand. It sent out a peal of sound more beautiful and terrible than anything I'd ever heard. It was at once love and loss, a blessing and a curse, life and death.

It hit me like a blow. I gasped and doubled over.

Aurelia. Aurelia, listen to my voice.

I was so close to the bell. So close. Mere inches away. But I could feel the Gray slipping away, and with it, my chance to retrieve it.

No. Not yet.

The voice in the distance was more insistent. *Aurelia!* But I turned from it and ran, the names of the sisters' flowers repeating in my head. *Galantha. Rosetta. Begonia.* I had to know what happened to them. *I had to go back. Galantha. Rosetta. Begonia.*

And then I was back in the castle at Syric, but not my mother's bedchamber; I had tumbled into the Hall of Kings, where portraits of generations of former Renaltan monarchs looked loftily down upon their progeny from their high-mounted gilded picture frames. I came to a stop under the last portrait down the line. Unlike most of his predecessors, he had a hint of a smile curling in the corners of his lips that made his eyes seem to twinkle. I'd spent so many long hours staring at his portrait, missing him madly. He was a handsome sight: blue eyes, sunny golden hair, a regal blue robe, and his sapphire crown. King Regus Costin Altenar, my father.

His mother and father's portraits preceded his: Queen Iresine and

King Costin. I never got to know either of them, for they died before I was born. But I was struck, for the very first time, by how much my father looked like Costin, and how little he looked like Iresine, with her ivory skin and red-rose hair, silver flower-shaped earrings glinting from her ears.

A pair of Tribunal devotees meandered down the hall: Magistrate Toris de Lena and his astonishingly beautiful companion, Isobel Arceneaux.

They stood together in front of my family's portraits, speaking in hushed tones that I couldn't overhear. When they began to walk out of the hall, a small sprite of a girl with tangled hair and too-large eyes careened past them before crashing into the wall of her grandparents' portrait.

Arceneaux was fixed in place, staring at the little girl with ice in her expression as she fiddled with the silver buttons sewn into her tribunal robes.

I watched as Onal came to see what the racket was and scolded me soundly for my recklessness, sending me away with a swat so that she could retrieve the fallen portrait and replace it on the wall.

She lingered there for several long moments afterward, and when she did move, it was only a few inches, so that she could gaze at my father's picture.

Her son's picture, as I now knew.

20

The Gray moved me again, a dizzying transition from the regal halls of Syric's castle into the heavy darkness of the Ebonwilde.

I was with Galantha and Mathuin in the Cradle once more, but some time had passed, perhaps hours. Galantha was sitting tiredly next to Rosetta's inert form, which was suspended in a disc of silver, when something caught her eye.

"No," she said, clawing at the edge of the silver disc, yanking plants up by their roots. "No, no, no, no. No bloodleaf. Not here. Not yet." But her efforts were futile, and as she realized this, she sagged, deflated. "It's not working," she said to Mathuin, looking up at the sky. "We have only until the comet has passed over, and it's almost gone on the horizon. I can't retrieve her from here. I have to go in."

"It's not safe, Gal," he said. "You have to keep the portal open." He sat up, pulling the leather strap of his pack over his head. "I'll go."

After a moment, Galantha nodded, lifting the bell from around her neck and placing it over his head. Mathuin crawled onto the mirrored plane and lay next to Rosetta's prone body. He put his hand on her face, touching his forehead to hers. "I'm coming to find you, Little Fox," he said, closing his eyes.

The Gray turned again, as if it wanted me to see where he would go.

It wasn't far.

We were back by the cottage again. Inside, the first scream sounded.

This time, Mathuin burst through the door, eyes burning like coals.

He grabbed the first weapon he could see—a dull kitchen knife by the water basin, where a handful of potatoes sat, half-peeled—and charged at the men who were holding Rosetta down. The first one was dispatched with ease as Mathuin embedded the paring knife into the back of the man's neck. But he lost his only weapon, and the second man was launching himself at him, letting out a scream like a war cry.

The attacker used his head as a battering ram and charged into Mathuin, knocking him to the floor. Mathuin was an artist, after all. Not a fighter. He was woefully outmatched.

I crouched near the spot where the first man fell. His eyes were darting around in terror, and he scratched helplessly at the knife as life leaked slowly away from him. I had no magic of my own here, but I could still feel the magic in *his* blood, calling me. Tempting me.

I had to at least try, I told myself, and I put my subtle hand into the pool. I couldn't feel the blood, but I could feel the magic.

"*Torquent,*" I whispered. *Twist.*

Shrieks. Thumps to the floor.

"*Dirumpo.*" Break.

Bones snapping, shattering.

"*Scissura.*" Rend.

There were no sounds from the soldiers anymore besides the gurgling of the blood in their lungs.

Mathuin stared at them. He'd won, and he had no idea how.

Aurelia. Aurelia. Come back, Aurelia.

No, I replied. *Not yet.*

Mathuin lifted Rosetta into his arms. "I've got you, Little Fox," he said, kissing her hair.

He took her to the clearing where he'd entered the Gray, laying the semiconscious girl out in the exact same position as her dead body, next to an anxious Galantha, who was holding the portal open from the other side.

"Come on, now, Rosetta," he said, curling up next to her. I could see the two realities in parallel, sliding closer and closer together, as if about to realign.

But there was a rustle from within the perimeter trees, and one of the Renaltan soldiers shambled into the clearing, his muscles twisted and his bones crooked. His eyes shone bright and malevolent from within his blood-caked face, his rage giving him the fuel to move when he should have died already three times over.

"Witches," he mumbled through a mouthful of shattered teeth.

Galantha became a storm of white fire and feathers, diving through the portal on her side only to appear on ours as a great snowy owl. She let out a terrible, earsplitting screech and plunged toward the soldier, talons open, sharp and gleaming. She made several swoops, screeching and slashing.

"Galantha!" Mathuin called. "The portal is closing behind you!"

Galantha made one final swipe across the soldier's neck, then shifted back to her human shape to push him from the perimeter of the Cradle into the arms of the waiting Ebonwilde. When he fell, his severed head rolled onto the edge of the mirrored plane and came to rest staring sightlessly at his own body.

On the portal plane, Galantha had crawled up alongside her sister, embracing her lifeless body on one side while Mathuin held her still-breathing body on the other.

"She can't cross over," Mathuin said. "She's going to die—again."

Above, the only piece of the comet remaining in the sky was its long, silvery tail.

Rosetta's second self took her last breaths suspended between her sister and the boy they both loved, between the material plane and the spectral plane, between the Now and the After. They'd managed to change the location of her death, but not the outcome. Her soul had already begun its separation from her cooling body—I could see it, just as I used to when ghosts haunted me. But now I saw it in striking detail, from both sides at once. From the spectral side, a hundred thousand silvery strings that had once been tethering the soul to the body suddenly released their hold. Free of their encumbrance, the strings flowed together into an amorphous shape that slowly molded itself into the form of a fox. Saffron, from the way Rosetta's spirit was looking at it, with surprise and sweet affection. The fox pranced around Rosetta's feet and then stepped away, waiting, as if to ask, *Are you coming?*

Rosetta's ghost was about to follow the creature when Galantha gave a wrenching cry. *"No!"*

From her side, she reached toward the spectral fox, her fingers tracing patterns so quickly, it was impossible to follow them, and the amorphous silver animal reformed itself as a sphere in Galantha's grasp.

Orb in hand, Galantha dragged Rosetta's spirit back to her physical body, pinning it there by etching a feral spell onto her skin with her nail. "As long as we have her blood, we can keep her soul and her subtle body together. Only her physical body has to die."

"Galantha—" Mathuin started.

"Give me her blood and the bell," she demanded. "I have to pass the wardenship on."

"You can't do this, Galantha. The blood will weaken you. You won't be able to hold the portal open—"

"The *blood* and the *bell!*"

He tried to lean away, but she didn't wait for him to remove it, grabbing the small vial that was hanging from his neck. She traced a pattern in the air above her sister's head and around her body, leaving trails of silver-blue light in its wake. From below, in the real world, and above, in the Gray, the knot of energy from the convergence of the ley lines amplified the spell, surrounding Rosetta in a cage of light. Then Galantha began to feed the silvery tether energy into it.

"What are you doing?" Mathuin asked, anguished. "Galantha . . ."

"A warden must ensure balance," she said. "This way, balance will remain." Then she lifted the bell in both of their hands and rang it.

The peal rippled across both planes, and the netting of silver and light that was cradling Rosetta tightened around her, crisscrossing her subtle body, embedding into her subtle skin, until it disappeared, leaving behind only a silver-white scar on the inside of her arm. It was an intricate, circular pattern. An exact copy of Galantha's spell knot.

"The Eighth Age," Galantha whispered, "the age of the Mother, has begun."

Mathuin reached across Rosetta to touch Galantha's chin. They were smiling at each other. She had done it.

And the comet's tail disappeared from the sky. The portal upon which they lay began to close.

In sheer desperation, Galantha stretched her hands against the retracting portal, pushing her sister and Mathuin across the border with all the power she had left. *"Vade!"* Go.

She was only whispering now, but her voice was deep and cavernous, as if echoing across the dimensions and back again. *"Ad Cunas,"* she chanted. *"Ad domum tuam." Back to the Cradle. Back to your home.*

This, her final spell, burst from her body, blasting Rosetta in one direction and Mathuin in the other in an explosion of blue-white light.

I closed my eyes at the rush of power. When I opened them again, the portal was gone. Mathuin, still wearing the bell, had been launched into the chaos of the Gray. Rosetta's subtle body and her soul had been pinned together and pushed into the material world. She was breathing, shallowly, next to her own corpse.

Galantha's body had been destroyed in the schism between two incongruent realities when the portal closed; there was nothing left of it besides a sprinkling of blood and some drifting dust. Her ghost smiled down upon Rosetta's two selves, one alive and irrevocably altered and one a dead shell. An owl of shimmering silver was already forming from her released quicksilver. It swooped and swirled in the air, and she followed it, fading into the distance.

I hoped that whatever waited in the After, beyond the in-between world of the Gray, was sweet and quiet. Galantha deserved to find peace.

The bloodleaf had taken root in Rosetta's blood, but it was Galantha's blood—the last traces of her left in this world—that caused the petals of the bloodleaf flower to unfurl.

Ten-year-old Begonia approached the edge of the clearing, eyes widening as she took in the sight. She dropped her basket, and a wealth of wild mushrooms spilled out by her feet as a white bloodleaf petal, lifted into the air by a lazy breeze, drifted down into her hands.

She would collect three petals that day. One, she would use on my father. One, I'd use on Simon, and the other . . . she'd use on me.

While the quicksilver girl slept on her mattress of bloodleaf, her little sister dragged the identical, red-haired corpse to the family plot in the trees behind the homestead.

She cried as she dug a shallow grave for one Rosetta, and when she was done, she wiped her eyes, squared her shoulders, and went off to wake the other.

I had to get back to Greythorne. That was where Galantha had sent Mathuin, however unwittingly. It had to be. That was *his* cradle. That was *his* home.

I tried to focus, imagining myself upon the Greythorne cobble.

The first thing I saw when I opened my eyes was the statue of a little girl holding a doll.

Onal.

A few turns later, I came to the snowy owl, wings and talons open.

Next was the fox, looking expectantly over her shoulder.

The last turn brought me face-to-face with Urso, blood dripping from his hands.

But they weren't Urso's hands. They were mine.

I was standing before a man on his knees. "Why, Aurelia?" Kellan asked, pleading with his soft brown eyes.

"Bound by blood, by blood undone," I replied.

Stop showing me this, I begged the air, the Gray, the Empyrea, any- one who was listening.

Aurelia! It was Zan in my head now. *Aurelia, come back. Hear me. Follow my voice.*

I still hadn't found the bell, but I wanted to get away from the Bleeding Dream. I tried to concentrate, like I had before. To will myself out. To reunite with my body on the other side. But my head was fuzzy. My eyesight was beginning to dim.

Aurelia. Please come back.

I could almost feel Zan's hand on my hand. But it was just my mind, using its last moments to remember happy, lovely things.

Zan touched my face. I couldn't see him, but his fingers were light on my skin. I could feel the life draining from me, and I felt my spirit peeling away from the fetters of my body so that it could finally fly free like a bright, brilliant bird taking to the sky. I wondered, fleetingly, what shape my quicksilver tether would take. Who or what would lead me to the other side?

"Aurelia!" Zan's voice was louder now. Why was he yelling? And so close to my ear. Didn't he know how tired I was? Couldn't he tell how desperately I wanted to sleep?

"Merciful stars, Aurelia. Please don't do this. Please don't make me do this."

Zan. Why was he so sad?

I was so tired.

"Wake up," he whispered. "Please. For me."

I'd do anything for him, wouldn't I?

So incredibly tired.

"Open your eyes, Aurelia," he begged. "Fight."

He brushed his lips against mine.

A sweet, soft kiss.

I reached back for him, following the golden light of my vitality as it was drawn toward his. And for one fleeting second, I reclaimed my body and kissed him back.

21

Onal was pounding on my chest. *One, two, three. Again. One, two, three. Again.* Between each blow, she uttered a string of curses so creative and colorful, they could belong only to someone who had been honing a collection for a hundred years. When I was finally able to draw a gasping breath, she hugged me tightly to her bony body, a show of affection more substantial than all I had received from her over my lifetime combined. Nearby, Kellan was doubled over as Rosetta scribbled hexes into the air above him—an effort to sustain him as long as possible while Onal restarted my heart.

Zan was hanging back behind the others, trying to catch his breath. His eyes, when they at last rose to meet mine, were simmering golden cauldrons. He'd kissed me back from the brink of oblivion, but now the light of my vitality was roiling under his skin, too; a transaction that healed and haunted him both at once.

"We have to go," he said. "Now."

Over the edge of the tower, I saw them: boats with black sails were headed into the harbor. Emblazoned upon them was the seven-legged spider of the Castillion family crest.

"How did they get so close without anyone noticing?" I cried. "Why didn't you pull me from the Gray sooner?"

"We did notice," Onal said. "It's hard not to notice. And let me tell you, we tried everything. Why do you think we let Killer Touch over there *kiss* you? We were out of options."

"How long was I Graywalking?"

"Two days," Rosetta said.

"Long enough for Castillion to come out to the fjord," I said, near tears.

"I knew this city, and I know its ruins," Zan said. "They're unfamiliar with them. They won't be able to follow us." He directed us toward the old stone stairs that led down to the canal passage.

"Why are we going that way?" Kellan asked. "There's water that way. And ships."

"And a way out," Zan said, "that doesn't involve thorns."

"Stars save me, if you knew a way to get *in* here that didn't involve thorns . . ."

Zan grinned as he dropped down to the rocks below. "Always good to have a second way out. This way, our friends on the *Humility,* the *Piety,* and the *Accountability* will think we've gone toward the castle."

"It might not be a terrible idea," Kellan said, "but don't think I'm not still mad about the thorns."

This section of the old canal system was lower than the one that originated in the castle kitchens; the muck was nearly waist-high and wall-to-wall. It was slow going and arduous, and we all tired quickly, even as the sound of marching boots on the ground above ricocheted down the passage.

The tunnel slowly ascended from the mud. When we reached the juncture that would take us to the castle or away to the culvert, we went toward the culvert; Castillion's men were sure to have reached the castle already. Anything we had left behind in the library would have to remain there.

It was a relief to break out into the light of day, but the mud, caked onto our clothes, squelching in our shoes, and dripping from our faces, continued to weigh us down.

"We can't keep going like this," I panted, still exhausted from Zan's kiss and empty with hunger after two days in the Gray. I looked down at the track of muck that coated the ground in our wake. "We're leaving a trail that will lead them right to us!"

"Allow me," Rosetta said. "I can't turn you all into foxes, but I can do this."

Her fingers began to work wildly, tracing designs in the air. As she worked, the mud leached from our clothes in rivulets that flowed down to the creek bed.

When she was done, we were all dry and clean once again. We started striding again, but then I stopped.

"Wait," I said. "If you could do that, why did you have to keep dumping freezing-cold water on me back at the homestead?"

She shrugged. "I thought it was funny."

There was nothing left of my old hut other than its stone footprint. Kate and Nathaniel's house was still standing, but barely. The roof had collapsed into the kitchen, the windows were broken, and the paint was peeling, but the walkway and the flower beds were choked with late-blooming goldenrod and phlox.

Kate would have been delighted.

The road that she and I used to take when we'd walk arm in arm into town, however, was completely blocked. Impassable.

"We'll have to go east," Zan said. "Where the stairs up the wall used to be. I haven't been there yet to see how it fared, but we should be prepared for the worst."

"What's the worst?" Rosetta asked.

"Use your imagination," Zan replied.

"Don't have to," she said, and she shifted into her fox form and scampered ahead, turning only to give Zan a disdainful yellow stare.

"Where is she going?" he asked.

Onal said, "I think she prefers to know what's up ahead rather than imagine it."

We chased after the fox, crashing past the new growth of trees and into the section beyond, where burned-out tree trunks stood like black iron spikes against the craggy hill. Rosetta's fiery pelt flashed as she zigged and zagged between.

I tried to talk to Onal as we went. "I saw some things in the Gray," I panted. I was so hungry. So weak.

"You spent two precious days there," she snapped back. "I hope you got something out of it."

"It was about you," I said. "I saw you, Onal. In the past . . ."

I had to stop because we had come to the wall. It had crumbled into a high pile of rocks; the stairs were no more. We had to climb with our bare hands over the serrated shards of rubble, struggling to find footholds in the loose stone, losing three feet for every two we climbed when the rocks would begin to slide. From this vantage point, without the leaves blocking our view, the sails of Castillion's ships were clearly visible.

As were the lines of Castillion's men methodically combing through the ruins.

Fox-Rosetta was first to make it to the top. She skittered across the pinnacle, then froze.

From beyond the wall, there came an unsettling sound: the howl of a wolf.

Rosetta barely had time to let out a distressed squeak before the rocks slipped out from beneath her and she disappeared in a cloud down the other side.

We climbed faster, listening to barks and growls and whimpers coming from just beyond our view, not knowing which were coming from Rosetta and which were caused by her.

Kellan reached the top next; then Zan. I came up behind them, but Onal was still struggling to get past the halfway point. Down below on the other side, three wolves in varying states of decay were brawling with Rosetta, snapping and scratching, teeth bared and eyes burning as she darted under their feet, swiping where she could swipe and biting when she could bite. But she was one against three and obviously beginning to tire.

Without a blink, Kellan skidded down the rocks sideways, one foot ahead of the other, leaving a single-line scar in the gravel mountain. He tucked into a roll at the base and rose with his sword already drawn, then plunged into the fray with Rosetta, giving a guttural battle cry.

Zan followed suit, a dagger in each hand, tearing with one and blocking with the other, his black coat flying behind him as he stabbed and parried.

I threw my hand down to Onal. "Come on! Here! Take it!"

"I'm too old for this shit," she said, straining to reach.

"Just a little farther!" Her fingers were almost in my grasp.

Then the rocks slid out from beneath her, and she tumbled in a cascade all the way back to the bottom, where she went still.

I didn't want to leave the others to fight the wolves alone, but I couldn't abandon Onal. My eyes stinging from the dust, I hoisted myself back over the ridge and was just starting to go back down after her when a shrill whistle sang out from the dark line of trees. I peeked over the top of the rubble to where the others were fighting and saw six of Arceneaux's acolytes emerge from the forest. They were led by a seventh: I knew him immediately. Lyall, her second-in-command.

He had Rosetta, back in human form, locked tight in his grip, the curve of an iron knife pressed into the soft skin under her jaw.

He whistled again, and the wolves froze mid-fight and then padded obediently to his side. One wolf had white ribs jutting visibly from its sagging fur. On another, the musculature of its hackles was open to the air; even from here I could see the stringy, graying meat pull and release as it moved. The third wolf was the same one Zan and I had already encountered outside the Quiet Canary; his teeth gleamed in his half-bare skull.

"One move," Lyall said, walking Rosetta forward, "and I'll use this knife to separate her body from her soul. Now, put your weapons down."

"Don't!" Rosetta tried to say. "I can't be—" But her words were cut off as the iron knife pressed deeper into her skin.

Kellan and Zan obeyed, laying their blades down and rising with their hands in the air.

The half-skull wolf had begun to sniff the air, shivering in excitement. It licked its teeth and what was left of its lips and made a growling bark that almost sounded like a word:

Girl.

Girl.

The last wolf was at the base of the broken rocks, staring up at me, its ravaged face pulled into a monstrous grin. I looked at Zan, and he mouthed one word: *Run!*

I half ran, half tumbled down the rocks, and crawled over to Onal, who had begun to stir. She groaned as I tried to lift her. I felt the magic in her blood before I saw it, oozing from a terrible gash between her collarbone and her shoulder. I strained away from its call, tamping down the urge to use it and focusing instead on putting distance between us and the coming canine.

"Let me go, you clumsy barbarian!" she growled.

"Can't," I breathed. "Wolf."

It had just crested the top of the rocks and was staring down at us, red eyes glowing.

"In that case . . ." Onal said.

I hoisted her arm over my shoulder and we limped back the way we came, with the dog close enough behind us that we could smell the stench of it. It seemed to be slowed by some of its missing pieces, giving me enough time to focus my concentration on all my own cuts and abrasions and begin to chant the invisibility spell. "We are not seen. We are not seen." But I had been inert for two days; I was dehydrated and hungry, my blood sluggish to respond.

The wolf's confusion at our disappearance earned us a little bit of time and distance, but it didn't take long for my diminished power to sputter out.

Girl. Its coughing bark came again, like a taunt.

Girl. It was my imagination. It had to be my imagination.

Little miss.

I stopped in my tracks, the last of my pitiable invisibility spell dying on my lips.

And then the wolf laughed.

"Why are we stopping?" Onal hissed.

I didn't answer; instead, I released her carefully amid the black coiling roots of a burned-out tree. Then I turned to face the wolf.

He was waiting for me to recognize him, slowly stalking me, one step forward at a time. His tongue lolled, but the unnatural sound was not made with lips or teeth; it had come from deep within its infernal, festering body.

Little miss.

Where are my apples, little miss?

My hand was slick on my knife.

In the Gray, I'd observed Lyall with a collection of luneocite stones, saying that he'd had a good "spectral harvest."

This soul, so full of rot in real life, seemed to have found a more suitable skin to occupy.

That's why I could not see ghosts anymore. Not because the events at the tower had changed my ability. They were being *collected.*

I was facing what was left of old Brom Baltus.

We waited, each watching for the other to make the first move.

Brom, true to form, grew impatient and lunged, teeth bared. I dodged, slipping between two trees that were too close together to admit his bulky frame. The trees scraped away what skin remained on his flanks as he followed, chomping and slathering. His rotting claws left white scratches in the blackened wood. I buried my knife up to the hilt beneath his jaw and twisted, but it broke through the skull on the other side and stuck there. I couldn't pull it out without risking my hand on those teeth.

You can't kill what's already dead. Rosetta's words came back to me.

She'd used a feral spell to separate soul from skin; I had only blood magic that was already too weak to even hold up the invisibility spell.

That's when I felt it again, the surge of ready magic calling, asking, almost *begging* to be used.

As the wolf wriggled from between the two trees, I dove toward Onal. She screamed as I grabbed her wounded shoulder and drew her blood into my hands.

It hurt to hear, but I had to do it. This was the only way I could help her. Help *us.*

Brom was on me, toppling me over and pinning me to the ground just like he had in the Quiet Canary's stable.

I'll kill you, the echoing, wraithlike voice said. *That's the reward for witches and thieves.*

"I'm not a thief," I said, putting my bloody hands on his bony maw while I uttered the first spell I could think of.

"Apage!" I cried. *Be gone.*

Thief, the wolf howled as the black smoke of his soul began to trickle from his shredded skin. *Thief!*

I yanked my knife from under its slackening jaw, and then I stepped back, feeling a surge of triumph.

Until I looked down and saw my hands, smeared with Onal's blood.

Brom was right.

I was a thief.

That night, Onal and I slept in the Tomb of the Lost.

It was agony knowing that the others were out there, in Lyall's control, and I was not with them. The weight of my desire to go after them pressed relentlessly on my chest, suffocating and painful. But equally excruciating was my guilt for what I'd done to Onal. The wound was terrible on its own, but it was my use of her unwilling blood for magic that seemed to have caused her the most harm. She was weak and sick, as if I'd poisoned her. Onal barely spoke to me, allowing me only to dress and treat her wound because she could not do it herself. She did not even criticize my clumsy fingers or poor technique; that's how I knew I'd really done wrong. In normal circumstances, Onal would never have passed up a chance to give me an earful.

When the temperature dropped at nightfall, I was forced to weigh the choice between the possibility of revealing ourselves to Castillion's patrols and the prospect of dying of cold and becoming the first human tenants of the Tomb. I decided to risk the former to avoid the latter, and I made a small fire between us and cooked the last two of

Father Edgar's shriveled potatoes, scavenged from the very bottom of Onal's pack.

Her shivering abated a little, but not much.

The waterskin had only a few drops of clean water left in it—not enough to conduct a full scrying spell even if I had been inclined to use it that way. I did find a six-inch pool of standing rainwater in the cavity of an old stone where a column had once stood. While Onal rested, I nicked a finger and let the blood drop into the puddle. *"Ibi mihi et ipse est,"* I commanded. *Show me.*

I saw Kellan first. He was shackled to the back of a darkened wagon that jerked and jolted over uneven ground. Beside him, Rosetta sat with her head on his shoulder, looking wasted and wan. An iron chain was around her neck, and her hands were now fully encased in iron as well; she had no power to get them free.

Zan was alone on the other side of the cart, staring up at the oppressive black-canvas canopy, where weak daylight peeked in from a scattering of tiny holes in the fabric like dim stars.

The vision broke when I heard Onal begin to cough on the other side of the tomb in guttural, full-body wracks.

I hurried over to find that her bandages—scraps of dirty fabric torn from our clothes—had already soaked through; when I went to change them, I finally ventured to break the silence. "You know," I said, "I did learn how to absorb sickness and injury. If you want, I could try . . ."

She wheezed, "Sure, do it. At least I'll die quickly."

"What do you mean?"

"I may not be a feral mage like Rosetta, but I'm a daughter of wardens, and blood magic weakens me." Huffing, she added, "You thought you were helping me, using my blood on that wolf? Ha! You may as well have put me in my grave."

"If that's true, why does it not hurt me? I'm a daughter of the woods too, am I not?"

Her gaze swiveled to mine. "What did you just say? What nonsense. Why would you—"

"When I was in the Gray," I said slowly, "I saw what happened. I saw my father as a newborn baby, in the nursery back in Syric. And I saw his mother." I paused. "She was not Queen Iresine."

At the name, I saw Onal visibly stiffen. After a long silence, she said, "I never told anyone. Not my sister. Not even your father, Regus. That's why you're not weak to iron, why you age at a regular pace—it runs through the wardens' direct female line, and you were born to my son."

"Rosetta is desperate for someone to take the warden's mantle from her, to become the guardian of the Ninth Age." I was trying to sort all the mismatched pieces. "Does this mean . . . I could do it?"

"I don't know," Onal said. "But you could try, I suppose. If you found the bell, I could pass it to you—only two of Nola's descendants are needed to make the change. Though I don't know why you'd want to. It's a very heavy burden."

"Why didn't you tell my father who you were?"

"It was safer that way, for everyone," Onal said tiredly. "After Galantha died, Rosetta and I fought constantly and bitterly. So I left. I traveled around for a while before settling in Syric. I set myself up as an herbalist there and began gaining a reputation for good work when I was asked to come take a look at the queen. She'd been try-ing to have a child, but she kept losing them in the early weeks." She sighed. "It was just a job. I didn't expect to like her"—Onal's eyes shone—"let alone *love* her. But I did. I couldn't help it." She sniffed. "And she loved me, too. For the first time in my life, I felt seen. Val-ued. Cherished, even."

Gently, I said, "Oh, Onal."

"She loved her husband, King Costin, too, but it never felt like she was *torn* between us. There was no jealousy or animosity. But, even showered as she was in our love, she was still fading, and there was nothing we could do about it. She wanted a child—she *ached* for a child—and she was dying of the wanting."

"What did you do?"

"Everything I could. Everything. But no matter what potions I concocted, what remedies I tried—her body wasn't capable of carry-ing one of her own."

"So *you* gave her the heir that she wanted."

"Yes," Onal said. "I delivered her son. Their son." She paused. "Our son." Then, taking a deep breath, she asked, "What else did you see?"

"I think you know."

Onal looked away, tears standing in eyes I thought were incapable of producing them. "It was a tradition by then to take girls born to the crown and spirit them away. I think that's what they tried to do."

My voice was barely a whisper. "Did you find where they took her?"

Onal shook her head. "I found a burned-out carriage. There was nothing left." She cleared her throat, trying to rid her voice of the roughness that had crept into it. "Iresine died only two years later. I didn't get to say goodbye."

"But you went back. You became Father's nursemaid when you could have been his mother."

"It was the most I could ask for, and I was grateful for it. After Iresine died, Costin asked me to return. I stayed with him until his death. I made myself irreplaceable to Regus, then Genevieve, and eventually . . . your brother and you. Rosetta is my sister, but you . . . you have always been my true family."

"Are you trying to say . . . you love me?" I asked with a gentle, goading nudge.

"If I'd meant to say that, I would have said it," she snapped. "I'm still mad at you, Aurelia. What you did back there . . ."

"I made a split-second decision. It was a one-time mistake. I won't do it again."

"If it were the first time you'd made that mistake, I might believe it."

I looked down, ashamed.

"The Founder was once like you," she said. "A gifted blood mage. Probably wanted to do the right thing. But he, too, got into the habit of taking unwilling blood. And it destroyed him."

"I am *nothing* like him," I spat. "I'm not a monster."

"No," Onal said. "Not yet."

Our fire petered out before dawn, but it wasn't the cold that woke me. It was Onal, who was mumbling to herself as she stared out at nothing, glassy-eyed.

"Lily," she muttered. "Where is my Lily?"

I touched her forehead; it was slick with sweat. She was burning up. Her bandages were saturated with blood, and the skin around them was hot and swelling. An infection had taken hold at the site of her gash; if I did not get help soon, she'd die.

I put her other arm over my shoulder and hoisted her to her feet, marveling at how light she was, as if she were made of paper and string instead of flesh and bone.

"Where are we going?" she asked. "Are you taking me to my Lily?"

"Lily is with the Empyrea," I said gently, "but you're not joining her, Onal. Not quite yet."

I dragged Onal along with me through the trees. Castillion's men must have given up the search, because they'd pulled back and were returning to their ships. The first two — the *Piety* and the *Accountability* — had already left shore. Only Castillion's last, most ostentatious vessel, the *Humility,* remained in the fjord, and from the bustle of activity on board, it looked like it would not be there for long.

I hurried as fast as I could, yelling and waving my arms after I set Onal down on the rocky edge of the water. "Wait! Wait!" I called. "Don't leave! I need to speak with Castillion! Let us aboard!"

A man came to the bow of the ship. His hair was a strange white blond, combed back from his brow in a swooping wave, his trim beard a dark brown in contrast. Despite the color of his hair, he couldn't be much older than twenty-seven or twenty-eight. He was good-looking but not quite handsome, well-dressed but not pretentious, commanding but not intimidating. He regarded us with more curiosity than animosity.

He called, "What is your business with Castillion?"

"I seek to make a deal with him. My companion here is hurt. She needs a healer's help."

"And what will you provide in return?"

"A bargaining chip," I called back. "With the Tribunal. Because they have King Valentin. And you"—I dropped the pretense that I did not know to whom I was speaking—"will need something of equal value to trade for him."

Castillion's lips quirked to the side, waiting.

I lifted my chin. "You need me. Aurelia Altenar, princess of Renalt."

He smiled, just a little, before motioning to the men still on the ground to bring us aboard. He greeted us on the deck, his purple-black flag and its seven-legged spider waving high in the background.

"Princess," he said with a genteel bow, "welcome aboard the *Humility.*"

PART THREE

THE MEN OF GREYTHORNE WERE MEN OF HONOR. IT WAS THE
trait by which they were best known and of which they were most
proud. Since Saint Urso built his sanctorium and requested that King
Theobald name the Greythorne family as its guardians and the pro-
tectors of the province in which it lay, they had lived every day by the
motto *Do your duty, and you'll never have to go to sleep with regrets.*

As he opened the manor doors to face the bobbing torches, Fredrick Greythorne hoped that in this, his final hour, he would do right
by all the generations that had come before him.

Isobel Arceneaux, dressed all in white, was waiting for him at the
bottom of the stairs. Tribunal clerics had been arriving at the province
for days now, collecting at the edges of the manor and sanctorium
like ants clamoring after a drop of honey. There were Greythorne
civilians among the crowd too: men and women who appreciated and
applauded the Tribunal's viciousness, or those too scared to speak up
against it lest it turn on them. They all watched and waited, growing
in numbers, but never crossed the property line; Arceneaux was being
careful to obey the laws to the strictest letter. Adherence to the rules
was little more than a pretense, of course, but it was a pretense that
gave her near-unlimited power.

Arceneaux could execute the law with the exactness of a surgeon's
blade, killing with the same cut she proclaimed was a cure for pain.
And where was the lie? All pain ends with death.

She lifted her gloved hand to quiet the teeming mass at her heels as one of her acolytes removed the hawthorn-hilted family sword from the scabbard around Fredrick's waist. "Lord Regent," she said, "for three weeks, I have requested an audience with our king. For three weeks, I have been denied. Why are you keeping him from seeing his subjects?"

"I do only as my king wills," Fredrick replied, hands behind his back.

"And is it his will to sit alone in his gilded halls, without recognizing the people to whom he owes his service? His very position?" Her eyes narrowed at Fredrick. "Or is that you, imposing your will upon him?"

"I do only as my king wills," Fredrick repeated.

"Lord Fredrick," Arceneaux said, "I know that you and your lovely wife have not yet been blessed with children, even after all these long years of marriage. Perhaps you've come to feel a fatherly fondness for our young king. Perhaps," she said pointedly, "that misplaced affection has led you to believe that you can also exercise fatherly control over him."

Fredrick squared his shoulders. "I do only as my king wills."

She held him in her icy gaze for one moment, and then two, before turning to the acolytes at her side. "Seize him," she said. Then, "Lord Fredrick Greythorne, you have unlawfully restricted public access to our sovereign monarch and have exerted undue authority in his place. You are hereby stripped of your title as regent to the king and placed under arrest to face trial by fair tribunal."

She raised her voice. "Let it be known: The law states that in such grievous cases of wrongdoing as this, the accused must forfeit all claims to title and property. It is, by right, passed on to his rightful heir. As I mentioned before: Lord Greythorne has no children. And his wife, without having any blood claim to the land, is also unable to hold it. It would, then, have been passed to his brother, Kellan Greythorne, but he, too, has turned traitor to the crown and cannot inherit. Which means," she lifted her chin triumphantly, "that Greythorne and all of its surrounding property must be considered forfeit and must return to the crown, a transaction that will be managed and overseen by its Empyrea-guided judicial arm." She took one step up the stairs, then another and another. The top step was the last one, the demarcation of where public crown land ended and private Greythorne property began.

She stepped over it and turned, arms raised. "I hereby reclaim this house for His Majesty, King Conrad! Long live the king!"

A cheer went up below, and the crowd surged forward, hungry for more outrage, more scandal, more brutal justice.

Arceneaux waved her highest-ranking acolytes inside. "Arrest everyone inside," she told them, "but don't kill anyone. When you find the king, bring him to me straightaway."

She waved and smiled while torches bobbed.

Fredrick waited and prayed.

A few minutes later, Arceneaux's acolytes returned. "There's no one here, Magistrate. The entire manor is completely empty."

Her composure slipped ever so slightly with the curl of her lip when she turned to Fredrick and spat, "Where is the king? What have you done?"

Fredrick smiled and said, "I do only as my king wills."

As he was led away, he repeated once again the Greythorne family phrase.

Do your duty, and you'll never have to go to sleep with regrets.

23

spent the first several hours on Castillion's boat locked in the captain's quarters.

Under other circumstances, being alone in such a place would have been a welcome respite: I bathed in water warmed by the furnaces in the belly of the boat; ate tiny, flaky pastries decorated with icing that looked like the most delicate of laces. Castillion had confiscated my satchel—bloodcloth still inside it—and the luneocite knife from my boot, but provided me with material to read and paper upon which I could write or draw, were I so inclined. Everything was plush and pristine, crafted by artisans of great skill and even greater vision.

I hated every second of it.

I spent my time practicing the litany of abuses I'd unleash upon him when he finally deigned to see me, but the moment he did arrive at the door of my extravagant cell, I forgot them all and instead said, "Onal. How is she? Please tell me she's all right."

He closed the door behind him and sat down in the red velvet chair behind his desk. "Well," he said, "I have to be honest and tell you that she was in a very bad way when you brought her to us. It is proving to be too much for our ship's healer—but of course, anything more than a paper cut would be too much for him—"

I blanched. "She's not—?"

"She's not dead yet," Castillion said in a too-bright way that made me think he was trying to come off as encouraging and hopeful. "And we're headed toward Ingram's port. There's an order of Empyrean nuns that runs a sanctorium on the harbor. If anyone can help her, it will be them—"

"Nuns?" I asked incredulously. "You want to hand her over to *nuns?*"

"They're very good at their work," Castillion said. "They'll treat your friend with the utmost quality of care . . ."

"I'm not worried about *her*," I said. "I'm worried for the nuns."

He regarded me with his dark eyebrows knitted together, creating a series of furrows in his brow. "You're not exactly what I expected."

"And what did you expect?"

"Honestly?" He shrugged. "I thought you'd be prettier."

"With everyone calling you 'the silver-haired despot from the north,' I thought you'd be elderly."

"Can't believe everything you hear," he said.

"Can't disbelieve it, either," I said. "Or are you *not* a raving tyrant bent on domination of two realms and the destruction of thousands of years of tradition and history?"

"I much prefer the term 'forward-thinking political outsider.'"

"And that's what all the refugees are running to Renalt to escape?

Your forward-thinking ideas?" I paused, and repeated for emphasis, "To *Renalt.*"

"Change can be frightening," he replied, unruffled.

"Especially if it comes with an army."

Castillion considered me for a moment and then said, "Would you, perhaps, honor me with a walk around the promenade deck, Your Highness?"

Mere weeks ago, I'd spent hours poring over diagrams of this boat, memorizing the intricacies of its workings inside and out, but nothing could have prepared me for the reality. The promenade floor was made of polished mahogany and lined with plush carpets the same purple-black as Castillion's flag. Above the gallery, a network of tiny, faceted glass squares formed an arching skylight. At night, you'd be able to look up and see the stars.

There were dozens of people milling in the gallery, laughing with one another while a musician plucked away at a heavy gilded harp in the corner. They were dressed as though for a ball, the women in crushed velvets and clinging silks, arms dripping with jewels, while the men wore opulent formfitting jackets studded with gem-encrusted buttons. In the center of it all, a pair of women slow-danced in a beam from the skylight, one in a silver gown and the other in gold, like a sun and moon orbiting only each other. Small tables were scattered about, at which players tried their hands at dice, chess, and even a game of Girl, Goat, and Dragon.

Stars above, I thought. *I wish the Canary Girls could see this.*

The rumors of Castillion's ship of revelry did not do it justice. I doubted I could have earned enough to buy a stay here if I'd won a hundred rounds of Betwixt and Between.

And though we made an incongruent pair walking arm in arm, no one looked at us askance.

"All right," I said. "Now, where do you keep all your prisoners?"

"That is just gossip, Highness. I do not imprison people. Nor do I enslave them."

"No? I wonder, then, why these people refuse to look directly at us? Is it because they are exceedingly courteous, or because they're afraid of you?"

Castillion smiled, crinkling the corners of his eyes. "Perhaps it is you they fear, Princess. You're the blood mage who infiltrated Achleva and brought down its impenetrable capital. That's no small reputation."

"I'm getting too much credit," I said.

"Or too much blame?" He brought me to the edge of the starboard side. "I've heard a rumor or two saying that whatever caused the wall to fall also robbed you of your ability to cast spells."

"That's true. Whatever power I had before . . . it's all gone now."

He nodded. "I will admit, when I was given information that a fugitive might be hiding in the ruins of Achlev, you are not the one I expected to come across."

"You thought you'd find Valentin?"

"I thought I might find the horseman," Castillion said. "I only recently began to suspect that he and Valentin——"

"King Valentin," I corrected.

"——were one and the same."

I asked, "I suppose you were quite disappointed to find out your previous efforts to dispatch him were thwarted?"

He regarded me with heavy-lidded eyes. "A little, yes. But I am ever an admirer of an indomitable spirit."

"A strange sentiment coming from a man who has all but enslaved his own people."

If I thought this would goad him, I was wrong. Castillion didn't flinch at my criticism. Instead, he said, "I know that's what it looks like, Your Highness. But you've mischaracterized my enterprise. I seek to bring Achleva—and eventually, all nations—to a place of equilibrium. Of balance. Is that not something you also desire?"

Rather than answer, I released his arm and gazed up at his flag. "Your family's sigil is a spider?"

"It is not my family's sigil," he replied. "It's the one I chose for myself."

"A peculiar choice for someone who wants equilibrium."

"Not at all," he said. "What is a spider, if not the enforcer of equilibrium? Its entire life is about balance. About symmetry."

"And yet yours is asymmetrical," I pointed out. "Four legs on one side, three on the other."

"We can aspire to perfection," he said, "but we cannot achieve it without sacrifice."

"What, exactly, have *you* sacrificed?" I said bitterly.

He lifted his eyes to mine. They were thoughtful beneath his dignified brow. "More than you know."

"Should I feel sorry for you?" I asked.

"Please don't," he replied. "I prefer piety to pity."

"Ah, yes. I noticed that you named all your ships after virtues." I tapped the balustrade upon which I was leaning. "The *Accountability,* the *Piety,* the *Humility.*" I eyed his clothes. They were perfectly tailored to suit him: a velvet black suit coat embroidered with slate-colored thread, an overcoat of polished leather dyed the deep red-violet of mulberry wine, and a belt slung across his hips that had been embellished with pure gold. "That last one seems a little bit ill-fitting, don't you think?"

"I do have things to work on," he agreed. "It's a process. I have four more ships in the process of being built: the *Sobriety,* the *Acuity,* the *Veracity,* and the *Morality.* My wish is that someday I deserve to be considered a scion of each trait."

I snorted before I could help it. Then, to regain some of my dignity, I said, "Well, at the very least, thank you for taking care of my friend."

"Balance," he said. "You gave yourself up to me to help her. I will ensure that your sacrifice does not go unrewarded." He gave me a grave stare. "Arceneaux will kill you, you know."

"I know," I said. "And if she gives you Valentin, you will kill him, too."

He nodded. "I'm sorry for that."

It felt like he was telling the truth.

"You don't have to do it. You could make a bargain with him. A compromise. Just like he originally proposed!"

"There can be no bargain. Achleva *must* be freed from tyranny. It must be rid of its kings." The white waves of his hair ruffled in the chill wind coming in from the door as the boat picked up speed.

"And, as you just pointed out, Valentin was born to be king. That is his life's one purpose. Would you deprive him of it?"

"Better to deprive him of his purpose than his life. And I assume you will take his place? Calling yourself something else, no doubt. What will it be? Steward? Emperor? Lord Regent?"

This provoked a response, if a minor one: he lifted his chin in defiance. "I believe I was meant to guide the nation into a new order, but no. I will not rule it. The people will govern themselves. There will be absolute peace."

"How many people do you actually know?" I asked. "Because in my experience, most are not generally inclined toward peace."

He smiled. "I suppose they can seem predisposed to fighting . . . especially when someone is going around telling them that they must."

Si vivis, tu pugnas.

We walked to the outside deck. Mentally, I tried to reconcile the cold-blooded usurper who'd overtaken half of Achleva with this well-mannered man preaching peace and perfection. There was a confidence to Castillion's refined manner that made it easy to mistake his rationalizations for reason. In that way, he might be even more dangerous than the Tribunal, who wore their brutality like a badge.

"You look tired," he said. "Come. Get some rest."

"And where will you sleep?" I asked pointedly.

"Have no fear of me, Princess," he replied. "I will bunk in another suite for the duration of your stay on the *Humility*."

"That's kind of you," I said, still feeling suspicious.

"Do not make the mistake of believing my commitment to

morality as kindness. Kindness is weakness. Morality is fairness. I do what is moral."

"And murdering an innocent man for an unattainable ideal?" The magic in my blood began to spark, just a little. "Is that moral?"

"If it were truly unattainable, it wouldn't be."

He was so damnably unperturbable. I could toss out a million valid arguments against him, and he'd never budge in his conviction.

"What about Arceneaux and the Tribunal? You're fine to let them carry on as always? Is what *they* do moral? Is putting me into their hands knowing that they'll execute me moral?"

"I must think of the greater good," he said calmly, and changed the subject. "In recognition of your limited time, I will not seek to confine you while you're on this ship. You're free to wander the decks as much as you wish. I think you should." He breathed in deeply, closing his eyes as he filled his lungs with the frosty air. "Take as much of this world in while you can."

I didn't know if I should thank him or throttle him.

I chose neither and spun on my heel.

"Where are you going?" Castillion asked.

"To see Onal," I replied. "I find myself craving more sensible conversation."

"She's delirious."

I glared at him over my shoulder. "I know."

When I got to Onal's bedside, I was pleased to find that her fever had broken. The healer was hurrying out, a harried look on his face. "She's all yours," he said, relieved.

"What did you say to him?" I asked, taking the stool at her bedside.

"I asked for a drink," she said through cracked lips. "He gave me *water*."

"Foolish man," I said. "Did he provide you a suitable alternative? Brandy? Bourbon?"

"Nothing," she replied listlessly. "He said that Castillion doesn't allow spirits aboard any of his ships." She clucked her tongue. "Then I berated him for killing me, because this is obviously the After."

"Obviously," I said.

"What are we doing here, girl?" Onal asked softly.

"I did what I had to do," I replied, "to keep you alive."

"It was a poor trade."

"Of course it was," I said, giving her a tiny smile. "I know, I know. I'm a foolish girl, always making bad decisions and terrible mistakes."

She gave a deep sigh. "Well, you come by it honestly." Then she added quickly, "From your mother's side of the family, of course."

"Of course."

"What are we going to do, Aurelia?"

I shrugged. "I don't know. They're going to get you to a better healer as soon as we get to Ingram's port. But then it will probably be on to Gaskin; Castillion thinks he's going to make a trade with Arceneaux."

"Bleeding stars," she said. "How many more days until the eclipse?"

"Seven," I said.

"How are you planning on getting back to Greythorne by then?"

"I'll figure it out," I said.

She said, "I don't know if I'm going to make it that long, Aurelia."

"Stop feeling sorry for yourself," I teased as lightheartedly as I could. "Or I swear, I'll simply do away with you myself and tell everyone it was an accident."

She grinned and patted my hand. "That's my girl."

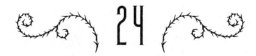

The Nothing Dream came to me that night.

It was still terrifying, even now that I knew it was not simply a dream but a glimpse into the Gray. But this time, the endless eventide did not change. It did not show me past or future. It remained a vast expanse of nothing.

When I woke, it was to a heavy fog curling against the cabin windows, obscuring the sky to the point at which I could not tell if it was dawn or dusk or sometime in between.

I dressed quickly, aware that the shift dress I'd borrowed from Rosetta's trunk was likely to stand out among the elaborate costumes of the rest of the ship's guests, but too stubborn to consider any of the prettier dresses Castillion had had delivered to the room. Then I went for the door, grateful when the knob turned without hindrance; he had kept his promise. While we were on the water, he would let me roam the decks as I pleased. I intended to explore the accuracy of my schematics, but curiosity drove me to the gallery first. Castillion and his ship intrigued me more than I cared to admit, and there was only so much I could glean from scouring his immaculately clean quarters. I wanted to talk to his overdressed guests.

The fog was icy and, on the decks, so thick that I had to walk with my hand against the wall or risk knocking into things as I passed. It took me three times longer to find the gallery than it should have, and I was chilled to the bone by the time I did.

The hall was full when I got to it, but there was no music playing, no cheery laughter. The guests played their games in eerie silence.

I was standing to the side, trying to make myself invisible, when a woman at the table nearest to me waved me over. She was with another man and woman, and they were all dressed in thick furs and brilliant fabrics. When they spoke, it was in hushed tones and furtive whispers.

The first woman, wearing a gown the color of citrines, said, "I was telling Loretta here that you are Aurelia, witch princess of Renalt. Killer of King Domhnall and destroyer of Achlev. She doesn't believe me."

"She's right," I told Loretta reluctantly. "At least about my name and title. The rest is . . . up for debate."

"An interesting character, at least," the man said, tipping his hat. "Castillion does love a good character. Do you play cards? We'd love to have you join in a game."

"What game?" I asked. I was really proficient only at Betwixt and Between.

"Serpents," the man replied. "Do you play?"

I shook my head. "But I wouldn't mind watching to learn how."

"I didn't know how when I first came aboard," Loretta said. "It's pretty easy to learn."

"When did you come aboard?" I asked as the man began to deal.

"About two months ago," she replied, picking up her hand. "After Aylward surrendered. I'm his cousin. Loretta Aylward."

"I'm Gretchen Percival," the first woman said. "Sister to Baron Lander Percival."

"Werner Humboldt," the man said, giving a slight nod of his head. "Fergus Ingram is my brother-in-law."

I nodded slowly. "So, you're all . . . ?"

"Hostages," Werner finished. "A way to ensure each baron's cooperation." He shrugged. "Not that Fergus would particularly care if I lived or died, but his wife—my sister—might."

"I thought a person could buy their way onto the *Humility*," I said.

Gretchen scoffed. "It's a pretty steep price. Just your freedom."

"And yet, you're here. Playing card games and dancing. Is it so bad?"

"A cage is a cage," Loretta said. "But he does feed us well, and he provides us with anything we could want or need."

"I thought he was . . . I don't know . . . your friend?"

"Dominic Castillion has no friends," Werner said. "Just his soldiers and us."

"It might be different if he ever came down among us." Gretchen laid down her first card, a serpent bent in the shape of a figure eight. "I've heard he used to love to play as a very young man, but he took too many risks and lost half his father's fortune, and the old man beat him near to death. So he vowed never to make such a mistake again, and devotes himself to virtue and moderation. But he does still seem very interested in it. He often sits up there, on the promenade, just watching."

Loretta grumbled at Gretchen's play and laid down another card, a serpent in the shape of a square. "Losing already," she said. "On the first play."

"What do you play for?" I asked. "I was just wondering how a man so obsessed with virtue would allow gambling on his ship."

"Ah," Werner said lightly. "But we don't gamble for money. We play for the sake of playing. We win for the sake of winning."

"That's a lie," Loretta said. "We trade what we have to trade."

"Usually a favor," Gretchen said.

"Or a secret," Werner added.

"It's always more fun on clear days," Gretchen said, moving cards around in her hand. "On the white days, everything is so much more subdued."

"White days?" I asked, looking up at the arched skylight. "You mean the fog? Does it happen often?"

"Not often, but enough." Werner played his first card, a snake in the shape of a spiral. "We used to have to stay in our beds on white days. We complained too much, so he eventually let us come back to the gallery and play as long as we keep quiet. No music, low voices . . ."

"But *why?*" I asked.

Loretta shrugged. "On white days, he goes up to the bridge alone and stays there for hours. No one is supposed to bother him. When the fog clears, he reappears and everything goes back to normal. As normal as all of this"—she motioned to the opulent surroundings —"can be."

Gretchen played another card: a snake in the shape of a circle. "Look at that," she said. "I win again."

"Secret or favor?" Loretta asked.

"Favor," Gretchen replied. "From both of you."

Werner began gathering the cards up again. "Do you want us to deal you in?" he asked me.

"No, thank you," I said. "I think I might use this . . . white day, as you call it . . . to do a little bit of exploring."

They exchanged glances. "Just make sure you stay far away from the bridge until the fog is gone," Loretta said, shivering. "Trust me."

✶

Castillion's fearsome forces, the ones who had overtaken half of Achleva in a few short months, were mostly kept on his other ships. Despite its cargo of hostages, the *Humility*'s defenses were spare, its soldiers few. And with the heavy fog hiding my movements, I made it belowdecks unaccosted and unquestioned.

The *Humility*'s plans, still rolled up and stashed away in my drawers at the Quiet Canary, were not as accurate in rendering the vessel as I had hoped; still, I was able to recall enough of the ship's layout to orient myself and reframe my once-abstract objectives within the now-tangible reality. This was no longer a hypothetical revenge scenario I could use as a distraction from my sorrow and as an outlet for my anger. This was about survival now.

I did not have time to be one of Castillion's hostages. I did not have time to dress up and act for him, to allow him to affect the role of kind and generous host. As I made my way deeper into the belly of his beautiful boat, I realized that his ship was a metaphor for him: once you cracked the pleasant veneer, the inside was all black coals and fire and suffocating darkness.

I'd gotten on this boat for the sole purpose of stabilizing Onal. With that accomplished, it was time to go about getting us off it.

The quietness of the white world above did not carry into the darkness of the decks below, but the sheer magnitude of sound—each cacophonous noise layered over the next—became its own kind of silence. The workers went about their business without speaking; indeed, it would have been of no use to try.

All I needed was one piece of the black rock. Just one. I shouldn't have been nervous, though; I was able to steal to the coal heaps, only a few feet away from the hot and hungry maw of the furnace, without a single look from any of the sweating, soot-stained workers. Their existence seemed to be bound to a single pair of actions, repeated into infinity:

Shovel the coal. Feed the furnace. Shovel the coal. Feed the furnace.

They did not look at one another; they certainly didn't spare any attention for me.

When I had a piece of coal in hand, I slammed it against an iron strut; the rock broke down the center into equal halves, the sound of the blow lost in the belowdecks din. One coin-size half went into my pocket. The other I tossed back onto the mountainous mound of fuel waiting for its turn to feed the fire. Then I hurried away, hoping to make it back above deck before the fog burned off and Castillion ended his vigil on the bridge.

The workers of the boiler room continued shoveling. To them, I'd never been there.

✳

The ease with which I'd gotten to the boiler room and back made me feel invincible and cavalier, and I had to make extra effort to temper those feelings. At the Quiet Canary, the gamblers who let themselves believe they couldn't lose were always mere steps away from losing everything. I could not afford to lose my few advantages to unearned audacity.

I measured my steps. I counted my breaths. I galvanized my resolve. Castillion was just a man. I couldn't lose to him; I still had a goddess to fight.

Onal was sitting up on her cot in the infirmary when I got there, staring listlessly out at the eddying mist. When the healer was out of earshot, I pulled a stool beside her bed and took her hand.

She stared at me as if I'd gone mad. "Am I a child? Do I need my hand to be held?" she asked, piqued.

"Shhh," I said. "I need you to look like I'm comforting you. Like we're enjoying each other's company."

"A tough task on the best of days."

"We're leaving. As soon as possible. I have everything ready."

She forced a smile as Castillion's physician walked by. Then she hissed, "Just how do you propose to make that happen?"

"The details aren't important. What's important is that you're well enough to handle it. It's not likely to be easy."

"Wouldn't be a plan of yours if it were."

"But before I go ahead with anything, I have to know: Are you up to it?" I scrutinized her face, looking for any signs of lingering fever or delirium. "If not, we can wait. The window is closing fast, but we could probably take another few days if we had to." Even as I said it, I hoped it wouldn't come to that. By now, Lyall would be almost to Greythorne with his captives.

Onal replied, "I'm up to it. Don't worry about me."

"Good." My relief was immediate. "Because I'm going to need your help."

I was leaving the infirmary for the captain's quarters when I first heard it: a strange whispering that seemed to be coming from deep within the blanket of fog. I turned on my heel and began to move hesitantly toward the sound. The white mist had grown colder now, closer to nightfall; its frigidness had become almost abrasive.

I shivered in the cool, blue-toned light, able to see only a step or two ahead of my feet as I walked the promenade toward the whispering. My breath sparkled with minute crystals of ice every time I exhaled. I knew this kind of cold too well. This was the cold of spirits manifesting in the physical world, robbing the air and water and earth of warmth and life to gain enough energy to exert themselves upon it. I'd been touched by ghosts enough times to recognize when it was happening.

But this . . . this was different. And far, *far* worse.

I came to a stop just below the spot I calculated to be the ship's bridge. I could go no farther or I'd risk frostbite. Already my lips and ears were numb, frost forming on my eyelashes. The whispering continued, harsh and scraping, and as caustic as the cold. But it was joined by another voice—a man's voice.

Castillion's voice. He was responding to the whispers.

A gust of icy air blew past me, and for one stunning second, I saw Castillion standing against the rail of the bridge, his white hair waving in the wind, his head and shoulders bent, his back bowed, as if he were carrying a considerable weight.

All around him, the white air churned, but nobody else was there.

And then, as if sensing my stare, he looked up.

I pressed myself against the nearest wall, heart pounding so loud, I was certain he'd be able to hear it. Without looking back, I retraced my steps to the captain's cabin, where I closed the door just as the fog was beginning to lift.

Now to wait for darkness to fall.

25

I was sitting at Castillion's desk when he arrived less than an hour later. He had a tired, weary look about him as he removed his over-coat and loosened the buttons at the wrists of his shirtsleeves. He'd regained his rigid posture, however; it was hard to believe I'd ever seen him the way I had, hunched and humbled. The true mascot of a boat named the *Humility*.

"Long day?" I asked him as lightly as I could. I had retrieved a deck of cards from the top drawer of his desk and was lazily laying them out in front of me, as if I were more interested in the illustrations than in actually playing the game.

"They're all long days," Castillion replied.

"Did you accomplish anything important?" I eyed him over the fan of cards in my hand.

"To a satisfactory degree," he said.

I stiffened. There was blood underneath his fingernails. I could feel the last gasp of its power as he removed a damp cloth from the water basin and began to scrub it away.

There was a cut in the side of his palm. A neat, narrow incision, just like the countless tiny wounds I'd inflicted upon myself over time, all for the purpose of casting a spell.

"You're a blood mage," I blurted.

"Not a very good one, I'm afraid." He tossed the cloth back down into the bowl. "I wanted to go to the Assembly when I was very young, but my father resented the institution. Didn't like that they'd built their fabled hall on Castillion land, never mind that it predated his claim by a thousand years. And that he could never actually find the building. It shows itself only to those who already know where it is, or those it *wants* to find it." He shrugged. "If I were the Assembly Hall, I wouldn't have wanted my father to find it either." Changing the subject, he said, "I heard you went to the infirmary today. Kept Mistress Onal reasonably occupied for a while. I can't imagine that was very easy."

"It was not," I said. "She's very tiring, I'll admit. Still, there's little a good game of Betwixt and Between can't solve. But you know that."

"I don't play," he said.

"Truly? You should let me teach you. If you value gaming to learn strategy, you've done yourself a disservice by overlooking this one."

"It doesn't seem to have served you very well."

"I never said I was very good at it." I forced a laugh. The evening bell was ringing; Onal would be in the gallery soon, shepherding Castillion's overdressed hostages onto the lifeboats lining the side of the ship.

"You recommend I learn from someone admittedly terrible?"

"Nothing but the worst for you." I tipped my face up to him. "What do you say, Captain?"

It wasn't my charm that won him over; it was too thin and forced to be truly convincing. It seemed as if Gretchen was right and he was still a gambler at heart.

He settled across from me.

"Are you sure Mistress Onal doesn't want to play as well?"

"I'm sure I don't want her to play. She plays very dirty."

"It seems to me that the best players always do, no matter the game."

"It depends on what you value most: integrity? Or ingenuity?" I shuffled the cards and placed the stack on the table between us. "What is right?" I dealt the first card to myself. "Or . . . what is interesting?" I dealt the second to him.

"There's a problem with your argument," he said. "It's based on the assumption that there *is* a right."

I passed out two more cards. "Isn't there?"

"There is no black or white," he said. "No right or wrong. Everything in this world exists in shades of gray."

I laid the last of our hands out, my attention catching on the word *gray*. "A funny way of looking at the world for a man who names his ships after virtues."

"Virtues exist in grays as well, each valuable only when balanced in the center of the spectrum. Too *much* humility becomes superiority. Too much piety becomes zealotry." He leaned forward. "Now," he said, "what shall we wager?"

"I thought your virtues didn't allow for gambling with money."

"I think I'll make an exception just this one time. After all, 'sobriety' is just another word for 'moderation.'" A smile spread across his face. "Unless you think you'll lose to a beginner?"

"You removed the only thing of value I had left to my name when you took me aboard. Outside of that luneocite knife now sheathed on your belt, I'm destitute."

"You have other things worth bargaining for," he said. "Your hair, maybe. Or your heart." He grinned, and I felt sure he was taunting me. "Your time."

"My heart is taken," I said. "And my time is short. In the gallery, they were playing for secrets or favors. The winner decides which it will be."

He lifted his brows. "Deal."

Halfway through the game, it became clear that I was outmatched. I had just played Clever Cassandra only to have him place the Hapless Traveler right on top of it. I took a deep breath for serenity, then confronted my smirking opponent with irritation. "You *have* played before, haven't you?"

"I said I don't *play*," he replied. "Not that I don't know *how*. But it was awfully kind of you to try to teach me."

"You lied."

"I led you astray by confirming your own beliefs," he said. "It's different."

"Shades of gray, and all that?" I asked, laying down the Angry Brother. Outside, the very first sounds of clamor were beginning to reach us through the door.

"Shades of gray," Castillion replied. "Even this game is a testament to that philosophy." He made a big show of placing his next card: the Daughter Defiant. "Betwixt and Between: neither one thing nor another."

I slid my second-to-last card over to him. "Lady Loveless." I leaned across the table, drumming my fingers on the pile of cards. "Your move."

He eyed me. "And what move can I make now that won't lose me the entire game? It seems as if you've got me backed into a corner, no way to get out."

"The great Dominic Castillion, unsure of his path to victory?"

"It's not *my* next move I'm unsure of," he replied. "It's yours."

"Then make your play," I said, "and find out."

He sat back in his chair, rubbing his chin. Then he threw his last card on the table. "The Two-Faced Queen."

I glanced from the woman's twin effigies to Castillion, who was still studying me. "Not bad," I said. "Would you like to see *my* last card?"

He kept his eyes on me as he reached across the table to where my final play was already laid out, ready to be made. Slow and deliberate, he turned the card over.

"The Two-Faced Queen?" he asked in confusion. "But how did you come by the same card as me?"

As he said so, his card faded into Sad Tom.

He'd been too focused on outmaneuvering my moves to notice the drop of blood I'd drawn by sliding my finger down the side of a card, or the spell I'd cast by muttering under my breath. Whip-fast, I grabbed his wrists and slammed them to the top of the table. *"Manere,"* I said. *Stay.*

I took out the chunk of coal and reached over to grab my knife from his belt.

"Aurelia," he said, and for the first time since meeting him, I heard anger in his voice, "don't do this. You're better than this."

I leaned in close, close enough that I could feel the rough brush of the stubble on his chin. "That's the thing," I said softly. "I'm not. Shades of gray, and all that."

The tip of my finger stung as I dug the knife into it and blood began to collect into a bead.

"I thought you said you couldn't use blood magic anymore."

"I led you astray by confirming your own beliefs." As the orb of blood on my fingertip grew heavier, I said softly, "Right after the wall fell, many of the Achlevan lords argued against Zan's reign. They said he was too merciful, and that made him weak." I looked up at him. "And then you came through. Slaughtering villages. Capturing anyone who stood in your way. I wonder, now, what most of them think of Zan's mercy."

I shook my head, then continued, "I don't know, truly, if mercy is a weakness. What I *do* know is that it is a trait that Zan and I do not share."

The drop rolled from my fingertip and onto the chunk of coal, leaving tiny specks of red across the desk and the scattered playing cards when it hit and splashed. Then I put my hand over it and imagined the coal's other half, waiting in the belly of the ship.

"*Uro,*" I said. *Burn.*

A groaning roar came from deep within the ship, juddering the timbers and rattling the glass in the lamps.

"What was that?" Castillion coughed as dust shook down into his face.

"That," I said, "was your furnace, blowing a hole in your hull."

"You're sinking my ship?" he asked, eyes alight.

"It's what's fair," I said. "A ship for a ship." I turned to go.

"Wait!" he called. "You won the game. Don't I owe you a secret?"

I turned back to him, his hands frozen on the desk, which was bolted to the floor. His shoulders were sagging, just like I'd seen on the bridge, but his eyes were bright.

"The ship I sank in Stiria Bay? It wasn't Valentin I was after. You were supposed to be on it too."

I tilted my head, considering him. "Why were you after me?"

"They told me—" He was almost laughing. "They told me that you would be my unmaking. I didn't understand what that meant until now."

I gave Castillion one last look from over my shoulder. The cards of our game were sliding between his splayed fingers as the ship began to tip forward.

Before I closed the door on him and left him to his fate, I said, "*Si vivis, tu pugnas.* The horseman sends his regards."

26

Most of the longboats had already been deployed by the time I got out. I half ran, half slid down the promenade deck as the ship tilted toward the water. Not everyone had heeded Onal's warnings right away, and those who had waited to board the escape rafts until after the explosion were now scrabbling after them in a disorganized panic that served only to hinder their getaways.

Many of the high-society hostages were among the last to board; they'd gotten too comfortable with their own incarceration, continuing to roll their dice while the people from the underdeck were already rowing away to safety.

Onal was waiting for me in one of the boats, the ship's physician and Werner Humboldt ready to launch it from the side as the ship groaned and lurched again. "There!" she cried, pointing. "She's coming! We can't leave yet!"

But the doctor wasn't listening. He was sweating as he tried to untie the rope while the other man screeched behind him, "No time! No time!"

I was no longer half running now; I was simply skidding. Objects loosened from above were pummeling me as I went down. The furnace chimneys were still belching black clouds into the night, and I coughed and rubbed my bleary eyes, hardly able to see.

The doctor finished cutting the boat away, and it hit the water with a jolt just as the ship tilted further and I tumbled down the decks. I was able to snag a thick rope on my way past and held on as it snapped tight. I swung around and crashed into the side of the hull and dangled there as the ship now protruded from the fjord at an exact perpendicular.

And then I let go.

I straightened my body into a spear, slicing through the water even as the cold choked out every other thought and feeling. When I broke the surface, I could hear Onal shouting for me, and I swam toward the sound of her voice. Above, an explosion sent tiny pieces of wood and debris raining down on us like missiles.

When I got to the boat, Werner Humbolt and Onal hoisted me into it and I huddled in the bottom, shaking violently. The doctor lay collapsed across the boat's bow, staring sightlessly at the sky, a piece of metal embedded in his skull.

Humboldt pushed the man's body overboard, grabbed the oars, and tossed one at us. "Paddle!" he yelled angrily. "Paddle!"

But I couldn't; I could hardly move.

He turned, the whites of his eyes showing bright in the dark. "Listen, you worthless sluts. If we don't get out of here right now . . ." He reeled his hand back as if to strike us, but one of the ship's chimney stacks broke and slammed into the water. The force of it sent us careening wildly, water crashing over our heads. Onal and I hunkered as low as we could, clinging to each other, but Humboldt was swept from his feet and away into the dark depths.

We had barely enough time to wipe the water from our eyes before we heard the creak of the second funnel as it, too, began to break away.

If it fell now, we'd be crushed beneath it.

I fumbled for my knife, my fingers numb and clumsy, but when I touched it to my skin, no blood rose to answer it. My hands were too cold, my blood too sluggish in my constricting veins.

With no blood, there could be no spell. With no spell—

"I'm sorry," I murmured to Onal. "I can't. I can't help us. I'm so sorry . . ."

"Stop blubbering," she said, shaking me. "Use my blood. Get us out of here. Do it now."

"But . . ." I tried to argue, even as my eyes came to rest on her bandages; they were soaked through. "You said blood magic—"

"*Now,*" she barked again.

The magic in her blood was calling for me to use it. Warm. Welcoming.

I threw my arms around Onal and answered its call. *"Ut salutem!"*

We collided with the edge of the rocky shore just as the second chimney stack went down, shattering the boat we left behind into a thousand pieces.

On the other side of the fjord, I thought I saw a shadow form: a cloaked rider on a tall horse. But I was too dizzy, too cold, too stunned to make sense of it.

As the black water of the fjord claimed the *Humility,* unconsciousness claimed me.

I dreamed about my mother.

She was sitting at her desk, her glossy chestnut hair spilling over her shoulders in spiraling curls. Her black mourning dress belled out in the front to make room for her swelling belly; Conrad would be born soon. She had one hand on her belly as she wrote, a stack of letters piled up beside her. They were all addressed to Brother Cesare.

She was so sad, and so happy, both at once.

"Mother?" I asked, approaching slowly. But of course she couldn't see me; I was the ghost here, not her.

She looked up and smiled brightly, but I realized she was not looking at me; she was looking behind me.

"Aurelia?" she said, rising to rush past me. "What happened?"

I turned to see a younger version of myself, all knobby knees and skinned elbows, dirt smudging my cheeks. There were tears shining in my eyes, but I was too stubborn to let them escape. Instead, young me said matter-of-factly, "I know I'm not supposed to fight, Mother. I know. But I heard them talking. They were going to push me into the pond and hold my head under the water."

"Who was saying that?" Her eyes were full of a fire I did not remember.

I stuck out my chin obstinately, unwilling to give up the names of my harassers. If we had punished everyone who teased or taunted me, there'd have been no one left to work at the castle.

She knelt in front of me. "You listen to me, Aurelia. I know I tell you to lie low. To be quiet, to not draw attention to yourself. Most of the time, that will work. But if it doesn't—Look at me! If it doesn't, you fight. Do you hear me? Save yourself. Promise me. *Fight*."

"I will, Mama. I promise." I spoke with two voices, both past and present.

Seconds later, that same girl was standing outside a hedge more than three times her height. Mother was no longer wearing mourning clothes, and a chubby, blond-haired baby was bouncing in her arms as she spoke with Fredrick Greythorne and Father Cesare.

"Kellan is young, but he's capable," Fredrick was saying. "I've never seen a boy with so much dedication."

"Is that him?" Mother asked, putting her hand up to shield her eyes as she gazed toward Greythorne's stables, where a young Kellan was leading a silver-white Empyrean foal across the garden.

"Yes," Fredrick said. "I promise you, if you put him to the task of protecting her, he'd rather die than fail."

In the next second, my young self was huddled in a dead-end corner of the maze, crying into her knees in the dark. Young Kellan leaned out from the other end of the corridor. "She's here!" he called over his shoulder before approaching me with the same conscientious calm he'd used in training his Empyrean foal.

"Princess?" he said, holding out his right hand. "Aurelia? Don't worry. I won't let you get lost again. I'll see you to the end."

My mother and his brother were waiting for us on the steps of the Stella. She hugged me tightly before turning to Kellan. "You did well, young Greythorne," she said to him. "You are going to be a great soldier, I can tell. Your queen thanks you."

Kellan beamed, first at Mother and then at me. But I was looking up at the statue in the fountain.

Father Cesare—who looked much the same despite being several years younger—came to stand beside me.

"What do you think of our patron saint, Your Highness? His name is Urso. It means 'bear.'"

"He looks like him," I said, pointing to Kellan.

"Urso had no family of his own," Cesare said, laughing, "but he loved the Greythornes, even convincing the king of that time to grant them the manor and the land around the Stella for cultivation."

The memory faded, but the statue and the sanctorium remained. I looked up at Urso with new eyes and finally understood.

Urso and *Mathuin* were both names for "bear."

Galantha's blood spell commanding him home had sent Mathuin back to the place of his origin; just a hundred years too early.

The church, the maze, the statues, the legacy of protecting witches . . .

Urso was Mathuin. Mathuin was Urso.

Which meant the Ilithiya's Bell was at Greythorne. It had to be.

I could save Kellan.

I surged into wakefulness with a gasp, then rolled over, coughing, hurting everywhere, bits of gravelly sand and debris shaking from my hair.

Onal.

I scrambled to the rocks against which she was sagging; she had pulled herself up to a sitting position to look out across the water as the first fuchsia streaks of morning began to stretch across the sky. She normally kept her iron-gray hair pulled into a tight bun, but it had come loose in the water and now cascaded down either side of her shoulders, just as long and thick as it had been when she was a child.

She turned her head toward me and said weakly, "My bag. There. Would you get it for me?"

I did as she asked, saying, "What do you need?"

"There's a little red bottle with a dropper. Yes. That's the one. I stole it from that fool of a physician. It's a marvelous pain reliever . . ."

"Onal," I said, sighing in exasperation. "This is belladonna." I gave it a sniff. "Highly concentrated, too. A mere drop or two of this will kill you."

She smiled widely. "Good girl."

I dropped the bag carefully and knelt next to her. She could barely lift the hand she used to pat mine.

"I did this," I said. "You were getting better. And you told me what using blood magic would do to you. I shouldn't have . . ." I trailed off, unable to finish.

"If you hadn't used my blood, we'd have been crushed," she said. "And we never would have gotten to see this." She nodded to where the first beams of sun were breaking into sparks of golden light and skipping across the water. "A much better way to go, if you ask me."

Tears were streaming down my face. I shook my head. "Onal, no. No."

Her hand went to the single silver button at the top of her collar. With a sharp tug, she yanked it off and laid it in my hand. I turned it over: it was in the shape of a flower. A lily.

"I had them made when I knew I was expecting. I gave two of

them to Iresine. Four, I sewed to my daughter's first gown. And this one . . . this one I kept for myself." She said, "That's what I was going to name her. Lily."

I nodded. "I'll make sure Conrad gets it. He can pass it down to his daughters, and they to theirs."

"It's not for Conrad. It's for you."

"But, Onal," I tried to argue, "I'm not going to . . . I don't have . . ."

"Stop moping. It makes you look like a sullen marmot. Listen to me." She pulled me by the collar. "You are my granddaughter. You are *not* going to give up. You are no delicate flower that wilts at the brush of wind. You are made of nettle, my girl. You're stubborn. And spiteful. And just stupid enough to keep fighting when smarter folk think there's no reason to try. *No one* is going to pull you up without getting stung. Do you hear me? Not Castillion, not Arceneaux. Not even the Empyrea herself."

She let go of me, then settled back against the rock. "I don't regret this," she said, her voice drifting. "I got to choose my end. Now go and choose yours."

I found an empty but mostly intact lifeboat farther up the shore and dragged it back, stopping every now and then to pick things to send her off with. Flowers were in short supply this time of year, but Onal wouldn't have appreciated them anyway. No, the bouquet I gathered was far less beautiful and infinitely more practical: valerian and yellow dock, dandelion and horehound.

Her body was lighter than I expected; it was hard to imagine how so large a personality had lasted so long in so thin a frame. I laid her carefully into the boat and set the herb bouquet under her pale hands. "Goodbye, you cantankerous old fiend," I said, touching her hair one last time before pushing the craft from the shore.

As it drifted away, I wondered what shape her quicksilver tether had taken to guide her to the beyond.

A badger, most likely. Or a wolverine. Something with teeth.

I nicked my hand again—too long, too deep—and the blood came swiftly this time. It dripped into the water at my feet, and I willed it out toward the boat. *"Uro,"* I said, and the blood became a trail of fire to the boat, where it hit the wood and caught, sending up flames the same bright, bold orange as their backdrop of morning sky.

I stanched the blood with my other hand and sat down in the rocks, water lapping at my feet. My blood began to slow just as the fire burned out and the last of Onal's boat sank below the surface. She was gone.

That was when the grief caught up with me.

Pressing my knuckles against my teeth to stifle the wail that was building up in my lungs, I rocked back and forth in the rushes, sobbing in great, heaving gulps.

For so long, I had convinced myself I wanted to be alone so that I couldn't hurt anyone, but now that I was alone—well and truly—I had no choice but to admit that Zan was right.

It wasn't for them. It was never for them.

It was always for me.

To protect myself from *this*.

Onal's words echoed in my head. *You are made of nettle, my girl. And just stupid enough to keep fighting when smarter folk think there's no reason to try.*

I dried my eyes, took a breath, and forced myself to my feet.

27

It took me four days to get back to the Quiet Canary, and the first two were spent following the fjord back to its apex, the ruined city and its needle-like tower. There was not much of value to be re-collected there; but I did find Madrona cheerfully munching forest grass not far from where I had left her upon first entering the city.

She was *far* less enthused to see me than I was to see her.

From there, we followed the River Sentis to its fork, then took the path that became the River Urso. I would have kept going all the way to Greythorne were it not for an image in my scrying bowl that sent me riding at full gallop southwest instead of southeast.

Conrad, sitting at a table lit by a single candle, a fan of cards in his hands. Across the table, his opponent's mouth was screwed to one side, the surest sign of her imminent defeat. Jessamine was never good at keeping her expressions under control.

The images of Kellan, Rosetta, and Zan were less promising. All I could discern was that they were being kept somewhere lightless and cramped, and that they were sick, hungry, and miraculously still alive.

I hoped that they would stay that way for a little while longer.

The red moonrise was coming, and now so was I.

As I approached the blessedly familiar tavern, it became quite clear, quite quickly, that something was different. Something was wrong. The windows were dark; the stables were empty. The Quiet Canary was finally living up to its name.

I knocked softly at the back door before opening it. "Hello?" I called into the dimness. "Hicks? Are you here?"

I heard a creak on the stair and had to duck when a fireplace poker came swinging at my head.

"Jessamine?" I gasped, jumping out of the way.

"Aurelia?" She dropped the poker and hugged me. "Thank the stars."

"What's going on?" I asked. "Where is everybody?"

As I said it, Jessamine put her finger to her lips to quiet me, then lifted her candle, motioning me to follow her into the gambling hall. All the tables and chairs had been moved to the walls, and the rest of the room was full of sleeping children by the dozens. I knew some of them: children from Greythorne. Some refugees, some the daughters and sons of the village folk. All of them younger than twelve.

Jessamine led me out again, pulling her shawl tighter around her shoulders. "The Tribunal took over Greythorne first, then started to spread out, raiding every house and farm in the vicinity, claiming they had the jurisdiction because they were looking for the missing king. They arrested almost everyone. It didn't feel like they were worried about the king—it felt like they were collecting prisoners. When they came here, Hicks had us girls hide in the secret cellar room, like you did. When we finally came out, everyone was gone."

"But the children. How did you . . . ?"

"They showed up on our doorstep not a day later, led by a little blond imp who reminded me a lot of you." Jessa's mouth quirked into a smile. "We've been taking care of them ever since."

"Where's my brother?" I asked. "Is he all right?"

"Yes," Jessamine said. "Better than all right. He's the reason any of these children made it here. It's thirty miles between Greythorne and the Canary, and he led them the whole way on his own. I still can't believe he did it."

"I can," I said. "Tenacity is a trait he inherited from our grandmother."

Delphinia came down the stairs. "Jessa? What's the—?" Seeing me, she gave a great sigh of relief. "Rafaella! Lorelai! It's Aurelia."

They all ganged up to hug me, and I let them. I basked in their affection. These wonderful, beautiful women had been there for me in some of my darkest hours, and now they'd done the same for Conrad. I didn't deserve their friendship, but what person with a truly wonderful friend ever could?

"I'd like to see him," I said finally. "My brother."

"He's sleeping in your room," Lorelai said, dimpling. "He likes that horrid little closet nearly as much as you do."

"Be warned, though," Delphinia added, "he discovered Hicks's collection of puzzles and knickknacks."

Rafaella said, "They're *everywhere.*"

Conrad was tucked into my old comforter, his curling locks splayed out on my pillow, his chest moving in and out in a soft, rhythmic motion. Someone—probably one of the girls—had cleaned up the glass from my smashed mirror, but that was the only way in which the room had improved since the last time I'd seen it. It was now covered on every surface with wooden toys and other whittled contraptions. I had to step carefully to get to the bed.

I touched my hand to my brother's hair. "Conrad," I said softly as he stirred and turned to look at me.

"Aurelia?" he asked sleepily, rubbing his eyes.

"Hello, little brother," I said.

"You're here." He yawned. "I told them you were coming, and now you're here. Are you going to Greythorne?"

"I am," I said.

"Are you ready?" he asked.

"No," I replied.

"You'll be fine," he said reassuringly. "You're brave."

"So are you."

He nodded. "I know."

I kissed his forehead and curled up next to him on the narrow bed as his eyes began to flutter closed once again, only to get a sharp poke in the ribs. I had to stifle a grin when I realized that, tucked under his blanket and hugged tightly to his body, was the funny little nine-sided box.

I wondered what sweet childhood treasure he might have hidden in there, but the thought lingered only for a moment before I, too, drifted off to sleep.

I got up before anyone else in the Canary did, slipping into an old pair of trousers and worn-in boots, braiding my hair into one long plait over my shoulder. I was just about to tiptoe from my room when I saw a folded piece of paper on my dresser. Tentatively, I unfolded it to reveal a charcoal sketch.

Zan had been drawing something the night I went in to him, drunk with sombersweet wine and emotion. Everything had happened so fast after that, all thoughts of his sketch were erased from my mind until now. That it was here waiting for me meant that he must have come looking for me after I tore from the room, only to find me gone.

My chest tightened, imagining it.

The picture was of the horseman, but not the fearsome version Zan had plastered across alleyway walls in Achleva. There was no billowing cloak, no mighty pose. His horse was not rearing back, hooves scraping the air in front of him. This horseman, his face still obscured by his hood, sagged under the weight of his cloak. His horse was weary. They were both battle-worn. Broken.

And yet they were still moving forward.

At the bottom of the page, Zan had written once more, *Si vivis, tu pugnas*. And I understood: this message was not a call to arms for the bold or the strong, or those burning with zeal to fight. It never was. It was meant to reach the hearts of those who are so tired, they can barely take another step, but they take that step anyway.

Like me.

I laid the drawing in the top drawer, alongside the rolled-up blueprints of the fallen *Humility* and the money I once thought would buy me passage aboard it. Then I took out Zan's ring, slipping it onto my finger, and the hand mirror. It was one of the less exciting prizes from my days of playing Betwixt and Between—small and brass-handled, cheaply made and tarnished on both metal and mirror—but it was exactly what I needed right now.

With the mirror in one hand and a lamp in the other, I tiptoed down one flight of stairs, then another, ending in the cellar. I was pleased to find that Jessamine hadn't sold all of my sombersweet wine; there were still a few bottles left on the table in the innermost alcove. I set my lamp down on the table and the mirror beside it while I grabbed one and popped the cork. The dank room was immediately filled with the smell of sombersweet, and for a minute, I could almost imagine myself back in the field at the Cradle.

The first swig had little effect. With the second, I began to feel a tingle in my fingers. I swallowed a third to make sure it was truly working, and I was about to lift the mirror when I asked myself, *What if my theory is correct? What if this really works?*

And then I downed a fourth drink.

It took a minute after I lifted the mirror for the reflection to change. When it did, it was a slow transition that started with my eyes. One minute they were mine, and the next, they were not. This time, she didn't even bother to match my braided hair or my linen shirt. She was wearing my coronation dress: red-violet, shot with silver threads.

One or the other, she whispered.

I spoke to her aloud. "Who are you, really? I know you're not me."

Daughter of the sister, or the son of the brother.

"Are you the Malefica?"

She made a strange hissing sound in response before continuing, *The firebird boy or the girl with star-eyes.*

"You're not the Ilithiya," I said, "because she died creating the world."

If it is he, the crone will be free. If it is her, the crone is no more.

I brought myself to the final question. "Are you the Empyrea?"

Her stare hardened. Instead of finishing her rhyme, she rasped, *Let the bell ring for you, Aurelia. Take up the mantle. The Ninth Age is yours.*

The mirror began to shake violently, the handle growing hot in my hand. Then the glass broke, and the only reflection left in the shards was mine.

28

A re you sure about this?" Jessamine asked, the cold morning wind catching her auburn hair. She had walked with me to the crossroads outside the Quiet Canary and was now shivering in her thin shawl; the Day of Shades had begun beneath an iron-gray sky. "You don't have to do this alone."

I hooked my foot into Madrona's stirrup and swung my other leg up over her saddle. "I do," I said, smiling softly. "But I wish I didn't."

"Be careful," she said. "The stories the children have been telling about Greythorne are . . . monstrous. If they're even a little bit true . . ."

"They're all true," I replied. "That's why I have to go." My eyes moved to the plaster-and-timber building still slumbering behind her. "Take care of my brother?" I asked.

"Until you return," Jessa replied.

"Don't let him bully you into giving him candy."

"I am a loyal citizen," she said with a wry shrug. "I'll do as my king commands." Then her smile faded. "When will you be back?"

I looked at the road stretching out ahead of me. "I don't know."

"*Will* you be back?"

I paused, and then said again, "I don't know."

Solemnly, she replied, "Empyrea keep you, my friend."

"And you."

✳

The wind was at my back the entire way to Greythorne, pushing me forward even as trepidation crept like a spider across my skin. The crops of flax had grown tall and coarse, and they waved somberly in the cold gusts, field after unharvested field.

The village depended upon the flax harvest to fuel its textile production, which kept the villagers fed through the winter. They'd never let it dry up and shrivel on the stalk.

But as troubling as the flax fields were, the sheep pastures that came after were much, much worse.

It was the smell that hit me first, rank and rotten. Covering my nose and mouth with my cloak did little to block it out. The more ground I covered toward the village, the stronger the stench got.

Then I saw the crows.

They were gathered by the thousands, pecking at the disintegrating corpses of Greythorne's flocks. The sound of my approach disturbed them, and they took to the air in a swirling mass of black feathers and clacking beaks, wildly winging across the sky.

When the curtain of crows finally parted, I got my first glimpse of Greythorne, eerily still in the far distance, save for a few sickly strings of rising smoke. The Day of Shades had arrived with no banquets or bonfires, no barrels of apples, no kegs of ale.

Madrona stopped two miles out from the village, balking along a border I could not see and that she would not cross. I had no choice but to climb down and go the rest of the way alone.

"Thank you, girl," I said, letting her nuzzle my cheek with her nose. "Now, off with you." I slapped her rump, and she bound off the way we had come, mane flying.

I walked the rest of the way alone.

I approached from the northwest, seeking the protection of the hawthorn thickets, though it made my progress slow. It was hard to know if the extra caution was warranted; no one seemed to be guarding the territory, Tribunal or otherwise. Had I an army at my back and a sword in my hand, I would have stormed the place with a war cry and won it with barely a fight. But I had no great weapons or strong warriors; I was unarmed and alone, a single girl running head-long toward her own downfall. And that was the *favorable* outcome.

I reached the edge of the refugee camp at dusk.

The smoke I'd seen in the distance wasn't from cooking or camp-fires. It was from the smoldering remains of collapsed tents and scattered clothing. Renalt's fleur-de-lis flag had been raised above the scene, the Tribunal's starred black banner flying below.

It wasn't enough to apprehend the immigrants—this was the work of those who wanted to see the Achlevan settlement and all it stood for destroyed. Decimated. And then were so proud of the havoc they'd wrought that they erected a flag in the ashes to claim it.

With an angry cry, I kicked the pole until it fell, landing at a steep angle against an overturned cart—my cart. The one I'd won from Brom and brought to the camp. Its load of once-red apples was spilled and spoiling on the ground.

Whatever reservations I had about making myself known were cast aside as I climbed up the wagon wheel to tear down the Tribunal's flag. I clutched it tightly, dragging it in the dirt to the center of the village, where the charred remnants of Achlevan spindles still sat in a blackened pile.

I didn't announce myself; I simply tossed the flag onto the ground, drew a bead of blood, and as it dripped onto the banner—landing at the center of a star—murmured, *"Uro."*

As the flag burned, I waited.

The villagers began to appear quickly and quietly, stepping from darkened houses and from behind stone buildings, their faces obscured by the grimacing, oversize animal faces of their Day of Shades masks. My breath caught, remembering my childhood terror at seeing the population of the village in these costumes for the first time. They'd been laughing, leering, dancing frenetic little jigs; a comical cavalcade compared to the absolute stillness of those assembled now. Within minutes, I was enclosed in a circle of monstrous caricatures: long-tusked boars' heads, open-mawed jackals, rabbits with glaring red eyes, and horses whose muzzles were warped into twisted grimaces.

"Grotesque, is it not?" I turned to see Arceneaux's long-limbed acolyte Lyall striding toward me from the direction of the old mill. He looked from mask to mask, his face a strange mixture of disgust and admiration. "A tradition so old, I doubt anyone in this region could recall its origin."

"The Day of Shades marks the time when the line between this plane and the spectral one is at its thinnest." My eyes dragged across the procession from ox to bear to crow. "These are representations of the quicksilver guides who take us across the Gray."

"Very good," Lyall said. "A proud tradition. I was very careful to note each soul's specific conjuration when I cut their tethers. Figuring out the particulars of this phenomenon will make a very intriguing future course of study after our current explorations come to a close. And I know it's an unnecessary flourish, dressing them up this way, but I did like the symmetry of it, replacing one kind of harvest celebration for another. And it has been a *marvelous* year for the collecting of souls."

I knew it then: These people were dead. Every last one of them.

They were standing right there in front of me, and they were *dead*.

I could see the signs now: mottled, purpling skin showing under collars and beneath cuffs, shoulders hanging at an unnatural angle . . . and on a few, burns in the shape of an unholy seal, a corruption of blood and feral magics both at once.

My stomach contracted, but I swallowed back the rising bile and asked, "Who are they now? Whose souls did you use for this" — my lip twitched — "experiment?"

"These" — Lyall gestured around — "are the Empyrea's Celestines. The best and bravest of the Tribunal's ranks, saved to be reborn on this day, to attend their queen as she begins her human reign."

"Their queen? You mean Arceneaux?"

"Arceneaux has earned the great honor of becoming the Empyrea's human vessel. And these Celestines . . . they will be her servants." From each pocket, he pulled several clear stones, and he held them between each of his fingers. Luneocite. *Soul stones,* Simon had once called them. "Some of them have waited a very long time for this moment. Their reward for lives spent doing Her work with honor."

He turned to lift the plaster stag's head from the body standing closest to him. Beneath it, old Mrs. Lister's decaying visage appeared, her shriveled lips pulled away from black-rimmed teeth in a perpetual snarl. Lyall frowned and settled the mask back over her head. "Some of the bodies we had to use are a *little* worse for wear. We're working on it."

I palmed my knife in my right hand, moving carefully in hopes that Lyall wouldn't notice, but his gaze snapped to me. "I wouldn't do that," Lyall said. "They'll smell it."

"And then what happens?" I asked. "Are these not the Tribunal's best and bravest? Do they not obey your command?"

"There are still . . . flaws . . . in the process," he said. "There's a certain amount of . . . degradation . . . that occurs to a spirit when it is not free or housed within the body to which it was born. Most of these spirits have been locked away in these stones for decades—even centuries. It may take a few more cycles of experimentation to bring them back to their full awareness." His eyes flashed. "But trust me when I tell you, right now you do *not* want them to smell blood."

"That puts me in a very difficult position," I said, pursing my lips, "as, at the moment, blood is the best weapon I have." I raised my small knife, no longer attempting to conceal it. "You're something of a scientist, aren't you, Lyall? Conducting your little experiments, never able to satiate your curiosity." At my feet, the Tribunal flag still smoldered. I edged closer to it. "But now you've piqued my interest in your studies too. You say they can smell blood? I'd like to see it for myself." I wrapped my hand around the blade and gave it a yank, wincing as the skin parted and the blood and magic began to freely flow between my fingers.

The effect was enormous and immediate. The villagers began to snap and slaver in their animal masks, some running toward me, others skittering across the ground on all fours. Their masks cracked as they crashed into one another in their struggle to reach me, chunks of plaster teeth and painted fur raining down into my hair and eyes as I ducked and rolled beneath the frenzied onslaught. As the masks began to break and fall away, I recognized their occupants. One was named Rowena, the wife of a sheep herder. Another was Niall, a man I knew from the Quiet Canary, a boisterous drunk who used to sing songs on the tables. I cringed when I sliced her neck, nearly retched when I drove my knife into his eye. *They're not them,* I told myself. *They're not them.*

"Burn!" I said, calling the fire up from the Tribunal flag and sending it in a column toward the stag that was Mrs. Lister and the rabbit that was revealed to be Elisa Greythorne, Fredrick's wife. I stifled a sob as she was engulfed in the flames, barely able to catch my breath before fending off a snarling scullery maid from Greythorne's kitchen with a strike of my knife's pommel to her temple. "Shatter," I demanded as an empty-eyed bear tried to claw my arm. All the bones in his body became shard-like splinters, and he gave a last yelp as he slopped to the ground, the bear's head rolling from the malformed face of Father Brandt. Then Father Harkness began to lumber over to me, his face half obscured in the disintegrating mask of a horse. I put my bleeding hands on his chest as he tried to dig at my eyes. "Rend,"

I said, and his chest opened down the center, his insides spooling out onto the ground.

"Find peace," I said, sobbing, to both of them. "I'm sorry. Find peace."

Gilbert Mercer was wearing the face of a ram; I turned his blood to acid and tried not to think of the sombersweet wine we'd shared even as his eyes boiled away in their sockets.

The jackal came at me next; I didn't have to see under the mask to know the name of the man to whom those knobby, callused hands belonged.

"Hicks!" I cried as I felt the flames leave my fingertips. "Forgive me. Forgive me."

Lyall was watching implacably, as if he were making mental notes. This was all an experiment to him. All of it.

With a cry of rage, I dove for him. My fury made me strong. I caught him around the waist, pulled him down into the dirt, and rolled with him through the rushes beside the mill and into the shallows at the side of the river.

Lyall pushed me off and rose, dripping wet, looking at me with new calculations going on behind his eyes. "Interesting," he said. "I'll have to gauge a subject's response to nonfamilial bonds when deciding which bodies will make the most suitable hosts for which spirits."

"You're dead," I ground out through my teeth. I stood up in the shallow water, facing him and the river.

"Look behind you," he said smugly.

I could hear the groans, the dragging footsteps on the shore, but I wasn't afraid.

"Look behind *you*," I replied, then raised my hand to command the mill's precariously hanging water wheel. *"Autem!"*

The wheel lifted with a screech of its old, breaking irons.

"Descendit!" I said, slamming my hand down. The blood from my newest cut sang free in response. Lyall screamed as the wheel plunged down and came to rest on his back. Blood ran from his nose and mouth into an eddying pool around him as he tried to keep his head up out of the river.

"No," he said, scared for the first time as the blood-hungry monsters of his own making stumbled toward the riverside after the nearer prey. "No!"

"I'll give your regards to Arceneaux," I said, "on her special day."

You can't kill what's already dead, Rosetta had said. *You have to exorcise it.*

Breathing hard, I gathered my strength and my magic, and cried, *"Et abierunt!"*

Be gone.

One by one, the dead began to collapse, the black clouds of their infesting souls dispersing into the air just as the last gasp of daylight disappeared behind the horizon.

29

When at last I made it to the manor's basement holding cells, my arms were covered with new scrapes and gashes, but there were five empty canine corpses left in my wake.

Rosetta blinked up at me with bleary eyes, both hands locked in iron mitts that looked like clubs.

"What took you so long?" she asked icily as I tried to force my knife into the locking mechanism on her binds, but my hands were clumsy in the dark. "And where's Onal?"

My movements stopped. "Gone."

Rosetta's expression tightened, but she nodded.

I asked her, "Where's Zan?"

She said, "Taken."

"Arceneaux came for him a few hours ago," Kellan said. "We haven't seen him since."

I tried to keep my face impassive as I kept working the lock, even as my heart twisted.

"Could you hurry it up?" Rosetta asked.

"I'm trying," I said before finally giving up. If picking the lock wouldn't work, there were other ways.

"Don't—!" Rosetta tried to stop me, but I'd already made the nick on my finger.

"*Occillo,*" I said, letting the blood drip onto the metal. *Break.*

The mitts fell off just in time for Rosetta to roll over and retch in the corner of the cell. When she turned back again, she was glaring at me, muttering, "Starsforsaken blood magic."

I let a second drop of blood fall onto Kellan's manacled left hand. "*Occillo,*" I said again, and the iron broke with a clink and fell to the floor.

"They were holding my brother with everyone they rounded up from the village," Kellan said.

"I went through the village," I replied. "I didn't see Fredrick. But Elisa . . ." I shook my head. "She didn't make it."

"They must have moved him," Kellan said. "We have to find him."

"There's no time," I said. "The manor is crawling with clerics, and the eclipse is going to happen anytime now . . ."

"Would you leave Conrad in the hands of the Tribunal?" Kellan asked. "Fredrick's my *brother.*"

I relented. "All right. We find Fredrick, and then we move toward the Stella. Arceneaux thinks she's going to become the human vessel for the Empyrea—that's where she's going to be. That's where she'll have Zan." I glanced at Rosetta, who was stretching her fingers. "We're probably going to need your magic. Are you ready?"

"I just spent ten days in irons and had a blood spell used on me. So, no. I'm not. But what choice do we have?"

Kellan knew the manor best, so we let him lead the way. On the first floor above the holding cells, we encountered two clerics. Kellan broke the neck of the first while I slit the throat of the second. He dragged both bodies out of the hall but didn't leave them behind until he'd borrowed one of their swords.

"Feel better?" Rosetta asked as he tossed it back and forth between his hands.

"Yes. Much."

We moved on stealthy feet, dispatching anyone wearing a black coat who had the misfortune of getting in our way.

We found Fredrick under guard in the manor's grand hall, surrounded by brass candelabras, each holding five lit candlesticks. He was sitting slumped in the chair meant to act as the interim throne during the king's residency at the manor. He looked ill, with purple bruises under his eyes, his cheeks gaunt and sallow.

"Kellan, no—" I tried to grab his arm, to keep him back, but he was already bounding into the fray. Within seconds, he'd brought down the two clerics closest to him, while the others ran to engage.

Rosetta and I exchanged pained looks. Then she shifted into her fox form while I readied my knife, and we both went in after him.

The battle was over quickly, and Fredrick had risen from his chair, his arms outstretched in welcome. "Brother!" he boomed. "Thank the stars you're all right!"

Kellan was stepping over bodies to get to him, eyes alight.

"Wait," I said. Something was wrong. "Wait!"

And then I saw it carved into the skin of Fredrick's forearm: the possession seal.

"It's not him!" I screamed. "It's not Fredrick!"

But it was too late. Fredrick had knocked Kellan's sword away and had his right hand locked in an iron grip. Kellan gave a guttural cry as the bones in his hands began to snap. Fredrick clamped his other hand around Kellan's throat and lifted him into the air, laughing. Kellan kicked and struggled, knocking one candelabra into the next, which fell into a tapestry behind the chair.

Not-Fredrick looked at me. "What are you going to do, Princess? You've already killed me once. Broke every single rule in the book to use my blood for your spell, and it didn't even work. Maybe the second time will take."

"Golightly," I spat as Kellan continued to writhe in his grip. "You look . . . different. Put him down, and we'll let you go on your way. No one will stop you or follow you."

"And leave my new home?" he asked. "I just got it. This"—he looked meaningfully around the hall, apparently not noticing the flames that had begun to eat away at the tapestry—"is all mine now. And I—"

Rosetta had crept up behind him and knocked him off his feet as she shifted back into her human form and tackled him to the ground. He lost his grip on Kellan, who dropped to his knees, gasping for air, while Rosetta smashed Fredrick's head into the floor and then drew her exorcism spell onto his back. Just as with the wolves in the woods,

Fredrick's body belched black smoke, twitched a few final times, and then lay still.

Kellan groaned and attempted to gather his brother's body into his arms, sobbing from the pain of his crippled right hand as he did. I tried to comfort him, but he shook me off. "He was my only family. He raised me. He took care of me. And then he tried to . . ." He squeezed his eyes shut, rocking back and forth.

"Kellan," I said gently, "Fredrick would never have hurt you. That wasn't him. This . . . shell . . . hasn't been him for a while."

Rosetta stood silently over him, obviously wanting to comfort him but lacking the instinct to know how.

Smoke was beginning to fill the room. "We have to go. Kellan, we can't—"

He took a deep breath and said, "I'm coming." Even here, in his darkest hour, Kellan clung to his cause. His duty. It was what gave him the strength to let go of Fredrick's body and remove the Greythorne family sword from the dead man's scabbard with his left hand, now that he could not use his right. He looked at me with the steely eyes of a soldier. "I told you I would see you to the end," he said. "And I will."

Kellan would guard me until his dying day. It was who he was. That devotion—that conviction—allowed him to leave his brother's body in that burning room and not look back.

finally figured it out," I said quietly as Kellan guided us through the maze. "The bell is here. At Greythorne."

Behind us, flames were beginning to appear in Greythorne's windows. Above us, the black shadow on the moon had advanced. Ahead of us, Arceneaux was waiting with Zan.

"Aurelia . . ." Rosetta began.

I continued, "I believe it's buried with Urso under the Stella, in the crypt. We'll find it, and then we'll ring it, and the bond will break, and Kellan won't have to—"

"Aurelia . . . listen . . ." Rosetta said again.

"Mathuin didn't *take* the bell," I said. "At least, he didn't mean to. Galantha pushed him through the Gray, and he ended up—"

"Aurelia!" Rosetta snapped.

"—here."

We had come to the Stella's plaza and were standing beneath Urso's statue.

Kellan and I both looked at Rosetta.

"I lied to you," she said.

"What?"

"I lied to you when I told you the bell could break your blood bond. It can't . . . The bell allows its bearer to walk the Gray without leaving her body behind. That is *all* it does."

She looked at Kellan, her yellow eyes shining with something that looked less like regret and more like . . . anguish. "It won't save you. It *can't* save you." Her chin trembled.

I gaped at her. "*Why,* then? What did I walk the Gray for all those times—what purpose did *any* of that serve?"

"I wanted the bell so I could destroy it," she said. "And in destroying it, let this *thing* in which my spirit is trapped finally, *finally* die. I'm a Warden of the Woods, descended directly from the Ilithiya's flesh and blood. I'm supposed to guard the natural order, to maintain the balance between the planes—and I'm not fully human myself."

"I know what you are," I said. "I know what Galantha did to save you. Would you take her sacrifice so lightly? Is the prospect of eternal life so terrible?"

"Eternal life?" she shrilled. "I'm not *living.* I'm a spirit bound to a quicksilver body. I don't eat. I don't sleep. I don't bleed. I can't have children. There will be no daughters to whom I can pass on my mantle." She advanced on me, tremulous. "I don't even have a reflection. I will outlast every living thing on this earth. You ask me what's so terrible about eternal life? Well, I ask you: What could be worse than living forever, alone in a dead world?"

I closed my eyes. "You put us on the wrong path, Rosetta. You gave us hope we didn't have. How could you do that?"

She wasn't looking at me. She was looking at Kellan. "I'm so sorry. I didn't expect to . . . to . . ." She didn't finish. She couldn't admit out loud that, sometime between their acquaintance and the end of their incarceration, she had come to love him.

Overhead, the clouds had thinned to wisps, gilt into silver threads by the bright white moon. The earth's shadow had already begun to carve away at the disc, turning it into the curved blade of a scythe.

Kellan said nothing to Rosetta, instead laying his brother's sword beside the fountain so that he could put his good hand on my cheek. "It doesn't matter," he said softly. "I knew this was a possibility, and I accepted it." Then he reminded me of the bloodcloth ritual: "Bound by blood, by blood undone."

I stepped back.

By *blood* undone.

Not by *death* undone.

The bond can be broken only by death, Simon said, *or something like unto it.*

The light was waning; only a sliver of moon remained. In seconds, the world would become red.

This was it. This was the Bleeding Dream.

I'd lived this moment a hundred times in the last months. I'd done everything I could to keep it from coming to pass, pushing Kellan away, separating myself from him and anyone else I could hurt, but with no luck. And now I'd walked right into it.

His hands. His beautiful musician's hands. Even as mutilated as his right hand was, there was still the possibility that it could heal. That it could hold his sword again. That it could give him the reputation he so desired: the brave knight, loyal to the kingdom and crown until the bitterest end.

It was that possibility I had to take away.

In one fluid motion, I kicked Kellan's knees out from under him and grabbed for Fredrick's sword.

Kellan put his hands down on the edge of Urso's fountain to steady himself, crying out as he hit his right hand too hard upon it. "What are you doing? Aurelia, wait—"

"I'm sorry." I sobbed, raising his brother's sword above my head. Then, "Bound by blood, by blood undone."

As I said it, the last bit of shadow covered the moon.

I brought the sword down on his right hand. It cleaved through his flesh and bone to the marble of the fountain underneath.

And the world turned red.

31

He screamed. When he looked at me, holding the bloody stump of his right arm, his eyes were full of rage and regret and a new emotion I never thought I'd see: hatred.

Kellan was a soldier. Born to protect. Bred to fight. The noble and loyal gryphon, and he was now rendered useless, his future felled in one fateful stroke.

Bound by blood, by blood undone.

I felt the connection between us snap.

His blood—Greythorne blood, Mathuin's blood—flowed into the inscription of the fountain, turning the chiseled words red and then dripping into the fountain itself.

Rosetta had gathered Kellan into her arms as he shook in shock, staring at the stump where his hand had been. She was whispering comfort to him, drawing spells into his skin, cauterizing the wound, taking away the pain, chanting him into a spelled sleep like she had for me each time I'd left my body behind to walk the Gray.

Better to deprive him of his purpose than his life. That's what I'd said to Castillion about Zan. And now I'd done just that to Kellan. I'd robbed him of his ability to fight. I'd betrayed him in a most heinous fashion. I'd stolen his noble end and replaced it with a lifetime of difficulty.

I'd also saved his life.

Rosetta looked up at me as the wind kicked up, her hair drifting and dancing around her face like flame.

"Take care of him," I said.

Magic from Kellan's blood was everywhere around me, crackling. I pulled it into myself and then, turning to Rosetta and Kellan, pronounced the same spell once uttered at Mathuin.

"*Ut salutem!*" I cried, pushing the magic toward them in a wave.

To safety.

★

I walked the steps to the Stella alone. It was not just the doors that were crimson now; the entire building was bathed in the color of blood.

Inside, Arceneaux was praying.

Her dark hair was free and loosely waving down her back, her hands clasped together in ardent passion as she lifted her voice in praise to the goddess in the glass above her. Her arms, now free of their gloves, were laced with the markings of rot.

Zan was suspended between chains running from each wrist to two marble pillars, arms outstretched, a starlike offering to the red-glowing glass Empyrea. Blood was flowing freely from wounds all over his bare torso and arms; Arceneaux knew she had to kill him to set her mistress free, but it appeared she wanted to take her time and enjoy the process.

"O Divine Empyrea," she sang, "I have done all you asked. I

am ready to become thy vessel. I know that my body is weak and human and frail, and that I am unworthy, but take it. Take it and make it thy own."

Zan groaned and tried to move.

Angrily, Arceneaux abandoned her prayer and stood, placing her decaying hands around his neck. "Silence," she ordered. "Submit now to the Empyrea's will."

I curled my fingers into a fist and walked up behind her.

"Let him go," I said quietly. Dangerously. I did not have to raise my voice here; the Stella Regina was built to glory in sound.

She dropped her grip just as Zan's eyes were beginning to roll back into their sockets. He sucked in a gasping breath, on the very precipice of consciousness. She turned to face me, and I was struck by how carefully she had cultivated her own image to match the Empyrea's as it had been rendered in the Stella's stained glass: long, dark hair; haunting blue eyes; a distant and disdainful countenance. But despite the trappings she'd donned—the diamond stars pinned to her free-flowing locks, her blazing white robes, the feverish gleam in her eye—she did not actually resemble the Goddess at all.

"I killed your favorite acolytes. And your 'Celestines.' And all of your clerics. Let him go, and I won't kill you."

"They are in the Empyrea's arms now," she said. "May she forgive them for their failures."

"Do you think she forgave Toris for his failures?"

She stiffened.

"You've been failed by all the men in your life, haven't you? Men who sought to rule you, use you, control you, discard you. Men who valued you only for what they could do with you or take from you. But not Toris. No. I daresay . . . you think he might have been the one person in all of this starsforsaken universe to actually give you purpose." I was inches away from her now, carefully gauging the twitch in her jaw, the tremor in her fingers, the hitch in her breath. "And I killed him."

She gave me a withering stare. "*You.* It's always you. Ruining everything. Taking what's mine."

"What have I *ever* taken from you?" I asked. "What do you have that I would ever want?"

"You should have been sent away," she said furiously. "Like the rest of us. You should have been cast aside into the garbage like we were. It should have been you to get passed from man to man so the kidnapper who called himself your father could make a few coins."

I was so close to Zan now that I smelled his blood, coppery sweet. If I could just get to him. Just touch him. I could give him my vitality. I could make this all end.

Then I saw her buttons.

Arceneaux's robe was decorated with four matching buttons, made of shining white gold, in the shape of a flower.

"Lilies," I said.

"What?" she asked flatly.

"Lilies." I looked up at her, into her eyes. "Your name was supposed to be Lily."

"Shut your mouth," she warned. "You don't know anything about me."

"That is what Lyall meant when he said this was your coronation. *You* were the daughter of a king."

"Daughter of a king and a queen. But what did it matter? They gave me away. Cast me aside."

"Iresine was not your mother," I stated surely, feeling the sweetness and bitterness of it both at once, like one of her herbal remedies. "Your true mother was Onal. She made those buttons for you. She was going to name you Lily."

Arceneaux was shaking. "Shut up."

"She wanted you. She wanted you so badly."

"No."

"But they took you from her. She never got a chance to say goodbye."

"No!" Arceneaux was growing shrill.

"They tried to make her believe she was crazy, that you didn't exist, but she knew better . . . She tried to track you down, but she found the carriage crashed. Burned to nothing. She thought you were dead."

"*That woman* could never be my mother. No. You're a liar."

"She died believing that you never lived past the day you were stolen from her." I went quiet. "She is one of the best women I have ever known. It is an honor to be her granddaughter. You have been given an *honor* to know that she was your mother."

She bared her teeth. "I am the chosen vessel for the Empyrea. I have no mother. I will be no crone. The Empyrea will take my body and then I will be the Maid forever as she rules over the world for all time."

"Take your body, and leave no room for you? You are about to *erase* yourself. Your consciousness, the thing that makes you *you*, will be gone. There will be no Isobel Arceneaux. There will be no Lily. There will be only Her." I leaned in closer, letting her feel the heat of my animosity. "And *She* is not the Empyrea. It is not the goddess of the stars that you serve; it never was. It's the goddess of the underworld. You're about to let yourself be taken over by the Malefica."

"You can call her by whatever name you choose," she said. "I know the goddess I serve."

"Your hands," I said. "You tried to hold her spirit once already, didn't you? On the night of the black moon, when Toris killed a city to set her free—"

"Toris failed too," she said. "I will not. Lyall figured it out. I've already marked myself with the seal. She'll come to me, and I will give myself to her completely. I will be a queen. I will be a goddess."

"You will be nothing," I spat. "You will be gone. Erased. Forgotten forever." Just an inch or two more, and I could lunge for Zan.

I wouldn't get the chance. Arceneaux's knife slid into my belly on the left side, in and out.

Stunned, I stared down at the wound, then grabbed her wrist with one hand while covering my torso with the other. The sigil she'd carved into the skin of her own arm was hot to the touch. Burning, even.

Zan, so close and yet now so impossibly far, was faltering. The Malefica's arrival in the material plane was very close at hand.

Arceneaux dropped her knife. "I shouldn't have done that," she said in disgust. "You just made me so angry. But I can't let you die. *He has to die, not you. I have to finish what Toris started.*"

I stumbled backwards against the altar. Pain made pinpricks of light dart across my sight, but her words struck me harder than her knife.

He has to die, not you.

One or the other.

I rolled over to face the altar and tapped in the exact sequence I once saw the Stella's priests complete. I didn't wait for the mechanisms to finish working before I threw myself down on top of it. With ropes whirring as they unspooled, I dropped into the darkness of the crypt below and felt the air crushed out of me on impact with the floor.

I scrabbled to Urso's sarcophagus, the only light a square of red from the altar opening in the chapel above. His stone coffin was carved in somersweet stalks: This had to be it. This had to be where the Ilithiya's Bell had been hidden for three centuries.

I put my feet against the stone alcove wall and pushed my back against the heavy lid, screaming as I further tore the wound in my side with the effort. The lid scraped ajar and fell to the side of the sarcophagus with a crash and a cloud of dust.

Inside, Urso's bones—Mathuin's bones—were resting quietly, arranged in a beatific facsimile of prayer. He had been buried with beads and baubles and a band of gold around his head dotted with stars in the arrangement of the constellation after which he'd named himself: the bear. But despite my frantic digging, there was no sign of what I was looking for. There was no bell.

No bell—but there *was* a book. From under his bony, folded hands, I pulled Galantha's green leather grimoire. It had been with them in the Cradle the night they raised Rosetta. It had to have come back with him then. This was no mere copy—it was exactly the same book I'd last seen with Rosetta in the library. It appeared to have been unmoved since it was laid in here, at Urso's burial.

I didn't have time to wonder at the mystery; Arceneaux had dropped into the crypt now, landing hard on her feet and twisting her ankle. Grimoire in hand, I tried to slip past her as she limped from the square of light. A shadow had begun to form behind her, and a red glow began to gather in her eyes.

I spun on my heel and sprinted to the door to the bell tower, blood marking my path in a serpentine stream. I threw myself at the door, and it gave way, sending me tumbling onto the wooden stairs.

"Where are you going?" Arceneaux screamed. But she knew.

I was going to the top of the bell tower. And then I was going to jump.

One or the other.

It was going to be me.

I couldn't be sure this would save Zan, but at least this would give him a chance.

Him, and all the world besides.

I had made it only to the second spiral when Arceneaux burst into the bell tower behind me. Her fingers were curled into claws that tore at my cloak. The black smoke was clinging to her skin now, burrowing below it.

"Where are you going?" she asked again, but her mouth spoke

with two discordant voices. I kicked at her, again and again, feeling the stairs heave and sigh with every move.

I was running out of strength, energy flagging. Even the magic in my blood seemed to have grown quiet and subdued with the imminence of my departure. But I remembered Zan's drawing of the tired horseman and took the next stair, then the next, without stopping until I reached the top.

Arceneaux, her eyes now black, caught my cloak in both hands. With a cry, I managed to wrench myself from her grasp and dash to the open window's edge, overlooking the whole of Greythorne, from the body-ridden village to the manor, now fully engulfed in flames. Heat and ash scoured my face as I climbed onto the edge.

The clock above my head turned to midnight, and the bells began to clang.

Up here the noise was piercing and ponderous, a wave of vibration that blocked out every sense, every thought.

I looked up at the carillons, their clappers all turning on the wire in the same prescribed order they had for nearly four hundred years.

Urso's bells.

No—Mathuin's bells.

And then I saw it. The last bell on the line, barely bigger than a thimble. It was made of gleaming metal and a wintry-white jewel fashioned into the shape of a sombersweet blossom. And against the sonorous tones of the most cavernous carillons, this bell's call was like a single drop of rain in a still pool, sending ripples out from all sides.

And finally, *finally,* I understood everything.

At the red moonrise, one of two dies. Those two lives were not mine and Zan's. Not mine and Arceneaux's. No.

They were *both* mine.

The Ilithiya's Bell had been here, waiting out the centuries in this drafty tower, for this moment.

Waiting for me. To give me this last, desperate chance.

So I reached out, and I took it.

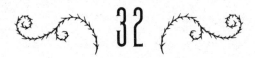

32

lifted the bell's chain over my head, and the minute the instrument's cool quicksilver touched my skin, I was launched into the Gray. But unlike the times I'd Graywalked before, I did not have to leave my physical body behind. With the bell, both parts of me — my physical and subtle selves — were one and the same.

I could feel the pull of the Gray's currents, too, as time and space eddied around my form like a river splitting for an impervious rock. I was still within that moment in the Stella's bell tower, but it was no longer one moment, not really — it was hundreds. Thousands. Forward and backward, there for the taking.

I knew where I had to go. I held the bell and concentrated, trying to re-create the Assembly in my mind. The mist stirred and solidified into a set of stairs before me.

I fumbled up the steps, hand to the side of my stomach, bell heavy around my neck. "Simon?" I whispered into the cavernous hall, but no one answered. All around me, headless gods and beautiful monsters warred in stone reliefs, darkened by age and draped in cobwebs.

This was, without doubt, the same room I'd seen when Simon had appeared to me at his death.

Had I come too late? Was he already dead? My strength was flagging; if Simon was not here, I wasn't sure an attempt to go back further to find him would leave me with enough strength to do what must be done when I did.

I was panting by the time I got to the top, dots swimming across my vision. I sank against a pillar, pain radiating from the wound under my ribs, robbing me of my breath.

"Simon?" I called again, louder. My voice echoed into the rafters, disturbing the pigeons roosting in the high buttresses.

I blinked to clear my blurring vision, the Assembly's sanctorium nave stretching seemingly endlessly before me, the meters extending into miles. And at its head, the coffin of glass rested empty upon the altar. Cael's coffin. The one in which he had been entombed for centuries before a hapless historian named Toris woke him and released him to wreak havoc upon the Assembly and the world. As my stumbling feet scuffed the dust on the floor, I could make out pieces of feral-magic sigils, like the ones in Galantha's book. But these were all the same, one after another. *Sleep. Sleep. Sleep.*

The mages of the Assembly couldn't kill him, so they did the only thing they knew to do: they put him here, locked him away in his luneocite box, believing that they were safe. That he was as good as dead.

But sleep is not death.

The night may stretch long, but it ends.

Slumber ends. Death does not.

Grunting with the effort, I made my way up the nave toward the casket, balancing myself against the splintering remains of the pews where skeletal Assemblymen remained bent in eternal supplication; whether they had died begging for the Empyrea's forgiveness or Cael's mercy was impossible to know.

Either way, their cries had gone unanswered.

I was almost to the casket, my feet unsteady and fingers shaking, when I heard a voice from behind me.

"Aurelia?"

I turned slowly to find Simon standing in the nave, an open book slipping from his hands as he stared at me. Even here, in this lost and lonely place, he was dressed in his fine satin brocade, black hair gleaming like a raven's wing. But despite his regal posture and his fine clothes, his cheekbones were prominent against his sunken skin, and dark circles framed his green eyes. "Simon," I said in a cracking voice, blinking away tears. Even knowing all I knew about the Ilithiya's Bell, even after all my experiences treading the Gray, it was a bewildering joy to see him again. Alive. Or, at least, not yet dead. "Tell me the day," I said.

"Aurelia, you're injured—"

"The *day*," I demanded. "I need the day."

"*Nonus*," he said, rushing to me as my knees began to buckle. "The . . . twentieth, I think. Why? What is happening?" He helped lower me to the floor, where I put my back to the altar, grimacing as he moved my cloak aside to inspect the gash in my torso.

"I can patch this up, I think," he said, "It won't be pretty, but at least—"

"No," I said breathlessly, pushing his hands away. "There's a lot to say, and very little time in which to say it. Listen to me."

"But you—"

I grabbed a fistful of Simon's tunic. "*Listen* to me! Zan didn't die in Stiria, Simon. He made it from the boat and onto shore. He knew Castillion wanted him dead, so he went underground."

Simon's eyes were shining. "He lives?"

"He does. But it was a temporary stay; he's going to die again unless . . ."

"Unless what?"

"Unless we stop it."

"And how do we stop it?"

"I have to die." I closed my eyes, letting my heavy eyelids rest for one moment, then two, before forcing them open again.

Simon said, "Which means I must also die?"

"No, Simon," I said, lifting my shaking, blood-sticky fingers to his cheek. "You already did."

His eyes dropped to the talisman around my neck, the sombersweet-shaped bell and its crystal-teardrop striker. "I know this relic," he said, eyes widening. "I've seen drawings of it. Mentions in old texts . . ."

Realization tugged the corners of his lips down, tightened the skin around his eyes. "I see. Where you've come from, Zan is alive. But *I* am not."

I nodded. Then said, "There's still time for you, Simon, if you want to save yourself. I can set you free. I did it for Kellan. I broke the blood bond between us." I shook my head as if to rattle the memories out of it, but they remained: the thud of Fredrick's sword. Kellan's cry. The snap of our connection, severed completely, shattered forever. "I could do the same for you. Now, before it's too late."

"My dear girl," Simon murmured, "I'm so sorry. For you, and your knight."

"You know what it takes to break it?"

He nodded grimly. "Yes." Then he swallowed. "If I don't accept your offer, how much time do I have, from this moment?"

"Days."

"And how do I go?"

"I die in Zan's arms," I said. "His life force, or godspark, or whatever the mages call it . . . his recognizes mine as his own. So when he touches me . . ." I let the sentence fade, unable to finish it. Here I was again, at the start of another loop: I was now telling Simon all the things he'd go on to tell me. "It's over before I know what's happening."

"It was never magic making you ill."

"No," I said. "It wasn't. Simon, I . . . I'm so sorry. It was so fast, so sudden . . ."

"You didn't know."

"But *you* do," I said. "There's still time to change your fate. I just have to find something you fear more than death . . ."

"The only thing I fear more than death is eternal life," Simon said. "And that is not something you can give me, even if I wanted it."

I thought of Rosetta and glanced up at the coffin above us. "You want to die?"

"Not particularly," he said. "Do you?"

I closed my eyes. "I must. I've been told too many times to count now. *One or the other.* It's me or Zan, and it can't be Zan. The Empyrea has spoken."

"And when have you ever trusted the Empyrea?" He rocked back. "You didn't answer my question. Do you want to die?"

I tilted my head toward the ceiling and opened my eyes. Above, the vaults had been painted in the indigo tones of the night sky and studded with golden stars.

"No," I said. It was the truth—*my* truth—spoken aloud for the first time. *Si vivis, tu pugnas.*

He nodded. "That's why you're here, isn't it?"

"When you came to me, after I . . . when you . . ." I cleared my throat. ". . . died . . . you told me to find a third way. *This* is the third way."

"What do you need?"

"First, I'll need you to make sure I get this." I pulled Galantha's grimoire from my cloak and pushed it into his hands.

Wincing, I dragged myself to my feet, leaning heavily upon the casket. I tried to wipe away some of the dust but succeeded only in streaking red fingerprints across the glass. Despite the grime and blood, I could still make out the silver surface upon which Cael had lain in stasis for centuries. "Then I'll need you to cleave my subtle body from my material one," I said. "And lock it in here until my consciousness can be sealed back into it."

Simon was stunned. "That's an undertaking of monumental proportions—"

"Two have done it," I said. "The Founder of the Tribunal and a Warden of the Woods. And now, me."

"They'll need blood to bring you back," Simon said. "Yours. And a blood mage who can use it. Outside of you and me . . ."

"I know of one other," I said. "And I have this." I brought out the empty vial that used to belong to him. "Can you help me fill it?"

Grimly, he took the tiny bottle, removed the stopper, and helped me make a cut wide enough to release a stream of blood before positioning my hand over the bottle to catch it as it flowed. When it was full, he replaced the stopper and laid the cord over my head. The glass clinked as it came to rest against the flower of the bell.

"If that blood is lost," Simon warned, "none of this will work."

"Don't worry," I replied. "I know the perfect person to entrust with its safekeeping."

He helped me to my feet. "Are you ready?"

I nodded, forcing myself into the appearance of bravery as he made a cut in his own hand and then clasped mine with it.

His voice, as he began the spell, reminded me of the carillons at the Stella Regina: deep, resonant, affecting and musical. I could feel his magic and mine both answer his call. And every word felt like a new wound, slowly eviscerating the unvisceral, cutting the physical from the metaphysical.

"Et sanguis meus tua . . ."
By your blood and mine . . .

". . . divinae luce . . ."

. . . and the light of the divine . . .

". . . et ego tres partes dividio."

. . . three parts I divide.

"Anima mea, visus, et substantia . . ."

Soul, sight, and substance . . .

". . . nunc in sanguine quod factum est . . ."

. . . by blood now undone . . .

". . . faciet, a sanguine rursus . . ."

. . . will, by blood, again . . .

". . . ut uniatur."

. . . be united as one.

"Merciful Empyrea," Simon said as he finished the spell.

I was not simply me—I was me times two: my spectral and material selves were now separate parts.

I commanded my spectral self to step away from me, and she—I—obeyed. We looked at each other for one second, blinking. Two sides of the same coin. The same but not the same. She had dark hair; I had light. She had blue eyes; mine were silver. I was cut and bruised and damaged; she was without scar or flaw.

Wordlessly, I lifted the lid to the luneocite casket and climbed into it, then leaned languidly back while I watched. I saw myself settling into the glass coffin at the same time as I actually did it. Only when my spectral self closed her eyes—my eyes—did my vision become singular once again.

While she rested there, I slipped Zan's ring from my finger and placed it under her clasped hands.

Simon laid the lid down over my spectral body, and I felt another tether snap—just like when the blood bond broke between me and Kellan. Only this time, it was the last thread of quicksilver connecting my selves that was dissolving.

"Bleeding stars," I said as I felt the silver melt away. It wasn't until it was leaving me that I realized how much a part of me it was. I had walked the Gray, Onal once told me, before ever taking a living breath in the material world. My silvery eyes and ashy hair were the physical manifestations of my unconventional path into existence—a quicksilver souvenir from the spectral world.

But now, as it drained in silvery trails from my eyes and fingertips, my material self looked as it would have if my birth had been easy. If I'd never been given bloodleaf flower before ever taking a breath.

I had my mother's eyes, my father's smile, and my grandmother's dark, thick hair.

There was no mirror that could give me my reflection now; she was safely resting in another kind of glass.

"By all the blessed stars," Simon said in awe. "Look."

A smoky shape began to coalesce before me, and with silver tears in my eyes, I held out a hand and a muzzle materialized beneath it. I smiled and then laughed, throwing my arms around her neck. Of *course* this would be the shape my quicksilver guide would take.

Falada.

She gave a soft nicker and gently nudged my bloodstained midsection.

"I'm not ready to greet the After just yet, girl," I told her. "I have a few stops to make first."

33

The stories said that King Theobald the Second had been sitting alone in the pews of the Stella Regina the night of his great Empyrean vision. He and his party had stopped on Greythorne land on their way to the Ebonwilde; they were supposed to be taking supplies to his men on the front lines of the fight with Achleva, but it was a hard summer with a poor harvest. And with winter waiting in the wings, he knew that despite their effort to scrape together this delivery, it would still not be enough. Achlev's wall remained as impenetrable as ever. *They* would never run out of food; inside those walls, it was ever summer.

The war was going to bankrupt them. He'd lose his title. The Tribunal was ravenous for more power, and they were not so scrupulous with lives — Achlevan or Renaltan.

"Merciful Empyrea," he said, casting a prayer to the skies, "tell me what I should do."

And in response, the earth beneath him began to shake, and the air within the sanctorium began to shimmer. From nothing, a glorious woman riding a horse so luminous and bright that it must have been made of silver and stardust galloped into view.

All those times I heard that story, I never could have imagined that the woman the old king described was actually me.

"King Theobald?" I asked, and he fell to my feet and kissed my boots. "Oh, my queen. My glorious goddess. Thou hast come down from your celestial throne to answer the prayer of thy servant. Tell me what I should do, most holy Empyrea, and I will listen."

I gave a hard sigh. "You want to stop the war? This is how you do it: You go to the king of Achleva and make a deal. The next daughter of your line will marry the next heir of his. Do you need to write it down?"

"No, most beautiful and wise Empyrea. Thy words have been seared into my memory. I will build you a monument, a tower to the heavens, greater than all—"

Apparently, Falada found my ancestor as tedious as I did and took us pounding off into the Gray without waiting to hear him finish.

When I returned to the *Humility,* Dominic Castillion had sunk back into his chair, head down on the desk between the hands I'd spelled into immobility, while anything not bolted down slid past him as the boat pitched slowly forward. When he caught sight of me, a fleeting look of surprise registered on his face before being replaced with a bewildering expression of worry. "You shouldn't have come back," he said. "You'll never make it now." Then his eyes grew wide at my bloodied clothes, changed hair, differently colored eyes.

"Aurelia." He gave a start.

"Favor," I said.

"What—?"

"The winner of the game gets to choose, secret or favor. You told me a secret, but I didn't ask for a secret." I put my hands on my hips. "So I'm here to collect my favor."

He peered at me, mistrustful. "I don't know if you noticed, but I don't have a lot of time."

"I know," I said. "If you agree to my terms, I'll save your life."

"Why?"

"So that you can save mine."

★

I left one burning ship to find another.

I left Falada on Stiria's shale shore, bathed in the orange glow of the ship burning, burning, burning on a plane of water black and still as obsidian glass. Zan was halfway to the safety of land, but his strength was flagging. He coughed and bobbed, clawing futilely at the surface until, at last, he disappeared under it.

It was dark under the water, the kind of darkness that can never be satiated, no matter how much it takes and takes. But I would not let it have this. I would *not* let the darkness take him. His body floated toward the empty depths, face obscured by his cloud of drifting hair and his swirling black coat.

Zan.

I strained toward him as my lungs began to burn and my limbs went numb. I wrapped my leaden arms around his chest and kicked toward the glimmering orange lights of the burning ship above.

I pulled him to the surface, coughing and spluttering frigid water, my hair streaming into my eyes, making it impossible to see, but I swam and swam, feeling my energy drained from the exertion, the water, and the touch of Zan's skin against mine.

When we reached the shore, I dragged his body up onto the black and rocky beach and pushed him to his back so I could pound his chest. "You already lived through this," I said angrily through numb lips. "So *wake up* already. *Si vivis, tu pugnas.* Fight, you fool."

Then he coughed water and phlegm, struggling to his side to spit it out. I hurried to Falada and climbed onto her back, wishing I could stay with him at this point and not go back.

But I couldn't.

I urged Falada forward as Zan wiped the water out of his bleary eyes. One step, then two. And then, with a triumphant scream, she reared back on her hind legs, kicking at the sky.

Zan watched as we rode away, our image burned into his mind, and I began to feel like maybe . . . just maybe . . . this might actually work.

I'd delivered the message to him so that he could deliver it to me.

While you live, you fight.

Conrad Costin Altenar, eight years old and the ascendant king of Renalt, was humming to himself in time to the creaks and jolts of his carriage. It was an old Renaltan folk song, meant to be sung in a melancholic minor key: *Don't go, my child, to the Ebonwilde, / For there a witch resides . . .*

I could see the moment ahead of us, and I steered Falada toward it, willing time to stillness so that we could reach it. The Ilithiya's Bell was warm around my neck, a force of radiant power of a scope I had yet to fully fathom.

Conrad could sense that something had changed. He climbed out of his carriage.

"Hello? Anyone there?" He gulped. "Lord Greythorne? Fredrick?" He pulled his knife from his belt, squinting. "Hello?" he asked again to the silence.

Falada broke through into the moment with triumph, her hooves scraping the air as she reared up in front of my brother, who froze, eyes bugging.

"Bleeding stars!" he yelped, swiveling on the toes of his pointed shoes and diving into the shelter of the hawthorns lining the road.

"Conrad!" I called. "Wait!"

He darted through the branches, nimble as a rabbit, but we followed closely behind. The thick-woven thatch was nearly impenetrable even for his slight shape; it should have been impossible for anything larger, but this was the Gray, and I had the Ilithiya's Bell around my neck, and it allowed us to slip through the brambles like smoke through a sieve.

I tried to change the landscape to something he'd recognize, and the next thing I knew, we were herding him toward the center of the maze. He dashed forward, screeching an incomprehensible combination of invocations, cries, and curses. "Conrad!" I yelled again.

We reached the center together. Falada neighed and reared, and I reached for my brother as I dismounted, pulling him tightly into the flying folds of my colorless cloak. He twisted and tried to pull from my grasp, but I clasped him under my chin. "It's all right. It's all right. It's me, little brother. It's just me."

His shaking and crying subsided. "Aurelia?" He looked at my bloodstained tunic. "Are you hurt?"

"In your time, I'm fine. This won't happen until much later."

"You're . . . not from my time?"

I shook my head and knelt in front of him. "I know this is strange, and I know you're scared. But I need your help, dear one. There's no one to whom I can entrust this task but you."

He nodded and slid his knife back into its sheath.

On our way back to the carriage, I told him as much as I could: the coronation, Arceneaux, the Gray. He listened solemnly, absorbing every detail without flinching. When we arrived back at the carriage, I asked, "The puzzle box I gave you, do you still have it?"

He retrieved it from inside the cab and said, "I almost have it figured out."

"Show me."

He demonstrated the sequence: twist, turn, tap. Then he said, "Wait! I get it now!" and added another tap and twist. The compartment popped open, revealing the wax-papered cinnamon candy I'd hidden inside.

He beamed up at me. "You got my favorite!"

"I'm going to need you to eat that candy," I said, feeling the prick of tears forming behind my eyes. "Empty it as fast as possible, because I have something else you'll need to keep in there."

"Right now?" he asked, brightening.

He was so sweet, this brother of mine. Sweet and smart and kingly and kind. "As soon as possible." I smiled wanly, knowing what was ahead for him, and hoping to distract him from the blood on my shirt and the pain in my eyes. "And then I'm going to tell you a story about a brave little king who hid an army of children in an ancient prophet's crypt to save them from a wicked queen, then led them on a journey of a thousand miles to freedom and safety."

"Does this story have a happy ending?" he asked.

I said, "Yes. Because you'll make it that way."

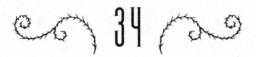

34

The bells were still humming when I returned to the tower.

Arceneaux was still moving in on me, seemingly unaware that anything had changed in the lightning-strike second that had passed since I first took hold of the bell. The Malefica's overtaking of her body was almost complete: only a thin sheen of black smoke still wafted around her body. Below the bell tower, the maze's portal spell knot was still open, but it would remain so without help only for as long as the eclipse lasted. And already, the red was fading into orange; in mere moments, the shadow would have passed and, with it, my chance.

Instead of fighting off Arceneaux's attack, I locked my arms around her and pulled her with me out the tower window. Together, we fell down, down, down, through the portal and into the reflected world of the Gray beyond it.

We rolled to a stop, and I pinned Arceneaux's hands to the ground. "What are you doing?" the voice that was not hers demanded.

"Manere," I said. *Stay.*

Then I lifted the bell and rang it over her head. "I declare that you, Isobel Arceneaux, daughter of Onal, descendant of Nola, the Ilithiya's true daughter, are now Warden of the Ninth Age, the Age of the Crone."

If the Empyrea wanted me to be the next warden, it meant I should not become the next warden. And that meant there was only one other candidate for the job.

"Isobel Arceneaux, Warden of the Ninth Age, you are now responsible for maintaining the balance between the planes, for ensuring the continuation of the Ilithiya's work, for the protection of all living things, large and small."

Isobel Arceneaux was gone now, fully erased to make room for the entity now occupying her body. Underneath her translucent skin, black veins writhed, straining to hold the spirit of a goddess never meant to exist in the material plane.

And now she never would.

She screamed incomprehensibly as I crossed through the portal one more time, making it back to the material plane just as the earth's shadow disappeared from the moon's surface.

Zan stirred as I pulled him down from his chains. "No," he said deliriously, trying to push me away. "You can't. Don't touch me."

"It's all right," I said. "Look at me." I brushed his hair back from his forehead, cradling his chin in my hands. "I'm choosing my own ending. I have to go one way or another. Why can't it be like this?"

I kissed his eyes, his jaw, his mouth. Each kiss was a drop of honey, a sparkling star. And each one revived him just a little bit more.

Zan pulled me into his arms as I weakened, clinging to him with my failing body even while knowing he was causing it to fail. In his eyes, impossible love warred against inevitable loss: He wanted to hold me tighter. He wanted to push me away.

He dropped his head down to my shoulder and said, voice breaking, "Don't leave me here without you. I can't do it. I can't."

I smiled weakly, feeling another wave of my life ebb away. "I know you can," I said. "And you'll have to. But not for long. Not forever." I touched the firebird charm, returned to its place on his leather cuff. "The frustrating thing about a firebird is that death never seems to stick."

His breath was coming fast, his eyes full of fragile hope.

I brought his forehead down to mine. "You told me once to stop running and finally let you find me." Then I moved my lips to his ear and gave one last coy whisper: "So come and *find* me."

EPILOGUE

Aurelia Altenar, princess of Renalt, was dead.

Her body was laid to rest in the crypt of the Stella Regina in the last open sarcophagus in the main circle of twelve, between the remains of the Stella Regina's founder, Urso, and her more recently deceased friend Father Cesare. There were few in attendance: the four beautiful girls of the Quiet Canary; Conrad, the little boy with the golden curls who was also the Renaltan king; Rosetta, the wild woman of the woods with yellow eyes and hair of flame; and two young men bearing mythical-beast-shaped charms, one on a necklace chain, the other on a leather cuff. Kellan, his right arm thickly bandaged and tied up in a sling, looked away, jaw tight, as Zan, Conrad, Jessamine, and Rosetta lifted Aurelia's body into the stone box and settled her into it, smoothing her hair around her face and settling her hands softly onto her chest.

"Do you have any last words you want to tell her, darling?" Jessamine asked, kneeling next to Conrad. "Do you want to say goodbye?"

"No," Conrad said with a shrug. "Close it up."

The adults exchanged surprised glances, but they did as he directed, and Aurelia's serene face disappeared into the darkness beneath the stone-slab lid.

Kellan turned his face toward Rosetta's shoulder. Delphinia sobbed as Lorelai and Rafaella comforted her. Jessamine took a drink of sombersweet wine and then laid the bottle at the foot of the coffin.

Zan said nothing. He just stared at the stone, measuring his breathing. *One, in. Two, out. Three, in. Four, out.* Behind the dark fall of his hair, his eyes glinted gold.

The somber gathering slowly dispersed, until only Conrad and Zan were left.

Conrad tugged Zan's sleeve, producing a pointy-ended box from within his cerulean cape. With a few twists and taps, the top sprang open. Inside it was a glass vial, filled to the top with rich, red blood.

"She gave this to me," he said, "so that I could keep it safe. And now I'm supposed to give it to you."

Zan took the proffered gift hesitantly, letting it dangle on its cord as he stared. It was a tradition among blood mages to leave a vial of blood behind for those they loved most. A last bit of their soul, their magic.

The young king said, "She's not dead, Zan. Not really."

Zan put his hand on Conrad's shoulder, crouching to look him in the eye. Carefully, he said, "It's hard to accept. I know. But your sister . . . she's gone."

"She's not gone," Conrad said matter-of-factly. "She's at the Assembly, sleeping. Waiting for *you* to wake her up." He tilted his golden head. "I did my part. Now it's your turn."

Conrad shrugged Zan's hand from his shoulder and went to catch up with the others, leaving Zan kneeling alone, shoulders slumped, next to Aurelia's stone coffin. Her last words echoed in his head, half invitation, half provocation.

Come and find me.

Zan closed his fingers tightly around the vial and got to his feet.

ONE YEAR LATER

The men, chiseling away at the side of the rock, had no idea if this search area would yield any new results. They were merely following their orders. It was not for them to question, just to obey.

After coming up short so many times, they were greatly shocked when a door appeared in the side of the mountain wall, creaking open as if to welcome them home.

Their lanterns cast spooky shadows on the ancient, cobweb-swathed carvings as they went from room to room until at last they found the entrance to the sanctorium chapel.

At the end of the nave, their lanterns caught the gleam of glass.

They raced back to the entrance and called down the mountain.

"Hurry! Hurry! Tell him the news! She's here! We've finally found her!"

ACKNOWLEDGMENTS

Bloodleaf developed over the course of eight years; *Greythorne* was written in eight months. It was a task that was often overwhelming, always daunting, and tested my belief in myself too many times to count. I owe so much to my editor, Cat Onder, who helped me navigate the ups and downs of crafting a sequel with aplomb. At the start of the journey, I could hardly fathom *finishing* the second volume of Aurelia's story, let alone loving it—but I do. So much. Thank you, Cat, for getting it (and me!) across that finish line.

Thanks and kudos also go to my agent, Pete Knapp. He is the kindest, most dedicated, most conscientious human . . . and a ferocious, passionate advocate for me and my work, even when I forget to copy him on 90 percent of my reply emails. You're the best, Pete. Truly. I thank the heavens daily for that query feedback giveaway. And to everyone at Park and Fine: I am so lucky to have such an incredible team on my side.

So much love to everyone at HMH Teen: Gabby, Mary, Sam, Zoe, Celeste, Alia, Tara, Lisa, Jessica, John, Anna, and the countless others working their tails off behind the scenes to put Aurelia's story into the world. Thank you SO much. Hugs to you all.

To Austin and Berni at CAA and Jen at Cavalry: thank you.

To Chantal Horeis: thank you for this gorgeous cover, and for capturing Aurelia exactly as I imagined her: full of determination and fight.

Debut year is always one of ups and downs, but I hit the lottery with the Novel Nineteens, and especially my fellow Utah Nineteens: Tiana, Samantha, Ruthanne, Erin, Dan, and Sofiya. If it weren't for you, I'd probably have spent a lot of my debut year hiding in the corner of my house in pajamas. Thanks for dragging me out into the world from time to time. Consider yourselves granted bookmark designs for life, ha. Thanks for the chats and goat GIFs, Sofiya. Someday Zan will grow on you, I swear.

And to the readers and indie booksellers and bloggers and You-Tubers and podcasters and Instagrammers who have showered me and *Bloodleaf* with so much love: thank you! I cry on a regular basis because of you. (In a good way, haha.)

I was lucky to have been born into a family of book nerds who were, and are, my first readers and biggest fans: Carolanne, Carma, Brandon, Melody, Stacy, Katey, and Tiffany. Their spouses, too: Zack, Steve, Kel, Mike, and Jesse. And my posse of nieces and nephews: William, Sam, Kaitlyn, Lucy, Pete, and Abby. Mom and Dad, thank you for raising me to love books. Hey, at least one thing stuck, right?!

And to my in-laws: Paula and Stan, it's impossible to overstate how incredible you are, and how thankful I am for your excitement for my books. Someday I'll make team shirts for *you* to return the favor. Amy: thanks for being my hype squad team leader. Logan, Marcus, Whitney, Sean . . . no one has in-laws like you: #blessed.

To my own little squad: Keaton, Jamison, and Lincoln. I love you so much, it hurts. Thank you for being there for me, for making me laugh, for showering me with hugs and kisses, for keeping me grounded. For closing the computer for me when you knew I needed a break and opening it when you knew it was time for me to get back to work. Guess what? I love you.